RENT AT YOUR OWN RISK

Sarah Kelling—A pretty widow and landlady in distress. Her Tulip Street townhouse attracted tragedy as well as tenants.

Barnwell Augustus Quiffen—A malcontent with a nasty mind. Someone he offended used murder to move him out before his lease was up.

William Hartler—An avid collector of antiques. He moved in with his Hawaiian treasures . . . and some very peculiar habits.

Theonia Sorpende—A most proper Boston matron. She had a scandalous way of spending her spare time.

Charles C. Charles—The very best of butlers. He's really a professional actor who makes Jeeves his role model.

Max Bittersohn—A one-man detective agency. He moved into the basement to protect the lovely landlady. Wouldn't he prefer to move into her heart?

Mildred Schuneman

The Withdrawing Room
CHARLOTTE MACLEOD

AVON
PUBLISHERS OF BARD, CAMELOT, DISCUS AND FLARE BOOKS

AVON BOOKS
A division of
The Hearst Corporation
1790 Broadway
New York, New York 10019

Copyright © 1980 by Charlotte MacLeod
Published by arrangement with Doubleday & Company, Inc.
Library of Congress Catalog Card Number: 80-920
ISBN: 0-380-56473-4

First Avon Printing, October, 1981

AVON TRADEMARK REG. U.S. PAT. OFF. AND IN
OTHER COUNTRIES, MARCA REGISTRADA,
HECHO EN U.S.A.

Printed in the U.S.A.

WFH   10   9   8   7   6   5   4   3   2

Chapter 1

"Damn it, Sarah, you can't do a thing like that! What will the family say?" Cousin Dolph's jowls quivered with empurpled outrage. Dolph went in rather heavily for outrage.

"Who cares what the family says?" Uncle Jem yelled back. Jeremy Kelling was not more than five years older than his nephew Adolphus, but relationships among the vast Kelling clan came in all sizes and assortments. "I've never listened to any of them, and I've lived a hell of a lot more satisfying life than the pack of you put together."

"Bah! You talk a lot, but you never did anything. If I had five cents for every woman you've—" Dolph recollected that he was in the presence of Sarah, whom he still thought of as a puling infant notwithstanding the fact that she'd been married and widowed. "Anyway, I wouldn't be a dime richer than I am now."

"The devil you wouldn't. If you're so flaming rich, why don't you stump up for Sarah's mortgage?"

Adolphus Kelling waxed even purpler. "What are you preaching to me for? Why don't you?"

"Because I didn't come in for old Fred's wad as you're about to. And I've rioted away my substance as fast as it came in on wine and wassail, as a sensible man should. And I've dipped into capital, too, and you needn't start yelling again because I don't give a damn. At least I wouldn't give a damn if it weren't for this outrageous mess over the mortgages. Sarah knows I'd give her the money like a shot if I had it."

Sarah Kelling Kelling, though many years younger and

7

a great deal smaller than either of the combatants, managed to raise her voice above the tumult. "Shut up, both
of you! I don't want anybody to give me the money. This
is my mess, not yours. I—I'm only grateful Alexander
didn't live to find out what was going on."

This was a lie, and Sarah's voice was none too steady
by the time she'd finished uttering it. Alexander would in
truth have been devastated to learn that his young wife,
whom he'd thought he was leaving amply provided for,
might wind up without so much as a roof over her head.
Yet to have lost him so suddenly and so dreadfully* was
a shock she still hadn't got over and probably never
would.

In a way, Sarah could not herself understand why she
was trying to make Dolph and Uncle Jem listen to this
idea of hers. It would be far easier to chuck the whole
business, let the bank foreclose, and be shut of both the
tall Tulip Street townhouse on Beacon Hill and the far
too large summer estate at Ireson's Landing, about twenty
miles north of Boston. Then there wouldn't be the agony
of waking up every morning and finding herself in the
house alone.

She wouldn't be a pauper in any case. Sarah still had
her own small income from the trust her father had set
up. She'd soon reach her twenty-seventh birthday and be
able to take charge of the principal which had escaped the
looting of the Kelling estate, although her father himself
had not. But to give up so easily, to haul in her horns and
slink off without a fight seemed too much like a betrayal
of the long, lonely battle Alexander had waged to save
something for her.

So she'd thought the matter over, weighed the fors and
againsts, and come up with what she'd honestly believed a
sober, dignified, reasonable solution to her immediate
problem. She might have known that no matter what she
proposed, she'd be precipitating a full-scale family fracas.

"You've got no more knowledge of finance than a goddamn tomcat," Dolph was informing Jem, neither of them
having paid any attention whatever to Sarah. "You ought
to know I shan't be able to touch a penny of Uncle Fred's
money for at least a year, and then there are all those
charitable bequests to be taken care of. By the time I've

* *The Family Vault,* Doubleday Crime Club, 1979.

paid the inheritance taxes and forked over endowments for fifty-seven different foundations and whatnot, I expect to be a damn sight poorer than I am now."

He winced at his own words. The thought of having to dip into his own pocket was always a painful one for Dolph. "Money isn't worth a damn these days anyway," he concluded sulkily.

"A fact which ought to bring you to your senses, if you had any, and make you realize how much more intelligent I was to blow mine while the blowing was good than you were to sit on yours and hatch a rotten egg," said Jeremy Kelling.

"Bah! And what have you got to show for all your carousing? Cirrhosis of the liver and a tail feather from one of Ann Corio's doves."

"And the fluorescent tassel off Sally Keith's left buttock," the retired roué added blandly. "Ah, those hallowed days around the bar at the dear old Crawford House, with Sally up there twitching and twirling! A bowl of chips, a pousse-café, and thou. Not you, naturally, you overstuffed lout. Did I ever tell you about Milly, the—"

"Will you two stop it?" shrieked his overwrought niece. "I don't want to hear about anybody's misspent or unspent youth, I want you to help me start a boardinghouse. And quit telling me I can't because I'm going to. Do I need a permit, or what? Dolph, you know everybody at City Hall. Can't you pull some strings?"

"Yes, Dolph, pull some strings," said Jem. "Strings don't cost anything. I know you'd never stoop to bribery because you're too damned cheap."

His nephew glared and decided to retire into outraged hauteur. "I daresay I could handle the formalities if Sarah persists in going through with this crackbrained scheme."

"I'd be a lot more crackbrained to let the High Street Bank grab my property without a struggle, wouldn't I?" Sarah was, after all, a Kelling herself, both by birth and by marriage to a fifth cousin once removed. "What's so crackbrained about a boardinghouse, anyway? Lots of perfectly respectable people have done the same. Look at Mrs. Craigie."

"Mh'h. I'd forgotten about Mrs. Craigie. Cambridge woman, right? And that Longfellow chap stayed with her. Wrote poetry, of course, but his people were all right, and he married an Appleton. Well, I suppose if you make sure to take the right sort—"

"The hell with that," said Jeremy Kelling. "Take the ones who don't squawk about the money. Stick 'em, Sarah. Make the suckers pay through the eyeballs for the privilege of living in a stately mansion in a fine old historic district and all that garbage. Put on a show. I'll pop in and play Autocrat of the Breakfast Table."

"Hell of an autocrat you'd make," sneered Dolph. "And what do you mean, breakfast table? You never even drag your rum-soaked carcass out of bed till noon. Degenerate old souse!"

"Truer words were never spoken, though I must say it's a refreshing change to hear any truth spoken by you," replied his uncle with the courtliness for which the Kellings were noted. "Getting back to this boardinghouse business, Sarah, are you in fact planning to serve meals?"

"I'm going to do breakfasts and dinners. That way I can ask a lot more rent, and since I'm used to cooking for the family anyway, I should be able to manage without much difficulty."

"I thought Edith did the cooking," said Dolph.

"All Edith ever did was sit and nurse her bunions and complain about being overworked."

Firing her mother-in-law's former maid, even though doing so cost a monthly pension she could ill afford, had so far been Sarah's one compensation for widowhood. "I've hired Mariposa Fergus in her place. You remember that adorable young woman who was such a prop and mainstay during the funeral? She and Charles are going to live down in the old kitchen."

"Who's Charles?"

"A friend of hers who looks like Leslie Howard and talks like a cross between Henry Higgins in *Pygmalion* and Sir Percy Blakeney in *The Scarlet Pimpernel.*"

"How the hell would you know? Leslie Howard's been dead since 1943."

"I used to see the reruns at the Brattle Theater. Anyway, Charles is alive enough, from what Mariposa tells me."

"My God, Sarah, you can't have a pair like that fornicatin' all over the back stairs. Can't you at least make them get married first?"

"I shouldn't dream of trying. Mariposa says she's tried

it both ways and this is more fun. And Charles would merely arch his eyebrow with aristocratic hauteur. He has the most fetching golden curls, but he's going to slick them down when he butles. His name is Charles C. Charles."

"The other C. being for Charles, I take it?"

"No, I believe it's for Chelsea. That's where he comes from. He's an actor by profession, but he's resting at the moment."

"That means unemployed, Dolph," explained Jem. "Like you."

"Oh no," said Sarah. "Charles works in a factory day-times and he's going to butle here during dinner for his room and board. He's been yearning to play Mr. Hudson ever since 'Upstairs, Downstairs,' and he's studying up madly on whether to serve the hock with the guinea fowl, though of course we shan't be having any. I do know scads of ways to fix chicken and hamburg, though, and I'm marvelous at pinching pennies when I grocery shop. I had to be, considering what Alexander gave me for a housekeeping allowance though he meant it for the best, poor darling."

Dolph shook his jowls. "Forget it, Sarah. You'd need at least a dozen boarders to make it work and you've only got three bedrooms in the whole damn house."

"Dolph, that's ridiculous. There's the other basement room, for one, that Edith used as her bedroom. I thought I might rent that to a student or something, since they'd have to share the bathroom down there with Mariposa and Charles."

"Never get a nickel."

Sarah ignored him. "And I'm turning the drawing room into a sort of private suite for someone old and rich who can't climb stairs. I've already had a door cut through from that powder room in the hall, and I've spoken to the plumber about putting in a stall shower there. I'm selling that McIntire escritoire to pay for the renovations. It's not under the mortgage, is it?"

"Don't ask," Uncle Jem advised.

"And what, pray tell, will you then use for a drawing room?" scoffed Dolph.

"Why the hell should she need one?" Jeremy Kelling sneered back. "Idiotic antediluvian custom anyway, the ladies withdrawing to sit on their bustles and gossip while the men stayed at the dining table and drank themselves blotto. When I start seeing double, I'd rather be sitting across from a daring décolletage than a red nose with a walrus mustache under it. Did I ever tell you about—"

"I'm sure you did," Sarah interrupted. "You're quite right, I don't need one. I'll use the library, as I'm doing now." The high-ceiled room where they sat, with its book-lined walls, its worn red velvet draperies, the portrait of the Kelling who'd founded the family fortunes over the mantel, and the dark old leather sofas and armchairs grouped around the fireplace was far and away the pleasantest room in the house.

"And I'll keep Aunt Caroline's room on the second floor for myself and turn her boudoir into a studio. I did all that book illustrating for Harry Lackridge, you know, and I'm sure I can get work from other publishers, to bring in a little extra money. And on the third floor there are Alexander's and my old rooms with the bath in between, and Mariposa has got one of her brothers-in-law, either past or present, I'm not sure which, to help me fix up those two in the attic that used to be maids' rooms and put another bathroom there, so that will give space for six."

"Ridiculous!" shouted Dolph. "Who's going to climb all those stairs?"

"Lots of people around the Hill live in fourth-floor walk-ups. Anyway, if I can't rent them, I'll move up there myself and rent the second."

"Don't you do it, Sarah," said Jem. "Take the best for yourself and put on the dog. Treat 'em like dirt and they'll eat out of your hand. Try to be a pal and they'll walk all over you."

"I hate to admit it," snorted Dolph, "but the old goat's right. You stick to your guns. Don't budge an inch for anybody. Speaking of which, where do you propose to find these hypothetical lodgers?"

"Advertise, I suppose."

"In the newspapers? My God, that's the last straw! What would Aunt Bodie—"

"Dolph," shouted his uncle, "if you don't quit dragging the whole damn clan into this, I'll get Egbert to poke you straight in the jaw." Egbert, Jeremy Kelling's man for all seasons, had been known to perform stranger assignments than this. "Boadicea's a fine one to talk, anyway. She'd rent her own bridgework if she could find any takers."

"I couldn't possibly care less about Aunt Bodie," said Sarah. "Furthermore, Aunt Emma's all for it. We talked over the whole plan while I was staying out there after —after it was all over. She's the one who thought of doing up the old maids' rooms, as a matter of fact. I'd forgotten those attic rooms were ever used for sleeping. She even gave me some blankets and linen."

"Then why didn't you say so in the first place?" Dolph snarled. "Emma's got a head on her shoulders, at least." That from him was highest praise. "Mabel will raise hell on general principles, I daresay, but who gives a damn for what Mabel says?"

"And I've also mentioned it to Anora Protheroe," Sarah went on, referring to an old and respected friend in Chestnut Hill, "and she's terribly relieved that I shan't be trying to stay on here alone. She's going to see if she can't get me a boarder for the drawing room. You know him, that Mr. Quiffen who's her husband's old fraternity brother or whatever."

"Quiffen? Must have met him sometime or other, I suppose, though I can't recall him offhand. At any rate, if he's a pal of George's he probably has sleeping sickness so he oughtn't to cause you any trouble," chirped Uncle Jem. "You see, Sarah, that's how you work it. Drop a word here and there to the right people and you'll find takers fast enough. I'll start alerting the tribe myself. How are you fixed for beds and stuff, by the way? Shall I do a little panhandling on the side?"

"No, thank you. I'm reasonably sure I can bring what I need in from the place at Ireson's. Mr. Lomax, our caretaker out there, has a friend who will lend him a truck."

"Uses it to lug fishheads to the glue factory, no doubt, and your mattresses will stink to high heaven by the time they get here," said Dolph with his customary optimism. "Well, then, Sarah, since you've made up your mind to cut your own throat, I'll see what I can do about getting you a permit."

Chapter 2

After this family discussion, if such it could be called, Sarah went into high gear. She got Mariposa to round up a few more brothers-in-law and sold the McIntire escritoire. She knew she was getting skinned on the price, but there was no help for that. Bills for labor and materials were piling up and she needed cash in a hurry.

Perhaps she could have kept herself going by selling off the family treasures one by one, but she saw no point in just surviving. Having people around her and work to do at least kept her from thinking too much.

Sarah was still handicapped by an arm injury that hadn't fully healed. She couldn't paint or wallpaper, but she could do small jobs and drive the 1950 Studebaker Starlite Coupe that had been bought new for Aunt Caroline and kept running like a charm by Alexander. That would have to be sold, too, if anybody was buying Studebakers these days. She had nobody now to do the repairs. Garaging and insurance at Boston rates would be far beyond her straitened means. She'd already made the grim decision to take the old car off the road at New Year's, but right now she must have transportation.

When she wasn't urging her work crew to yet more frantic efforts, she was dashing from the tiny, twisting streets of Beacon Hill—lined with unbroken rows of elegant and once-elegant townhouses in brick and brownstone, with their Bulfinch fronts and wrought-iron grilles, their window boxes so carefully tended in summer, so festive now with evergreen boughs and dried scarlet salvia—out to the deserted Victorian clapboard ark at Ireson's Landing on the North Shore. There, with the wind howl-

14

ing around her ears and the ocean pounding on the rocks in the distance, she roamed her vast, overgrown estate with Mr. Lomax, the caretaker, marking trees for him to cut and sell. With firewood at something like a hundred and fifty dollars a cord, the proceeds ought to pay his wages and, God willing, leave something over toward the back taxes. Sarah and Alexander had talked of selling off some of the land but she couldn't do that now on account of the pending litigation. She could and did pillage the house to furnish her empty bedrooms. If she managed to rent the estate next summer, Mr. Lomax would have to borrow the truck again and bring back all the beds and dressers, no doubt, but by then she'd either have money enough for replacements or else have made such a fiasco of her boardinghouse idea that she'd have to pitch a tent out here among the chipmunks and live on roots and berries.

Going to bed totally exhausted every night had its advantages. Sarah had no time to brood over Alexander, though she missed him fifty times a day. She couldn't keep calling the workmen from their more vital tasks to help her spruce up battered chairs and chests, hang curtains, do all the puttering odd jobs he'd performed so expertly and enjoyed so much. Charles and Mariposa did their best, and it would have to be good enough.

After dinner when Sarah was too worn out to work any longer, she would put on high heels to raise her five feet three inches to a more imposing stature, don a black crepe dress of her mother's that was old enough to be back in style had any true Boston lady ever given more than a passing hoot for the vagaries of fashion, sweep her light brown hair into a twist that lent a few years and an air of dignity to her small, pale, squarish face, and grant interviews to prospective tenants.

Jeremy Kelling had been right about applicants. Once the news got around that the same Sarah Kelling who'd made headlines a month ago was now opening her home to paying guests, she had them camping three deep on her doorstep. Her chief problem was to weed out the insolvent, the impossible, and the sensation seekers who didn't really want to move in but couldn't resist a chance to gawk. For this she relied heavily on the superior worldly wisdom of her household staff. About 80 per cent of the hopefuls never got past the vestibule. Those who did got a shrewd going-over from the apparently impassive maid and butler. A muttered, "Honey, this baby's for the birds," from Mariposa wiped out a beautifully dressed lady who was an ardent volunteer for one of Dolph's inherited charities. The merest flicker of Charles's eyelids turned away several others whose references and manners appeared impeccable.

Her assistants themselves were impeccable and then some. The pair had insisted on providing themselves out of Charles' paycheck from the plastics factory with uniforms suited to their positions as they conceived them. Mariposa had elected to set off her trim figure and vivid coloring in bright orange topped by a frilly white cap with long orange velvet streamers. Charles was the epitome of what the well-dressed Eaton Place butler should wear, up to and including the white cotton gloves, though his were in fact drip-dry nylon which he felt Mr. Hudson would have pardoned since Mariposa made him wash them himself. His dress suit had come from the costumer's with certain embellishments, but Sarah had persuaded him to save the red ribbon and the row of medals until he was either made ambassador to somewhere or offered a bit part in *The Merry Widow*.

Indisputably the uniforms lent cachet to the establishment. The mere sight of Charles in full panoply was enough to discourage most of the ineligibles. Those who did manage to run the barricade, having been formally announced by Charles and then served a minuscule glass of sherry on a silver tray proffered by Mariposa in her beribboned cap, were far less apt to quail at the rates Sarah quoted.

The three had decided together that it would be easier and what Charles referred to as better theater to assemble the cast of boarders all on the same day rather than have them trickle along one by one. Since it was fiscally vital to set the day as soon as possible, the Tulip Street house began to look like the setting for a Keystone Cops movie with people flying in all directions at impossible speeds.

Sarah developed quite a talent as a nagger. When she flagged, Jeremy Kelling was ready to take over. Either because of his expert chivvying or because they couldn't endure to stay and hear any more of his reminiscences, the plumbers, carpenters, electricians, and decorators made well-nigh superhuman efforts to meet their deadlines.

Cousin Dolph was as expeditious and no doubt a good deal more obnoxious in getting the required license. Thanks to the plethora of applicants, Sarah had her boarders all chosen well before the last nail was driven and the last curtain hung.

Mrs. Theonia Sorpende was to have Sarah's old room. Mrs. Sorpende was a stately, handsome, middle-aged lady of brunette complexion, almost overpowering refinement, ineffably gracious manner, and a surprising streak of dry humor. She said she wouldn't mind the two flights of stairs a bit, and added with a ruefully amused glance down over her Junoesque contours that she could use the exercise. She was a widow and dressed the part in a simple black dress and coat, though she had relieved the somber costume with a wine-colored velvet turban and matching handbag and gloves. She had few acquaintances in Boston and would be living very quietly. The name she gave as a reference was Mrs. G. Thackford Bodkin, a friend of Aunt Marguerite's in Newport. With Mariposa making thumbs-up signs behind the lady's back and Charles so far forgetting himself as to mouth a fervent, "Hubba, hubba!" Sarah dispensed with Mrs. Bodkin and accepted Mrs. Sorpende on the spot.

Alexander's room would be occupied by a Miss Jennifer LaValliere, who probably would not be living very quietly. She was another who needed no investigating since her grandmother lived just around the corner and had served on committees with Aunt Caroline. She was perhaps attractive, if one could have seen beyond the frizzy hair and the assortment of garments awful enough to be no doubt the ultra chic of the moment. Sarah hoped the moment would soon pass.

Miss LaValliere had caught the career bug and was doing a business course at Katy Gibbs, which had also given her a plausible excuse to get away from her vigilant parents in Lincoln. What she'd wanted, of course, was an apartment of her own in town. Mrs. Kelling's boardinghouse was a family-approved compromise that couldn't have been wholly acceptable to a nineteen-year-old with advanced ideas, but the girl was taking it well enough. She seemed to be an agreeable little thing on the whole. Sarah couldn't recall that she herself had ever alternated with such blinding rapidity between ultramundane sophistication and fits of the giggles, but at Jennifer's age she'd already become a married woman with two big places to keep and a blind, deaf tyrant of a mother-in-law to cope with.

On the top floor she was putting Mr. Eugene Porter-Smith, an elderly gentleman of about twenty-seven. He put Sarah in mind of W. S. Gilbert's ballad of the precocious baby although he was by no means a fast little cad like that disreputable infant and certainly not about to die an enfeebled old dotard at an impossibly early age. He worked for Sarah's third cousin Percival as an accountant. Percival vouched for him as a model of rectitude and what Percy didn't know about recitude wasn't worth knowing. Moreover, Mr. Porter-Smith was into, as he said, mountain climbing and proved it by taking the three flights in high gear without a single puff.

Mr. Porter-Smith looked decorous enough, at any rate, with his neat three-piece suit and his sand-colored hair slicked back from a thinnish face that was neither attractive nor ugly but merely present in the usual place. His frame was spare and wiry, his height perhaps five feet nine or ten, his pale blue eyes sharp and inquiring. Mr. Porter-Smith was obviously a man who liked to know things; in fact he spouted information on any given subject at such a rate that Sarah suspected him of reading the encyclopedia in his spare time, which was surely a habit no landlady could disapprove.

Her other attic room was assigned to Professor Oscar Ormsby, a burly, hirsute man of fifty or so who wore hairy tweed suits and brown turtleneck jerseys and taught aerodynamics at Massachusetts Institute of Technology, just across the river. When Sarah apologized for the room's being so high up, he grunted, "Hadn't noticed."

That was about all Professor Ormsby did say except to grunt again as he wrote the check for the first month's rent in advance, which Charles and Mariposa had drilled Sarah always to insist on, and ask what happened if he didn't show up for meals.

Sarah and Mariposa had that one all worked out. "If you call the house sometime during the day and let us know you're going to be late, we'll keep something hot for you. If you don't call, you'll be free to go to the kitchen when you come in and help yourself to a snack from the refrigerator. If you choose to eat out, we can't give you a refund but we do allow you to bring a guest free of charge any time within the month. With proper notice, of course. If you haven't missed a meal but still want to bring a guest, there is a ten-dollar charge. In advance," she added, responding to the frenzied pantomime Charles was going through behind the professor's back.

Uncle Jem had set the fees, and while they were indeed far from cheap they were still lower than the cost of maintaining an apartment and much less than living at a hotel and eating in restaurants. Costs of food, salaries, utilities, and maintenance would have to be deducted from the gross, but Sarah figured that with careful management and her monthly allowance from the trust, she'd clear enough to stay afloat until she knew where she stood with the bank.

Her basement room was the only one not yet ready to let. Sarah was still in a quandry about whom to put there. She'd abandoned the idea of students. They might not mind sharing a meager bath with the maid and butler or object to their occasionally somewhat rowdy behavior offstage since Charles could hardly be Mr. Hudson all the time. However, they might intensify the rowdyism and that would never do. Her upstairs tenants were paying for class, and class they were going to get. She'd just have to wait for the right sort of applicant, whoever that might be. If she didn't, Mr. Quiffen would be sure to raise a stink.

Barnwell Augustus Quiffen, George's old fraternity brother, had indeed taken the drawing room. Anora and George had brought him to look at it themselves. It was the first time they'd been in the house for ages, and Sarah couldn't help thinking that away from their own everblazing fireside they looked like a couple of pigmy elephants gone astray. With both of them clad in baggy gray tweeds, with George's soft rolls of flab and Anora's short gray hair and white bristles about her mouth and chin, it would have been hard for a stranger to say which was the man and which the woman.

Barnwell Quiffen was a perfect Tweedledee, ovoid in shape and about to have a battle. He glared around the beautifully proportioned, spacious room, sniffed at Anora's exclamations over Sarah's excellent redecorating job, and snapped, "Where's the desk? I told you this would be a waste of time. Of course it won't do! I can't live here without a desk."

"Get him a desk, Sarah," said George sleepily.

"Quit fussing, Barney," said Anora. "Sarah, Barney needs a desk to write his poison-pen letters on. What about that one in the library? You won't want it there anyway, will you?"

"No," stammered Sarah. "I was wondering where to—"

"Well, then, just move that little table out and move the desk in. Come on, Barney, Auntie Anora's got a nice, big, gorgeous desk for you to feel important at. Show him, Sarah."

They trooped across the hall to the library and solemnly inspected the handsome burl walnut desk that Alexander's father and his father before him had sat behind. Sarah didn't much like the idea of this fussy little man's taking their places, but obviously she wasn't to have any say in the matter. At any rate, she'd have to put it somewhere or her lodgers wouldn't have room enough to sit.

Quiffen grudgingly admitted the desk would suit his purpose well enough, but where was the filing cabinet to go with it? He must have a filing cabinet to hold his important correspondence.

"Get him a filing cabinet, Sarah," droned George.

"Here's one right here," said Anora. "What's in it, Sarah? All that old committee nonsense of Caroline's, I suppose. Chuck it out."

So Mr. Quiffen got his filing cabinet for his important correspondence, which Sarah vaguely recalled consisted mostly of writing letters to the papers about what was wrong with everybody and everything in and around Boston. If a light bulb flickered on the Cleveland Circle platform at Park Street Station, if a red tulip popped up in a bed in the Public Garden where only yellow tulips were supposed to grow, if (though this was unlikely to happen) a trombonist at Symphony hit a B-sharp where a B-natural was called for, Barnwell Augustus Quiffen would leap to take pen in hand and regret to inform.

Mariposa then served tea, Charles being still at the factory, and Mr. Quiffen thawed sufficiently to recite excerpts from his family tree, at which Anora roared, "She's not planning to use you for stud purposes, Barney. Drink your tea and leave the poor girl alone. She'll get enough of you after you move in."

That, Sarah thought, was more than likely to be true. She'd had nearly enough of old Barnwell Augustus already. However, his readiness to make out a check in advance for the stipulated month's rental, which amounted to a good deal thanks to Uncle Jem's agile arithmetic, made her decide that perhaps, after all, she might be able to endure the man. Since the Protheroes had managed to stay friends with him all these years, he must have some redeeming features. If she failed to discover them, she could at least depend on Anora to shove him into line when he got too far out of hand.

Chapter 3

Despite everybody's good intentions, Sarah's renovations didn't get done overnight. Work that had started in late November was still incomplete when she realized that the holidays she'd been dreading were actually upon her. This was all to the good. Whatever her many relatives might think of her scheme, and Dolph's reaction had been among the politest, they couldn't fault her for attending to business instead of accepting their sometimes well-meant invitations. Nobody expected cheery cards or gifts from a new-made widow. She ate a stodgy Christmas dinner with Aunt Appie and Uncle Samuel in Cambridge and spent a surprisingly riotous New Year's Eve on Pinckney Street with Uncle Jem, Egbert, and Dolph, who got tiddly on champagne and recited all he could remember of "Gunga Din," which fortunately was not much.

On Sunday, January 2, Mariposa swept up the last of the shavings. On Monday, the third day of a new year that couldn't possibly be any worse than the one just past, Sarah found herself seated at the head of her own dining room table wearing her mother's slate blue dinner gown and Granny Kay's bluebird brooch, being served in her public role as mistress from a dish she'd prepared in her private capacity as cook, by Charles doing his impersonation of a perfect Scottish butler in a noble English household.

Sarah herself had a sense of total unreality about the performance, but her lodgers appeared satisfied that they were getting the genuine article. All except Professor Ormsby, who stuck to his hairy tweeds and brown turtleneck, had dressed for the occasion. Mr. Quiffen was cor-

22

rect in black tie. His clothes were probably even older than Sarah's gown, since he also was of a caste that didn't believe in discarding anything that still had good wear in it just because the garment happened to be a few decades out of style.

Mr. Porter-Smith, on the other hand, had blossomed forth in a wine-colored suit with satin lapels wide enough and shiny enough to skate on. The ensemble was completed by a matching tie the size and shape of an Amazon butterfly, and a ruffled pink shirt.

Even he, however, was outshone by Mrs. Sorpende. She was dressed in black as usual, a long-sleeved, long-skirted gown of dull black crepe beautifully fitted to her ample though by no means unpleasing figure. This she had artfully enhanced by an emerald green chiffon scarf that veiled but did not quite conceal the low-cut neckline. In her elaborately dressed black hair was set an aigrette of green ostrich tips and jewels which, had they been real, would have given Sarah cause for alarm about burglars.

Charles was trying to remain correctly impassive, but Sarah could sense his inward rejoicing at having such a classy dame to pass the crackers to. Professor Ormsby happened to glance up from his soup and once having glanced continued to gaze. No doubt Mrs. Sorpende's alluringly draped corsage was an agreeable change from wind tunnels.

Poor Miss LaValliere, though a pretty enough child in spite of the fact that she had subdued her frizz into a sort of Early Andrews Sisters hairdo, was hopelessly outshone. She was wearing a conventionally indiscreet tubelike affair of some clinging substance, but not even Charles bothered to peek down her unfettered décolletage since it was obviously not worth the bother. Perhaps she was trying to discourage the treatment of woman as a mere sex object, Sarah thought. If so, she could hardly have chosen a more effective way.

Be that as it might, Jennifer LaValliere was pouring badly needed money into the Kelling coffers and it was Sarah's job to keep the girl happy. She started being gracious, whereupon Mrs. Sorpende and Mr. Porter-Smith both followed her lead. Miss LaValliere's suddenly becoming the focus of attention annoyed Mr. Quiffen, who started acting like a superannuated and very spoiled baby. This landlady business was going to be more complex than Sarah had bargained for.

Luckily she'd had plenty of experience at sticky family gatherings. She placated the old man by letting him bore her to excruciation with a diatribe against the Metropolitan Boston Transit Authority. He rode the MBTA a good deal, it seemed, for the express purpose of finding fault with it. His tale of being trapped for half an hour outside Kenmore Station on the first hot day of summer with the air conditioning not on and the heat in the car going full blast might have had more punch if it had been told eight months earlier. However, Sarah endured his whinings and snarlings with a practiced look of keen attention, an occasional shake of the head, and a few murmurs which Mr. Quiffen might take for whatever he chose to take them for.

In fact, she hadn't the faintest notion what he was saying most of the time. She was wondering if the beef stroganoff would hold out until everybody had got a fair share. She hadn't realized professors of aeronautics ate so much. Thanks to some fancy footwork on Charles's part, though, disaster was averted. If Professor Ormsby wound up with a great many noodles and a very little beef the second time around, he didn't appear to notice, but shoveled in the last forkful with the same gusto as the first.

There was homemade apple pie for dessert. "The apples came from our trees at Ireson's Landing," Sarah told the company, and they made suitably reverent noises. Little did they ken that they'd be eating plenty more of these apples before the winter was over. As soon as she'd been able to think straight enough to start planning her boardinghouse, Sarah and Mr. Lomax had scooped up every one that was still salvageable.

At the end of the meal, Mr. Porter-Smith touched his napkin to his lips with a gracefully Edwardian flourish and said, as Sarah had been betting with herself that he would, "My compliments to the cook."

Without batting an eyelid, Charles replied, "Thank you, sir. I will convey them on your behalf."

They adjourned to the library to drink their coffee, they dispersed, and Sarah went upstairs to take off her dress and collapse. The first major hurdle was over.

For the rest of the week Sarah was kept as busy as she'd been getting ready for her lodgers. Now she must find out their needs and crotchets, keep the larder stocked, think up ways to feed Professor Ormsby and still wind up on the profit side of the ledger. As he never showed any sign of noticing what he ate provided he got enough of it, this was not too difficult.

As for the others, Jennifer LaValliere tended to pick and nibble. Mrs. Sorpende always said she shouldn't, then did. Mr. Porter-Smith was so overcome by the grandeur of Charles and the value of the Kelling silver and china that he'd no doubt have eaten a slice of old boot with relish if it were served to him elegantly enough. Mr. Quiffen gobbled, glared around the table to make sure nobody got a better portion than he, quarreled with anyone who'd quarrel back, and made himself generally obnoxious at every opportunity.

Letting the Protheroes bully her into taking George's old buddy in as a boarder had been a sad mistake. Worse, it was a mistake she need not have made. Only a day or so after Sarah had got herself trapped into putting up with Barnwell Augustus Quiffen, she was visited by William Hartler.

Mr. Hartler was as cheery as Quiffen was nasty, which was saying a good deal. He beamed, he chuckled, he reminded Sarah of those delightful parties at Aunt Marguerite's where he and she had got acquainted and Sarah recalled that Mr. Hartler himself had been the main reason why those particular gatherings had been less Godawful than the rest.

On those occasions, he'd always had his sister with him. Sarah recalled her vaguely as a gentle, self-effacing soul, even shorter than he and a good deal thinner. Her name was Joanna, but she and William had called each other by ridiculous nursery nicknames even though they must both be seventy or close to it. She'd appeared devoted to her brother and it was Sarah's impression that she'd kept house for them since neither, to the best of Sarah's knowledge, had ever married. Then why was William alone now?

"Oh, Joanna's flown the coop," Mr. Hartler told her. "She deserted me to spend the winter in Rome with an old friend from boarding school. Do her good to get away for a change, but it's pretty ghastly for me, I can tell you. We got rid of our place in Newport and put our things in storage. We plan to find an apartment here in Boston when she returns. In the meantime, I'm bumming around on my own and making a poor job of it. I tried a hotel but that cost a fortune, so now I've got a room over on Hereford Street, which means I have to go trailing out to a restaurant to get anything to eat. It's no fun. No fun at all. Living here with you would be ideal for my purposes. Good food, good company, lovely home, ground floor. I'm not supposed to climb stairs, you know. Doctor's nonsense about my heart. Other than that, I'm fit as a fiddle."

Sarah believed him. Mr. Hartler could have posed for Thomas Nast's drawing of St. Nick with his tummy and his twinkle, except that he was clean-shaven and not smoking a pipe and withal as spruce and tidy an old gentleman as any landlady might want occupying her front parlor suite.

"And it would be so convenient for my work," he sighed.

"Your work?" Sarah asked in some surprise.

"Volunteer work, of course, but it's important. Most important! I'm tracking things down for the restoration of the Iolani Palace. In Honolulu, you know."

"As a matter of fact, I do know. Edgar Driscoll had a fascinating feature story about it in the Boston *Globe* a while ago and we had a letter back when my husband was alive, asking whether we had anything to donate from the royal visit in 1887."

"And did you?" cried Mr. Hartler eagerly.

"Nothing of consequence. Queen Kapiolani and Princess Liliuokalani never stayed with us, but they did pop in for tea one afternoon."

"Here? In this very room?"

"Oh no. They'd have been entertained in the formal drawing room."

"Mrs. Kelling, could I see that room? Just for a moment?"

Sarah shook her head. "I'm terribly afraid you can't because it doesn't exist anymore. I've had to turn it into a bedroom. That's the room you'd have had if you'd only come a little sooner."

For a moment, Sarah thought Mr. Hartler was going to burst into tears.

"I feel as if St. Peter had just slammed the pearly gates in my face," he said with a rueful smile. "To think that I might have been sleeping in the very same room where those two wonderful, vibrant ladies sat and drank tea! Mrs. Kelling, I'm shattered, utterly shattered. I only hope the fortunate person who occupies it now realizes his great good fortune. Would it be someone I know, by any chance?"

"His name is Quiffen, and he's a friend of the Protheroes. You've met them, surely?"

"The Protheroes, yes, though only in passing as it were. But Quiffen? No, I can't say that name rings a bell. Perhaps I could find a way to scrape his acquaintance," he added, brightening a little. "If I were to explain what it would mean to me—I don't suppose he'd be amenable to a spot of bribery and corruption, by any chance?"

He said it with a whimsical smile, but Sarah wasn't altogether sure he didn't mean it. "I'm afraid not," she said firmly. "Mr. Quiffen is very well off and he appears to be perfectly satisfied with his accommodations. For the moment, at any rate."

Mr. Hartler took the hint she couldn't resist throwing in. "Ah, then if you think there may be any chance whatever, I implore you to keep me in mind. The Harvard Club will always find me. They'll take a message at the switchboard. Wonderful people. Most obliging. You're quite sure it wouldn't do any good for me to explain the circumstances to this Mr. Quiffen?"

"Quite sure. I really shouldn't try it if I were you, Mr. Hartler."

If old Barnwell Augustus thought anybody else wanted the room that badly, he'd dig himself in like a badger for sheer cussedness, and she'd be stuck with him forever. One could only wait and pray.

Chapter 4

Sarah had established the pleasant routine of gathering her boarders in the library half an hour before dinnertime for sherry and chat. This helped her get them to the table on time in a mellow mood, and gave Charles breathing space to change from working clothes into his butler's rig-out. It also provided an opportunity to dull people's appetites with some inexpensive but hearty hors d'oeuvres if the meal was going to be a trifle on the lean side, as it was on this particular occasion.

Mariposa was circling the room with a tray of Sarah's hot, delicious, filling, and surprisingly economical cheese puffs. Sarah was pouring wine for Mrs. Sorpende out of a cut-glass decanter she'd been tempted to sell but was now glad she'd held on to. Though they were filled from gallon jugs of the cheapest drinkable sherry she could find, the decanters did seem to have a favorable psychological effect on the flavor.

All of a sudden it occurred to her that the gathering was several degrees more amicable than usual. Nobody was fighting with anybody. No whiny voice was pontificating about some niggling point in which nobody else except possibly the encyclopedic Mr. Porter-Smith had the vaguest interest. Momentarily puzzled, Sarah stopped short with the decanter in mid-air and looked about. Mrs. Sorpende continued to hold out her glass with an air of sweet patience. Sarah recollected herself.

"I'm sorry. It just this moment dawned on me that Mr. Quiffen isn't here. He's usually so punctual."

"Been hoping he'd get stuck in the subway again, myself," grunted Professor Ormsby, taking several more cheese puffs and settling himself where he could ogle Mrs. Sorpende's décolletage in comfort.

Tonight, that elegant lady had enlivened her favorite black gown with a huge red silk poppy, and set a high-backed Spanish comb in her hair. Sarah thought not for the first time that Mrs. Sorpende would make a far more impressive landlady than she, and asked her to do the honors with the decanter.

"Could I ask you to take my place for a moment? I want to run out to the kitchen and see how things are getting on."

Actually she was wondering if Mr. Quiffen might have sent a message that nobody had remembered to give her. As a rule, both members of her multi-talented staff were punctilious about such things. In fact, Charles liked nothing better than to make a stately entrance with a slip of paper on a silver tray as if he were carrying the good news from Ghent to Aix. Tonight, though, he might have got held up at the factory while Mariposa was preoccupied with the cheese puffs.

No, she found Charles bustling up the cellar stairs, white-gloved and ready to roll. There had been no message.

"Then we shan't hold dinner for him," said Sarah crossly. "Mr. Quiffen knows the house rules. He'd be the first to squawk if anybody else kept him waiting."

Mr. Quiffen did not call and he did not come. They ate without him and found the experience a most agreeable change. Only Sarah could not escape the little worry that was nagging at her. It was so very unlike Mr. Quiffen not to make any kind of fuss whatever.

Perhaps she ought to call Anora Protheroe after dinner and see if Barnwell Augustus was out there. He might have got waylaid into hearing George's bear story, which went on for hours and from which once a victim was trapped there could be no escape. Sarah's nerves were still too raw from her own recent tragedies to tolerate any unexplained absence, even Mr. Quiffen's, without some degree of apprehension.

After dinner they went back to the library for coffee. Sarah used the Export China that had been brought back by one of her seafaring ancestors after a successful deal in nutmeg graters, chamber pots, and other products of an advanced Western technology. The cups had the double advantage of being so small that they saved a good deal on coffee and of giving Sarah an excuse to drop an occasional nugget of family history, thus contributing to the atmosphere her lodgers were paying for.

Jeremy Kelling had already joined them twice for dinner. On those occasions the anecdotes had been a good deal more picturesque. Sarah wished Uncle Jem could be here tonight to help her out of her preoccupation. However, he'd gone to some kind of old Barflies' Reunion at a suitably disreputable saloon for which the group had been forced to search far and wide, urban renewal having hygienized all their old haunts out of existence or into respectability.

Luckily, she could escape before long. Sarah had let it be known that exactly half an hour after she'd served the coffee, she would either adjourn to her upstairs lair or go out to whatever social engagement she might have, though since she'd opened her boardinghouse she hadn't been invited anywhere. She did so tonight, leaving the others to continue socializing in the library or get on with their own plans for the evening.

As it happened, nobody was going anywhere. The lodgers were all still in the library enjoying their unaccustomed congeniality when the telephone rang at about a quarter past nine. After several rings, when it became clear that Charles and Mariposa must be in their basement quarters reading good books, listening to Bach *partitas,* or more probably doing something else, Sarah came back downstairs to answer it.

According to old-fashioned custom, the original instrument had been installed in the front hall. This was the one she answered. As the library door was open, her boarders could hear, and the babble of conversation died suddenly as she gasped, "The police station? Yes, this is Mrs. Kelling. Yes, he does. Mr. Quiffen is one of my boarders. No, I'm not acquainted with his family, but I can find out who they are. Why? What's happened to him?"

They told her. She put down the receiver and entered the library with a face as white as the linen damask tablecloth she'd have to iron tomorrow. "I'm afraid we have some bad news. Mr. Quiffen has been in an accident."

"What kind of accident?" demanded Mr. Porter-Smith.

Sarah swallowed hard. "He appears to have fallen under a subway train at Haymarket Station."

"What the hell was he doing at Haymarket Station?" That was a stupid question. Oddly enough, it was Professor Ormsby who asked.

"I have no idea," she replied.

"Is he badly hurt?" was Mrs. Sorpende's more reasonable inquiry.

"He—" Sarah found she could not go on.

"You mean he's dead?" squealed Miss LaValliere.

"I—I believe it happened very quickly."

"Naturally it would have to," said Mr. Porter-Smith. "When you consider the weight and velocity of a subway train—"

Sarah had no desire to consider any such thing. "Excuse me," she interrupted. "I must call some friends and see if they can tell me who are his next of kin. Mr. Porter-Smith, you might pour us each a little brandy, if you will. I'll get the decanter."

"Please allow me." The young pontificator switched without effort to his role as mountain climber. He was out of his chair and across the room in a bound. Sarah showed him where to find the brandy and the liqueur glasses. Then she escaped to the kitchen, where there was an extension telephone, and dialed the Protheroes'.

George was, as she'd expected, three sheets to the wind and fast asleep by this time. Anora was awake and every bit as shocked as Sarah had thought she would be.

"Barney wasn't such a bad old wart when you got to know him," she snuffled, "and we'd known him forever. George is going to take it hard." As to relatives, Anora had to stop and think. "Barney never married. Or anything else," she added forthrightly. "He could never find a woman to suit him, and if he had, she'd have known better than to get stuck with such a pest. I expect you've had your hands full. But Barney wasn't any worse than a lot of others, no matter what they say."

The parents were long gone, of course. There had been a brother, but he was dead, too. However, Anora was pretty sure she could produce a nephew and a cousin or two.

"I hope you can," sighed Sarah. "Otherwise this may wind up as my responsibility. Frankly, Anora, I don't think I could cope."

"Of course you couldn't and why should you? George is one of the executors. Poor old Barney was going to be one of his. They used to go on about which would get to plant the other. George can stir his stumps for a change. Maybe it will buck him up a bit to learn he's the survivor instead of the survivee. I hope Barney's rent was paid up."

"Until the end of the week. If his heirs are anything like him, I daresay they'll demand a refund, since today is only Wednesday. I'm sorry, Anora. I know you cared for him."

"Yes, but that doesn't cut any ice. I know what Barney was like. You should have heard the way he carried on after your Uncle Fred died and he found Dolph had been given the chairmanship of one of those ridiculous foundations instead of him. Anyway, whatever the nephew says, don't give him a nickel. You've got to be tough if you're to succeed at that landlady wrinkle of yours, Sarah. As soon as we've got poor Barney safely underground, I'll see whom else I can dig up for you."

"That's sweet, Anora, but I already have one. Do you recall that nice Mr. Hartler we met at Aunt Marguerite's? His sister is in Rome and he's alone here in Boston, desperate to get the room. I'm sure he'd move in tomorrow, unless this thing about Mr. Quiffen turns him off."

"Why should it? Old people know other old people are going to die. We know we are, too, though we don't believe it till it happens and maybe not then, if you can put any stock in that parapsychology twaddle. What do you want to bet Barney's lodging a complaint with St. Peter right now? Or more likely trying to hunt up a nasty-minded medium to put a hex on the Secretary of Transportation. Whatever happened, I'm sure he brought it upon himself. No doubt he was bending over to inspect the rails or something that was none of his business in the first place, and wondering whom he should write to about it. Now, Sarah, you go lock his bedroom door right this minute. Don't let a soul set foot over that threshold until George and Barney's lawyer get there. Especially the relatives. Those Quiffens are all cut from the same bolt of cloth, and pretty shoddy material it is, if you ask me."

"Darling Anora, I do love you so!"

Sarah had been properly brought up not to get sloppy

with people, but she'd also learned the hard way that it was no good bottling up your feelings until suddenly you had nobody to tell them to. Maybe that fat old woman out there in her overheated, overfurnished cavern of a house with her fat old servants and her fat old drunk of a husband would forgive being told she was loved.

At any rate, Mrs. Protheroe replied in a gruff but not snappish tone, "Now don't you fret yourself about this business for one minute, Sarah. Take a little brandy and a hot bath, and get some rest."

Sarah obeyed and was glad later that she had. Almost at the crack of dawn, a sharp-nosed, thick-waisted, middle-aged man who could be nobody else but Barnwell Augustus Quiffen's nephew was on the doorstep, set to go through his uncle's possessions before the landlady pinched all the goodies. Or so his supercilious expression implied until Charles, who had taken the day off from the factory because he thought Mr. Hudson would have wanted him to, proffered a silver salver and straightened out the caller with a lofty, "I will tell the mistress you are here. Would you care to present your card?"

As Mr. Quiffen did not have a card and was much shorter, less attractive, and infinitely less impressive than Charles, he was thus put at a disadvantage and meekly allowed himself to be herded into the library.

Sarah, having anticipated an early-morning visit, was ready and waiting, but she let the man cool his heels for five minutes or so before she descended the stairs, correct in black-and-gray tweed and a discreet strand of pearls. Having picked up a few tricks from Charles, she entered the room with exactly the right degree of hauteur.

"Mr. Quiffen?" She held out a limp hand and permitted him to touch the first two fingers. "Allow me to express my sympathy on your sad loss. This has been a shock to us all."

"I'm going to write a mighty stiff letter to the Metropolitan Boston Transit Authority, I can tell you." No question about it, here was a Quiffen. "Now would you show me his room?" the nephew added almost in the same breath.

"Your uncle had the suite directly across the hall."

Sarah was about to add that he wouldn't be able to get into it, but the man was over there trying the knob before she had a chance, so she merely sat down and waited. In a moment he was back, his nose twitching as his late uncle's would no doubt have done in a like circumstance.

"I can't get in. What's wrong with the door?"

"Naturally I instructed my manservant to lock it as soon as we got word of your uncle's death," Sarah replied calmly.

"Then would you kindly instruct him to unlock it again?"

"Certainly, as soon as Mr. Protheroe arrives with the other executor. I assume you have made the necessary arrangements to meet him here?"

"Protheroe? That old—why, I never—"

The nephew began gobbling like an infuriated turkey. Sarah touched the small silver bell at her elbow. Charles, who had been lurking in the wings enjoying the show, entered on cue.

"You rang, madam?"

"Charles, would you telephone the Protheroe residence? Present my compliments and inquire whether Mr. Protheroe plans to come here this morning. If so, find out what time we may expect him to arrive, and give Mr. Quiffen that information. Mr. Quiffen will then either wish to make a proper appointment and return later or wait here in the library, depending on Mr. Protheroe's plans. If he chooses to wait, have Mariposa bring him some coffee. And now, Mr. Quiffen, I must ask you to excuse me. I have some things to do."

Giving his comeuppance to this not very pleasant man who had so obviously expected to barge in and stamp all over her afforded Sarah no cause for rejoicing. She'd sent Charles out for the morning papers and found as she expected that they'd pulled out all the stops. The late Barnwell Quiffen had "fallen or jumped" in front of the train. Altogether too much was made of the fact that he'd been staying with Sarah Kelling, to whom they'd already given more publicity than anybody but a movie starlet could ever want.

The brief statement she'd reluctantly made last night had been twisted beyond recognition. "Penniless Socialite Forced to Turn Ancestral Mansion into Boardinghouse" was among the less offensive headlines and "Kelling Murder Curse Strikes Again" undoubtedly the worst.

Sarah had made a formal apology to the survivors at the breakfast table, and assured them that their privacy would be guarded in every way possible. However, they'd all known her recent history before they'd agreed to take up residence with her and she got the distinct impression they were not particularly bowed down by being in the midst of another sensation, especially Professor Ormsby, who'd only grunted and helped himself to yet another fried egg.

Miss LaValliere and Mr. Porter-Smith were no doubt basking in the interest they could stir up among their respective classmates and fellow employees by now. Mrs. Sorpende, on the other hand, had looked genuinely distressed and expressed a fervent hope that the late Mr. Quiffen's fellow boarders would be able to avoid any personal contact with the press. Mariposa and Charles applauded the feelings of this true gentlewoman and Sarah again felt a private surge of gratitude at having Mrs. Sorpende to set an example for the others.

Having wadded up the papers and thrown them away and dealt with the importunate Mr. Quiffen, Jr., she turned her attention to more pressing matters. She was cleaning an upstairs bathroom when Charles ascended the stairs three at a time without losing a jot of his Hudsonian aplomb to announce that Mr. Protheroe was on his way, that a cousin of the late Mr. Quiffen had already joined the nephew in the library, and that the new arrival had his attorney with him.

"Oh, gosh," said Sarah, that having been the strongest oath she'd been allowed to utter during her carefully guarded childhood. "Maybe I'd better call up the troops, myself."

She ran over her short list of possibles. Uncle Jem would come like a shot, but he'd be of no use in a situation like this. He and old George would get off in a corner with her only bottle of whiskey and swap reminiscences of bears and bares while the battle raged about them as it was shaping up to do.

She might get somebody from her own lawyer's office, although she'd have a problem persuading any of the Messrs. Redfern to drop his writs and rush over here at a moment's notice. She'd also get stuck for a fee and her financial position was sticky enough already. It would have to be Dolph. Her cousin might be a bit slow on the uptake sometimes, but when it came to a case of bellow and bluster, she'd back him against any Quiffen alive. Sarah leaped to the phone and sounded the alarm.

After delivering himself of the anticipated remarks about having told her from the first that this scheme of hers was totally insane and did she have to keep dragging the family name into the papers, Dolph said he'd be right over and was. He even took a taxi. Altogether it was quite an assemblage that greeted George Protheroe when he arrived, blinking like the dormouse that had been dragged out of the teapot, and being bullied along by his wife. Sarah took Anora off to meet her household staff, leaving the men to fight it out among them with Dolph yelling louder than all the rest as she'd been proudly confident he could.

Anora and Mariposa were buddies from the moment they met. The three women were drinking tea and holding a strategy session on household matters at the kitchen table when Charles came in to inform them that the gentlemen, which his tone implied was rather a loose term for some of them though it wasn't his place to say so flat out, had taken an inventory of the possessions in the late Mr. Quiffen's room. Charles had taken it upon himself to point out that several of the inventoried articles belonged in fact to Mrs. Kelling and Mr. Adolphus Kelling had personally deleted those items from the inventory list.

It had been ascertained from Mr. Quiffen's files that his will was in the hands of either Mr. Snodgrass, Mr. Winkle, Mr. Tupper, or Ms. Pickwick of the firm bearing that name in Devonshire Street and the gentlemen were about to hie themselves thither. Mr. Protheroe was desirous of ascertaining the whereabouts of Mrs. Protheroe since he assumed she would wish to accompany the party, and what message should be conveyed to him?

"My God," said Anora, "is he always like this?"

"You better believe he isn't," giggled Mariposa.

Anora said she was too old not to believe anything, gave them all her blessing, and waddled after her husband. Sarah went back upstairs and cleaned another bathroom. Now, please God, they'd have a little peace around here.

Chapter 5

Sarah was scrubbing potatoes for dinner and wondering how soon she could decently let Mr. Hartler know she had the vacancy he was waiting for when Charles came into the kitchen.

"A person wishes to see you, madam," he announced.

"A person?" Sarah put down the potato she was washing and dried her hands on a dish towel. "What kind of person? Male or female?"

"I am unable to state, madam. The person is wearing a great many concealing garments and also carrying two decrepit paper shopping bags stuffed with trash."

"What for?"

"I have no idea, madam. I have instructed the person to wait in the vestibule while I ascertain whether you are at home."

"Why not in the front hall or the library?"

"This does not appear to be the sort of person one would wish to admit inside the house, madam."

"Oh, come off it, Charles! Neither was that last lot of Quiffens. Are you trying to tell me this is one of those poor old souls who go around fishing through the trash bins on the Common?"

"The person would appear to fall into that category, madam."

"Did this person say what the person wants with me?"

"The person claims to have information of interest to you."

"I can't imagine what it might be, but I suppose I'd better come. Leave the paper bags in the vestibule and bring the person into the front hall. As soon as I get the potatoes cooking I'll find out what the person wants. Most likely a handout."

Sarah hustled the potatoes into the oven, took off her apron, and went to meet this enigmatic person. When she caught sight of the visitor perched on the tip-edge of a hall chair, she understood Charles's unwonted confusion about sex. Her uninvited caller was bundled into such an assortment of outerwear, including khaki army pants, rubber boots, a sailor's peacoat, and a knitted balaclava helmet that not enough of the presumed human being inside was visible to afford a clue. However, if this was one of those pathetic derelicts who wander the streets and sleep in doorways, its standard of dereliction must be remarkably high. The coat was threadbare but not unclean and had all its buttons firmly sewn on. The pants showed signs of having been pressed in the not too distant past. The navy blue balaclava was expertly darned in wool that almost matched, and the boots were wiped free of slush.

"Good afternoon," she said to the helmet. "I am Mrs. Kelling. I understand you have something to tell me?"

A hand in a much-mended cotton glove pulled the knitted mask away from the mouth, revealing a somewhat wrinkled but well-washed and by no means unattractive woman's face. "How do you do, Mrs. Kelling. I'm Mary Smith. Miss Mary Smith, I suppose I should say. I didn't give my name to your man there because he'd have thought it was an alias, which it isn't. My dad was a Smith and my mother a Mary and I can show you my birth certificate with more years on it than I care to count. You must think I'm a real crackpot butting in on you like this, but I've got to find somebody who'll listen to me and you're the only one I haven't tried. You see, I was there. I saw it happen."

"Saw what happen, Miss Smith?"

"The murder."

"Oh, dear!" Sarah repressed a moan. Ever since the remains of a long-vanished ecdysiast had turned up in the family vault on the eve of Great-uncle Frederick's burial, she'd been pestered by a wide assortment of cranks. She'd hoped she'd seen the last of them, but evidently she hadn't. Yet Miss Mary Smith, in spite of her ragpicker's getup, didn't look like a crank.

"Yes, it was the worst thing that ever happened to me," the woman agreed, evidently thinking Sarah was offering sympathy. "I still get the shivers every time I think of it. I was on my way home with my day's gleanings. Since my retirement I've developed sort of a hobby, as you might say, collecting papers and cans to recycle. I can't take glass because it's too heavy to carry. Helps the ecology a little, or so I like to think, and gives me something to do. But I'm not here to talk about that."

"Please, won't you take off your things and come into the library?" Sarah still wasn't sure whether Miss Mary Smith was a nut, a reporter in disguise, or the perfectly sane elderly woman she appeared to be, but she thought she'd better find out.

"I don't want to impose on your good nature." Nevertheless, Miss Smith rolled up her helmet into a neat cap and began struggling with the toggles of her peacoat. "I will just slip off this jacket, though, if you don't mind. Otherwise I won't feel the good of it when I go out. I never used to mind the cold, but now it seems to go right through me. That's why I bundle up in any old thing I can lay my hands on. Anyway, if I'm going to be a ragpicker I might as well look the part, eh?"

"Here, let me help you." Sarah managed to extricate Miss Smith from the top layers and led her into the library, where Charles had already lit the fire and laid out biscuits and sherry for the evening gathering.

"What a lovely room!" Miss Smith arranged her dilapidations in a thoroughly feminine manner and took the glass of sherry Sarah poured out for her. "Thank you, Mrs. Kelling. I certainly didn't expect such royal treatment after the brushoff I've been getting from everybody else. Of course I ought to have known better than to rush up to that policeman the way I did, dressed like a tramp with two big bags of garbage in my hands, but that's me all over. I never think how I look till it's one step too late."

"My whole family are the same way," Sarah agreed, "and they never give a hoot, so why should you? But do please tell me—"

"Why I barged in on you like this?" The sherry was giving Miss Smith more self-assurance. "It's going to sound foolish, but just a little while ago, I picked a paper out of a litter basket. There was your name and picture staring right out at me, and it said where you lived and everything. It struck me all of a heap, like an omen or whatever you want to call it. So being, as I said, the kind who leaps before she looks, I picked up my junk and waltzed myself on over here. I'm sure that man of yours didn't want to let me in and I must say I can't blame him. But I do think a citizen has to take some responsibility, don't you?"

"Of course," said Sarah, still nonplused.

"Well, there you are, then. I wasn't about to let anybody get away with a horrible thing like that, but the policeman just brushed me off and the reporters thought I was looking for an easy buck and told me to go home and sleep it off as if I were some old drunk, which I wouldn't be even if I could afford to which I certainly can't. Though this sherry is a real treat," she added politely.

"Anyway, being a senior citizen, I get to ride the T on the cheap fare, so I was down there on the platform waiting for my train. It's good pickings around Haymarket, you know, on account of the tourists and all. Some of them slip me a quarter now and then, and if you think I'm too proud to take it, you can think again. I can't afford that sort of nonsense anymore.

"But as I started to say, I was standing beside the track and this stout elderly man in a dark blue overcoat was standing next to me. He gave me a nasty look and edged back as if he was afraid I had lice or something, which I don't in case you're wondering. Of course I couldn't help noticing. I may have had to shed my pride since I started trying to live on Social Security but I've still got my feelings. Then the train came along and everybody started shuffling forward, you know how they do. The station was mobbed, as you'd naturally expect at that hour. So anyway I was still turned toward this fat man in the overcoat, giving him a look as much as to say I'm as good as you are, you old goat, because I don't care to be treated like dirt under somebody's feet. And I distinctly saw a pair of hands come out of the crowd and shove that man down on the track, right in front of the train."

"Oh no!" cried Sarah. "You couldn't."

"There," said Miss Smith. "I didn't expect you'd believe me any more than the rest. But I'm telling you, Mrs. Kelling, I had my eye right on this Mr. Quiffen and I know he was the one because they had pictures of him in both the *Globe* and the *Herald* and I tore them out and I've got them right here in my coat pocket. I never carry a purse because it's an invitation to be mugged, even an old derelict like me. And I have very good eyesight for my age and that's not the sort of thing a person could forget. And I tried to tell the starter and I tried to tell the conductor and I—but I've been through all that, so now I've said my piece I'll go away and not pester you again. And thank you for at least not laughing in my face."

"But I'm not laughing at all," said Sarah. "The awful part of it is, I can believe you because I know how obnoxious Mr. Quiffen could be. He had a natural gift for making enemies. I know of only two people in the world who had a good word for him and they're such old sweeties they'd like anybody."

Miss Smith nodded. "That doesn't surprise me. He was always writing the nastiest letters to the papers, mostly about dumb little mistakes anybody could make. I'd read them and think how somebody was going to get in trouble with the boss over that letter, and wonder if this Barnwell Augustus Quiffen had the faintest idea what he might be doing to some poor slob with six kids to support."

"I'm sure he neither knew nor cared. If I'd realized what he was like, I'd never have let myself be talked into taking him on as a boarder. But please don't broadcast that, Miss Smith. I haven't said that to anyone else, and I shouldn't have said it to you."

"Don't fret yourself," the woman replied. "I have nobody left to tell. I don't visit my old neighbors anymore because I wouldn't want them seeing what I've come down to and thinking I was after a handout, and anybody who knows me well enough to say hello to now thinks I'm just another harmless nut. Then you do think Mr. Quiffen might have pestered somebody into doing something desperate to get rid of him?"

"I don't know that I think so. I simply can't say it's impossible. You didn't happen to catch a glimpse of the person you say pushed him?"

"All I can swear to is a pair of dark leather gloves and the cuffs of a dark overcoat. That's not much to go on, because no doubt half the men in the crowd were wearing leather gloves and dark coats. I'm not even sure it was a man, though the gloves and coat seemed more like a man's than a woman's. I may have jumped to the conclusion that it must be, I suppose, because men are more apt to be violent than women. But there was so much confusion and milling around, and I was right next to him and I was scared I'd get pushed under the train, too, and I was trying to get back and people were pressing me forward. It was such an awful moment I couldn't think straight, or I might have had sense enough to try for a better look."

"How could you have? It must have been utterly terrifying."

"Well, I hope I never have to go through another one like that," Miss Smith agreed. "And it was no accident, Mrs. Kelling, and I'm sure he never did it on purpose, either, no matter what the papers say. I mean, here's this pompous old prune, which is a fine way to speak of the dead and it's as well my poor mother isn't alive to hear me, but that's what he was. And he wasn't thinking about anything except keeping his distance from me so I wouldn't contaminate his nice overcoat. And mind you, he wasn't moving forward, he was stepping back. And I saw what I saw and I'd swear to it on a stack of Bibles, no matter what anybody says."

Miss Smith drank off the last of her sherry and set down the glass. "And now I must go along, and thank you very kindly."

"No," said Sarah. "I can't simply let you go like this, after what you've told me. First, you've got to promise that you won't make any further attempt to tell anybody else this story. If someone did in fact push Mr. Quiffen under that train and you're the only person who's willing to come forward and say so, then don't you see that you constitute a threat to the murderer?"

"Why, I—"

"You say you didn't see the face, but how can he be sure of that? How can you, for that matter? You might remember more than the gloves and the coat sleeves once you've got over your shock and had a chance to think about it. You've already called attention to yourself by trying to tell somebody in authority what you saw. I hope you realize that being brushed off as a crank was the luckiest thing that could have happened to you. If your name had appeared in the papers along with mine, you mightn't have stayed alive long enough to come here this afternoon."

Miss Smith laughed incredulously. "You make me sound pretty important."

"You are important. Decent citizens who have the courage to act on their convictions are always important.

Miss Smith, you must listen to me. You may think I'm trying to shut you up because I don't want the story to get around that one of my lodgers has been murdered, but believe me, I'm not. If this boardinghouse business flops, I stand to lose my property, but I could live with that. What I could not bear is the thought that I'd sent you out into the dark and got you killed."

"Mrs. Kelling!"

"I'm speaking from experience. Give me your address so that we can keep in touch. I'll let you know anything I can find out, but I most earnestly beg you, for your own protection, to keep acting like a harmless crank and trust me to handle the matter from now on. Will you promise?"

"I might as well, I guess. At least you stand a chance of getting somebody to pay attention, which is more than I do. Look, have you got a back door I can sneak out by? I don't want to embarrass you by running into one of your other boarders."

"You wouldn't embarrass me, but there's always the nasty little odd chance one of them might recognize you and guess what you're doing here. I'll call you a taxi."

"No, don't do that. I live over in the project. If anybody around there saw me coming home in a cab, they'd think I must have money hidden in my room. Let me go on the subway same as I always do."

"All right, if you must, but you're not going alone. I can't go with you myself right now because I have to cook dinner, but you must wait till I see what I can arrange."

Sarah touched the bell and Charles came running.

"Charles, fetch Miss Smith's parcels from the vestibule and her wraps from the closet, and show her down to the back door. She is doing valuable secret research for the Ecological Commission and we mustn't let anybody know she was here. I'm sure I needn't explain, Miss Smith, that you can rely absolutely on the discretion of my staff. You'd better wait inside until your escort arrives. We sometimes have prowlers in the alley, I'm sorry to say, and Charles's duties will keep him upstairs. I'll try not to keep you too long, but I beg you to be patient."

Charles couldn't resist this appeal to his sense of drama. He led Miss Smith and her bags of ecological research down the back hall in furtive majesty. Now Sarah's problem was to find the woman an escort.

Cousin Dolph had already done his good deed for the

day. Anyway, Sarah couldn't see him tootling out to the
project with a woman who looked like a walking ragbag.
Uncle Jem couldn't go because he was already booked to
show up for dinner and keep the boarders' minds off Mr.
Quiffen. He was no doubt getting decked out in his antique soup-and-fish right now, thinking up a few more
picturesque skeletons to hang on the family tree and
warming his vocal cords with a couple of quick martinis,
knowing he'd get no cocktails from his impecunious niece.

Egbert might possibly be persuaded, but Jem's valet
was getting on in years himself, and had enough to cope
with as it was, riding herd on his wayward employer. Mr.
Lomax would be just the person, but he was an hour's
drive away at Ireson's Landing. Miss Smith couldn't be
left dithering in the alleyway door all evening. There was
only one person Sarah could think of who might realistically be asked to perform such an errand.

If only he wasn't in Hong Kong or Uxbridge or some
other outlandish place! No, he was at home. Sarah could
have cried with relief when she heard his voice on the
phone.

"Mrs. Kelling! I've just been—"

"I know, reading about me in the papers. I'm terribly
sorry to bother you again, Mr. Bittersohn, but I'm in a
desperate rush to find somebody willing to escort an elderly lady wearing six sweaters and a balaclava helmet
home to a very tough neighborhood without getting her
killed on the way. I don't suppose you could possibly—"

"Where is she?"

"Right now she's waiting down at the alley door. You
remember, the one you were guarding that night when
Great-uncle Nathan's campaign chair collapsed under
you?"

"I have tender memories of that occasion. Will you be
with her?"

"I doubt it. I have to cook dinner for my boarders. But
I'll nip down and tell her you're coming. Would you mind
giving her your name and telling her Sarah Kelling sent
you? If you'll come to lunch with me tomorrow, I'll be
glad to explain what it's about. Mariposa has the day off
and Charles will be working so I'll be able to talk freely.
Charles thinks she's a spy for the Ecological Commission,
by the way, so if you run into him, please don't disillusion
him."

"I wouldn't dream of it. Who's Charles?"

"Charles C. Charles, my butler. That is, he's—oh, I'll have to explain when I see you. You will come?"

"I'm on my way."

The line went dead, and Sarah hung up, not without a twinge of regret. It had been rather pleasant talking to Mr. Bittersohn again, even under such circumstances as these. But what other sort of circumstance did she exist in lately? She did wish she could at least wait with Miss Smith until he came, but she was already late with her dinner.

Sarah did take a moment to run down to the shabby, ill-lit back entry with a hastily collected plate of hors d'oeuvres and tell her strange guest, "Mr. Max Bittersohn, a very kind, trustworthy man, is coming to take you home. He'll give you his name and say Sarah Kelling sent him. Don't go with anybody else. Here's something to nibble on while you're waiting. I'm sorry to leave you, but something's boiling over on the stove."

"Think nothing of it. What'll I do with the plate?"

"Leave it on the chair."

Sarah was already halfway up the stairs as she spoke, for the cooking was indeed in a perilous state and her food budget too tightly calculated to allow for calamities. Alexander would be proud of the way she was managing. Darling Alexander! Why was she thinking of him at this hectic moment? Was it because she felt the tiniest bit disloyal at being so glad Mr. Bittersohn was again coming to the rescue?

Chapter 6

"Mr. Bittersohn, how very nice to see you again."

Sarah's greeting was conventional enough, but her voice held a degree of warmth that Cousin Mabel would undoubtedly consider excessive. As Cousin Dolph had remarked, who gave a damn about Mabel anyway? Furthermore, Mabel wasn't here. It occurred to Sarah that she'd made rather a point of telling her guest that nobody else would be, either. Her cheeks were pinker than they'd been for weeks as she shook his warm, square hand.

"I've been meaning to drop you a note of thanks for all you did—"

"After you solved my case for me?" His smile was as attractive as she'd remembered it, not the teeth-showing kind but an amused curve of unusually well-shaped lips. Mr. Bittersohn was not so handsome as the late Alexander Kelling, no man could be that, but his somewhat rugged features were still pleasant to look at. Sarah noticed with inward amusement that his exuberant waves of dark brown hair were springing up again where he'd tried to slick them down, and she still couldn't make up her mind whether his eyes were gray or blue.

"I did no such thing," she protested. "Here, come into the library and let me give you a drink. I never dare bring out the whiskey when my boarders are around for fear they'll all want some. Like the gentleman dining at Crewe who found a large mouse in his stew."

She was babbling and she knew it, but what did one say to a man who'd saved one's life and gotten his reward by being asked at a moment's notice to escort Miss Mary

46

Smith and her shopping bags back to the project? "You like scotch with a twist and lots of ice, don't you?"

"Great." He didn't seem to know what to say, either.

"My Uncle Jem taught me to bartend when I was six, so I'm quite good at it. How's that?"

Bittersohn took a sip. "Perfect. Aren't you going to join me?"

"I certainly am."

Sarah poured herself a smaller drink, and added water. "You know, when Miss Smith told me yesterday about what happened, I was so taken aback that I don't think it sank in properly. Then I had dinner to cope with, and Uncle Jem joined us and stayed and stayed as he always does once he gets over the agony of pulling himself together to come. Naturally everybody was egging him on because he really is a marvelous storyteller in a highly censorable sort of way, so it was awfully late by the time I got to bed and I went right to sleep. This morning of course there was breakfast to fix so I honestly hadn't time to think about what she said till a little while ago. Do you think she could possibly be telling the truth?"

"I might if I knew what you're talking about."

"But didn't she tell you?"

"Miss Smith told me a good deal about her one-woman save-the-environment plan but I don't suppose that's what you're referring to. She did mention something when we got to that dump she lives in about being glad I was with her and not having realized what she might be letting herself in for till Mrs. Kelling pointed it out to her, but Mrs. Kelling told her not to say anything to anybody else so she wasn't about to."

"But I didn't mean you. Here, have one of these cheese things while they're hot. I appear to be in my accustomed state of utter confusion. I expect I ought to start at the beginning, which is the financial mess you know all about. Probably you weren't surprised to read in the paper that I'd turned this place into a boardinghouse. I couldn't think of any other way to keep afloat till this business with the High Street Bank gets settled, if it ever does. I couldn't bear to knuckle under without putting up any kind of struggle, and keeping up appearances on a shoestring is all I'm trained to do."

"I thought you were a commercial artist."

"Well, yes, I suppose I am but I've never made any

real money at it. I do intend to look for work, but so far I haven't had time to get a portfolio together. I'm always having to rush off and call the plumber or whatever just as I think I'm going to start."

"Don't you have any help in the house?"

"Oh yes, I've been awfully lucky there. Mariposa, that darling woman who used to clean for us, has come to stay."

"The one with the dog and the boy friend?"

"You remembered! The dog has gone to live with her brother in the country, I'm happy to say. Rover was the sort that needs lots of roving space. The boy friend is still with us. He's the Charles I mentioned on the phone. Charles is really an actor but he's resting, as they say, so he's keeping his hand in by doing a superb impersonation of a butler. I don't even have to pay him, except room and board, because he also has a job on some assembly line attaching gadgets to widgets. I must say I dread the day when Charles's agent finds him another role. Can I fix your drink?"

"I'm fine for the moment, thanks. So where does Miss Smith come in?"

"She showed up out of the blue yesterday about tea-time. Tell me, Mr. Bittersohn, what was your general impression of her? I know one might assume at first glance that she must have a bat or two loose in the belfry, but do you honestly think she does?"

"A crowded subway train isn't the best place to judge," he replied, "but my off-the-cuff impression is that Miss Smith is a gallant old sport trying to make the best of a lousy deal. She told me she worked all her life for one of those upper-crust department stores that have been driven out of business by inflation and the big chains. They paid peanuts and she had an invalid mother to support, so she never got a chance to put much away. By the time her job folded she was too old to get another, and the Social Security check that was supposed to take care of her declining years doesn't stretch beyond a ten-by-ten room in a fleabag and a can of sardines once a week."

"Then how on earth does she live?"

"Makes a game of survival. Collects newspapers out of trash cans and reads up on who's doling out free meals to senior citizens. Then she peddles the papers to a junk-man for carfare to get to the grub. She told me she has some very nice clothes she wears when she goes out in company; I'd just happened to catch her when she wasn't dressed up. And she insisted on paying her own dime for the subway. I was tempted to ask her out to dinner and a show, but I thought I'd better not try to get fresh on such short acquaintance. Miss Smith looks as if she might be a stickler for the proprieties."

"Don't you believe it," said Sarah. "She'd have taken you on like a shot. She told me she'd got beyond any nonsense about false pride. So have I, that's why I was so brazen about hurling you into the breach. There simply wasn't anybody else, and I didn't dare let her go off alone. I think she's perfectly sane, too, so when she told me her story I couldn't take the risk of not believing her."

Sarah drank a little of her scotch. "I'm sorry. I thought I'd be able to talk about this easily enough, but it's—I'm just so sick and tired of horrors!"

"That's okay, Mrs. Kelling. Take your time. Maybe I can guess. Putting the newspapers and the subway together, would I be correct in assuming that Miss Smith's story had something to do with this Mr. Quiffen who boarded with you and fell under the train yesterday?"

"Have you ever been wrong? Miss Smith's story is that she and Mr. Quiffen were standing next to each other at the front of the platform. They were more or less exchanging glares because he didn't like being near someone who—well, you saw her last night—and she didn't take kindly to being regarded as a walking pestilence. Would you?"

"Was he that sort?"

"Oh yes, very much so. I got him foisted on me by some old friends who thought they were doing me a big favor, but I realized he was a mistake from the beginning. If he couldn't find an excuse to be nasty, he'd go looking for one. If I'd had him on my back for another week or so, I daresay I might have been tempted to do what— what Miss Smith claims she saw somebody else do."

"Shove him under the train?"

"So she says. She insists she distinctly saw two hands wearing brown leather gloves reach out from the crowd and deliberately push him onto the track at the moment the train came out of the tunnel."

"Is that all she saw, just the hands?"

"That and an impression of dark coat sleeves. Of

course the train wouldn't have been able to stop the instant it hit him, and she was right next to it with everyone milling and shoving. She was afraid she'd be pushed under the wheels herself. You know what it's like in the rush hours. I expect whoever did it just stepped back and got lost in the crowd."

"Or turned to the guy behind him and yelled, 'Quit shoving,' so that in case anybody else happened to be looking he could claim it wasn't his fault. It's unlikely anyone would have paid any attention. People are concentrating on the train, or maybe guarding their handbags and wallets for fear of getting their pockets picked, or trying to keep their bundles and briefcases from getting knocked out of their hands. It's not a bad way to get rid of somebody if you have the nerve. You'd simply give him the push, let the crowd close in around you, step back and get on the first train going in the opposite direction, and be away before anybody realized what was happening. Did Miss Smith report what she saw?"

"She tried hard enough. I gather she must have made quite a scene. She claims she told the starter, the conductor, the police, and even some reporters, but none of them would pay attention to her. That's why she eventually came to me. She happened to pick up a newspaper that had one of those 'Tulip Street Curse Strikes Again' stories with my name and photograph. She took it for divine guidance or something and beetled straight on over here, shopping bags and all. It was a dreadfully reckless thing to do, and naturally I was terrified for her after what happened that other time."

"You know that wasn't your fault."

"I know it wasn't, but I can't help feeling it was. Anyway, Miss Smith was totally oblivious of the fact that she's a noticeable sort of person with her shopping bags and all those ragged clothes peeking out from under one another. And Mr. Quiffen's heirs, or what I presume are his heirs, had been here earlier like wolves on the fold, and my boarders were due in for dinner. I had to get her out of here and I couldn't think what else to do, so I called you. After this episode I daresay you'll be having your telephone number changed."

Bittersohn smiled again. "Don't bet on it. Let me ask you an embarrassing question. Did you want to keep your boarders from seeing Miss Smith because she looked so crummy or because you were afraid one of them might recognize her as having been the witness who made the fuss? I take it you're ready to believe Miss Smith's story yourself."

"I have to, don't I? As to the boarders, I couldn't have cared less about how she looked. I could always have introduced her as one of my rich relatives. I was only concerned that one of them might recognize her as the person who'd tried to be a witness."

"Anyone in particular?"

"No, but you see, I don't know them. They all came with recommendations of one sort or another, and we had preliminary interviews and all that, but what does that prove? I haven't seen enough of them yet to form any valid opinions about what they might or might not be capable of, and Mr. Quiffen had got everybody's back up at one time or another. We haven't actually been pelting each other with mashed potatoes at the table, but that's mainly because Charles and I and Mrs. Sorpende, who's a darling woman, have been ganging up on him whenever he threatened to become totally unbearable. What sort of relationship he might have had with any of them outside the house, of course, I have no idea and couldn't very well ask."

"You say his heirs were here. Did he leave a lot of money?"

"I think he must have, from what my friends told me. I can find out exactly how much and how it was left if you want, because George Protheroe is an executor. It was George's wife Anora who sicked Mr. Quiffen on me in the first place. She told me to soak him plenty since he could well afford it, and she added that he'd make sure I earned it, which was the truth, goodness knows. I called her last night because I didn't know how else to get in touch with his people. They were all here this morning, including the nephew and a cousin ready to cart off whatever they could get their hands on. Luckily, Anora had warned me to lock his door and keep it locked till George arrived."

"Did she?"

"Yes, and if you're thinking what I think you're thinking, you might as well forget it. The Protheroes don't need to steal from anybody. Furthermore, when I saw what a delegation I was collecting, I decided I'd better have a representative of my own present, so I called my Cousin Dolph. They went charging through that door in one seething mass, so I can't see how one of them could have pocketed anything of Mr. Quiffen's without getting jumped by the rest. Shall we go in to lunch?"

"In the kitchen?"

"No, the dining room." Sarah recalled that the last meal she'd cooked for Mr. Bittersohn had been breakfast, and that he liked his eggs the consistency of old leather. That was one small part of her adventures she'd never mentioned, even to Aunt Emma.

"We're very high-toned these days," she went on with a self-conscious attempt at airiness. "I'm sorry we can't give you the full treatment, with Mariposa buttering your buns for you and Charles being grand in his butler suit, but perhaps you can come to dinner one night soon. Please help yourself to the salad, as the footman happens to be off today. I hope you like chicken."

"My mother should hear you ask that. She's one of the old chicken soup crowd."

"That's true, it's supposed to be a cure for all ills, isn't it? I'd better make some, and keep my remaining boarders healthy."

"Tell me about them."

Sarah was surprised to realize how little she had to tell. "Well, there's Jennifer LaValliere. She's the young granddaughter of a woman who lives here on the Hill, and she's going to Katherine Gibbs. At least I presume she is, because she brings home a textbook now and then. And a Mr. Porter-Smith, who does something or other in an accounting firm that one of my third cousins has an interest in."

"What's the name of the firm?"

"Come to think of it, I don't know. Kelling and somebody or other, I suppose."

"How old is this Porter-Smith?"

"Getting on for thirty, I should say."

"Oh?" said Bittersohn in what struck Sarah as a rather deliberately noncommittal way. "Good-looking guy?"

She shrugged. "So-so. He's rather alarmingly well dressed but pleasant enough in a chatty sort of way. Anyway, I knew Percy wouldn't send anybody who's fiscally irresponsible and that's my chief concern right now. Then I have Professor Ormsby, who teaches aerodynamics at

MIT and a charming lady named Mrs. Theonia Sorpende, whom I think I mentioned before. She and Professor Ormsby are both on the middle-aged side and he appears to be quite struck with her. Mrs. Sorpende's what my Uncle Jem calls a fine figure of a woman."

"Where did you collect her?"

"She found out about me from some friend of Aunt Caroline's sister Marguerite, so she called and asked if she could come and see the room. And she was such a delightful change from most of the others I'd been seeing, and she liked the house and didn't mind the stairs, so I took her on."

"Without checking her references?"

"Well, actually, no. I just grabbed her before she could change her mind. Mrs. Sorpende's a widow with no children."

"How do you know?"

"She told me so. Otherwise she doesn't talk much about herself."

"Doesn't she?" For some reason Bittersohn didn't look altogether happy. Perhaps the chicken wasn't up to his mother's standard.

Chapter 7

Sarah's guest ate for a moment in silence. Then he asked, "How did your boarders react to Quiffen's death?"

"They made the right noises when they heard the news, all except Professor Ormsby, who seldom says much of anything, but nobody acted particularly shattered. To be quite frank with you, I think we were all a little bit relieved to be rid of him, in spite of the shocking way he went. And right now, much as I'm upset about what Miss Smith told me, I'm wondering how soon I can decently rent his room again, because I'm so desperately hard-up for the money. What do you think, Mr. Bittersohn?"

He shrugged. "How soon could you find another tenant?"

"Oh, I have one already. He's quite an old man, like Mr. Quiffen, but much pleasanter. Oddly enough I got him through Aunt Marguerite, too. He was bitterly disappointed when he found I didn't have a place for him because the drawing room is exactly what he wanted. It has its own bath and it's on the first floor. He's not supposed to climb stairs, you see, and he wants to be back on the Hill. I believe he and his sister used to live around here somewhere before they moved to Newport. Then they decided they wanted to come back here, but she was invited to visit an old friend in Italy for the winter so they broke up their other place and put everything in storage. He's tried a hotel and the regular sort of rooming house and hates them both. I told him I'd let him know when a vacancy came up because I already had a hunch Mr. Quiffen and I were going to part company before long. But of course I never dreamed it would happen like this."

"What's this other man's name?"

"Hartler. William Hartler. You may possibly know him, since he's more or less in your field."

"Is he? I don't think I've ever heard of him."

"Well, actually he's not a professional like you. He's simply trying to track down some things for the Friends of the Iolani Palace."

"The Hawaiian royal treasures? They've got some very good people working on that project. This chicken is excellent, by the way. Ever see the Iolani Palace yourself?"

"No, I've never been to Honolulu. Or anywhere else, for that matter. My father always took the 'Why should we travel? We're already here' line, and Alexander and I never could afford to travel even if we'd been able to leave Aunt Caroline. You've been there, I suppose?"

"Once, on business. I was tracking a guy who'd stolen a nice Degas from some people in Brookline. Also a Puvis de Chavannes, though why they wanted that one back is beyond me." Bittersohn was a one-man detective agency specializing in the recovery of stolen art objects and jewelry, either for the desolated owners or for insurance companies that suspected the desolated owners might have arranged their own burglaries in order to collect on the policies.

"How did the palace come into it?"

"Oh, that was a stroke of luck. When the guy found out I was on his tail, he panicked and tried to get rid of the paintings by peddling them to the curator, making believe King Kalakaua had presented them to a great-aunt of his. Unluckily for him, the curator's an acquaintance of mine and knew what I was there for. Also, the Degas happened to be a late one, painted in 1899. Kalakaua died in 1891 and his sister Liliuokalani, who succeeded him, reigned for only three years, until the revolution of 1893."

"What a lot you have to know!"

"Knowing is what I get paid for. Want to come to the art museum with me sometime? I could bore you stiff with my profound erudition."

"I'm sure you wouldn't," said Sarah, and, for some reason, blushed. "But imagine anyone's getting a Degas

and a Puvis de Chavannes for a present. Did King
Kalakaua actually do things like that?"

"Oh yes, he was no piker. I wish you could see that
palace. It has a hundred and four rooms."

"So Mr. Hartler was telling me. He's promised to show
me photographs, though I hope not of all the hundred
and four. He seems tremendously caught up with this
project. That's the main reason he wanted to come back
to Boston, where he thought the pickings would be better.
You know, I expect, that Queen Liliuokalani married
into a Boston family. Mr. Hartler claims to be connected
with the Dominises through his mother, though he didn't
explain how. Anyway, when she was still a princess,
Liliuokalani and Queen Kapiolani, who was Kalakaua's
wife, visited Boston. That was in 1887, when they were
on their way to Queen Victoria's Golden Jubilee. Everybody wanted to entertain them and they gave the most
marvelous presents in return. When I told Mr. Hartler
they'd actually been to tea in the very room he could have
had if Mr. Quiffen hadn't already taken it, I thought he
was going to break down and cry."

"Maybe we'd better find out where this Hartler was
when Quiffen got the push," said Bittersohn, only half
joking.

Sarah laid down her fork. "You certainly know how to
brighten one's day, don't you? It can't possibly have been
Mr. Hartler. He wouldn't have been able to climb down
the stairs, for one thing, and he's much too old."

"How old?"

"Older than Mr. Quiffen, anyway, from the look of
him, and a good deal frailer. He walks with a cane. Mr.
Quiffen was stout and strutting and had this Horatius-at-
the-bridge way of planting his feet. It must have taken a
fairly hefty push to knock him flat. Still, I suppose one
shouldn't take anything for granted."

"Well, don't worry till you know you have something
to worry about. I know somebody who's been involved
in the palace restoration. He's out of town just now, but
I'll have a talk with him as soon as we can connect, and
see what he knows about Hartler. In the meantime, you
might as well go ahead with whatever plans you want to
make. No doubt Hartler will be panting on your doorstep pretty soon anyway. He reads the papers, too, I ex-

pect. You don't happen to own any of those royal treasures yourself, by chance?"

"Which Mr. Hartler wants to steal as soon as he moves in? I wish I did. I'd sell them like a shot. We did have a gorgeous peacock feather fan with the Hawaiian coat of arms on a silver plaque in the center, but when the Iolani Palace people started canvassing Boston families for donations, Alexander thought we ought to give it to them, so we did. I don't suppose the fan was worth much compared to most of the other things. King Kalakaua is supposed to have spent a hundred thousand dollars on furnishings alone, and of course that was an enormous sum in those days. Then there was all that royal family jewelry that had been handed down from one generation to another, and a staggering amount of other stuff."

"I know, and much of it auctioned off for peanuts after the revolution," said Bittersohn.

"Yes, and all us Yankee horse traders right in there bidding our heads off," Sarah added. "I shouldn't be surprised if some of the Kelling jewels came from there, but we'll never know now. At least I have Granny Kay's bluebird, thanks to you."

She touched the exquisite enameled brooch with the ruby eye and the one magnificent baroque pearl dangling from its beak that was all Bittersohn had managed to salvage for her out of the once-fabulous collection.

"And I do have a photograph of the fan. Alexander took it before we sent the fan off, because he thought we should keep some sort of record in the family. I can show you that if you like. Or are you like my Uncle Jem? He says he only likes pictures of fans if they have fan dancers behind them. Mr. Bittersohn, what am I going to do about Miss Mary Smith?"

"The best thing you can do for that woman is to stay as far away from her as possible and concentrate on running your boardinghouse. Officially, you know nothing about Mr. Quiffen's death except what everybody else knows. He was just somebody who rented a room from you and met with an unfortunate accident. You take it for granted you're entitled to rent the room again as soon as his things have been removed. How far in advance did he pay his rent?"

"Only through the end of this week."

"Then there's your answer, right? Tell this Mr. Hartler

he can move in Monday, or whatever day is convenient for you. The longer the room stands empty, the more likely he is to have found another place and the harder time you may have filling it. By the way, you still haven't told me who's living in the basement. You've got those two rooms down there as I recall, plus the little one with the furnace and laundry business. Does the maid have one and the butler the other, or what?"

"At the moment, it's a case of 'or what,' " Sarah told him. "Mariposa and Charles share the old kitchen, which is the larger and looks out on the little back yard where they plan to make a garden next spring if we're all still here. I hope to rent the front room that used to be Edith's bedroom as soon as I can get it fixed up, but I'm in a quandary as to who'd take it. I don't much want students because as you must have gathered, this whole enterprise is based on snob appeal. I took a chance on Jennifer La-Valliere because she has family nearby and if they heard of any goings-on they'd ship her back to her parents in a hurry and she knows it. But if I got the sort who smoked pot and played disco records and whatnot, they'd blow the scene, as Charles might say in an unguarded moment. I've got to have somebody who's willing to go along with the stately home act, yet not mind having to use the cellar stairs and share a bath with a couple who are just good friends."

"Them wedding bells shall not ring out, eh?"

"Not according to Mariposa. She appears perfectly happy as she is. Anyway, she's not quite sure about her last two divorces. She's been getting them through some mail-order operation in Uruguay and it does sound a bit chancy, wouldn't you say?"

"I don't know that I'd say chancy." Bittersohn was eying the last mushroom on his plate. "It's a shame I have no snob appeal."

"Oh, but you have tons!" gasped Sarah. "Mr. Bittersohn, you—you wouldn't possibly consider—oh, dear, I know you already have a place and I'm being—pretend you didn't hear me. I'll get the dessert. Do you care for cheese with your apple pie?"

"Cheese costs money, doesn't it? You know, if you happened to be considering me as a prospective tenant, you could deduct the cost of this meal as a business expense."

"How could I ever think of you as a business expense? But as a tenant—Mr. Bittersohn, are you serious?"

"You need a tenant who's trained to keep a straight face under any and all conditions, right? And I need a place to hang out when I'm in town, don't I?"

"But you already have one."

"Wrong. I've had one. They're turning the building into condominiums and I either have to buy a scroungy apartment I have no desire whatever to own or get out by the first of the month. You wouldn't want to see me sitting in the middle of Bowdoin Street with all my worldly goods, namely two suitcases and a genuine hand-carved teakwood back-scratcher presented as a token of esteem by a grateful client, would you?"

"Of course not, but—I can't believe it!"

"So call up the real estate agents. I'll give you their number. They'd sell you my place this minute, if you don't mind paying an arm and a leg for two crummy rooms overlooking several acres of pigeon droppings. I may be homeless by the time I get back there, for all I know. Mrs. Kelling, I don't smoke, I don't shine my shoes on the bedspread because my mother brought me up right, I don't own any disco records and wouldn't play them if I did. I pay my rent a month in advance because I never know when or for how long I'll be called out of town, and whatever you charge couldn't be any worse than I'm getting stuck for now. I'd need to install a private phone, which of course I'd pay for myself. I sometimes have slightly weird visitors at odd hours, but I could make them come and go by the alley door in order not to tarnish your image. I'd as soon be in the basement because I'd probably feel more at home with the hired help than the paying guests. Do we have a deal or don't we?"

Sarah hesitated, then laughed. "Go give those sharks your notice and pack your back-scratcher. Your room will be ready for you by Monday morning."

Chapter 8

It took a good deal of doing, but by Monday morning, fresh white paint was dry on the walls of what had been part of Edith's lair for so many grievance-filled years. The room looked twice as big and bright as it ever had before. Sarah and Mr. Lomax had brought in the best of what they could glean from the now-depleted house at Ireson's Landing: a pine chest, a comfortable armchair and hassock, a couple of lamps, a sturdy table and ladderback chair that she hoped would be an adequate substitute for a desk. Mr. Bittersohn must have to do some kind of paperwork in that strange profession of his.

She'd splurged on a new mattress and box spring, got Mr. Lomax to screw wooden legs into the frame, then sat down at the old Singer and run up some bright red print pillow covers to make the bed look more like a studio couch and brighten the faded blue denim spread. She'd made little curtains to match the pillows, and put pots of nephthytis and sansevieria on the high, narrow, sidewalk-level windowsills, knowing nothing less hardy would survive there. Charles gave the worn old brick floor a good scrubbing and waxing, and Mariposa laundered the least faded rag rugs Sarah could find at Ireson's. By the time Sarah had everything in order, her two helpers were insisting this was the best-looking room in the house and they ought to charge more rent.

"Mr. Bittersohn is a very distinguished man in his profession," she replied primly. "We could hardly expect him to live in a dump."

"Classy guy, eh?"

"Very classy, but not a bit stuffy. You'll like having him here."

"You like him yourself?" Mariposa asked a shade too innocently.

"He saved my life not long ago, among other things. I owe him a debt of gratitude."

"We still collect the rent, though, don't we?" Mariposa took the family finances much to heart.

"Certainly we do. I'm not that grateful."

In fact, she was. However, Sarah had known by instinct that Mr. Bittersohn would have been horrified if she'd so much as hinted at his getting the place for nothing, though she knew people with far greater pretensions to gentility who'd have leaped at the chance. She'd compromised by naming a lower price than she'd meant to charge. Mr. Bittersohn had insisted it ought to be much higher, and named his own. At last they'd split the difference and come up with what Uncle Jem had set as a reasonable rate in the first place. Sarah had broken down and told him so, whereupon they'd laughed and parted with mutual satisfaction.

At least Sarah hoped the satisfaction was mutual. On her side there could be no question. The more she watched Professor Ormsby wolfing his food and listened to Mr. Porter-Smith enumerate the mountains he had climbed, the more impatient she became to have Mr. Bittersohn at her dinner table.

As for Mr. Hartler, he'd been on the doorstep with an armload of belongings almost before Sarah had got around to telling him he could come. Getting his room ready had been no problem. Mr. Quiffen had barely lived in it long enough to track up the rug. The heirs had been only too happy to remove the dead man's personal effects.

Anora had approved Sarah's taking quick action. So had George, once his wife had managed to prod him awake long enough to get official consent for the clearing-out of Mr. Quiffen's possessions. Even Dolph showed a grudging admiration of his young cousin's acumen in not being done out of a week's rent for which she might otherwise have to sue the Metropolitan Boston Transit Authority. Dolph had already been considering legal action on the grounds that Quiffen would have wanted it that way.

Doubtless Dolph was right. Barnwell Augustus Quiffen had been an incredibly cantankerous, vindictive old man. The problem would be not to find out who'd had a serious grudge against him, but to sort out one from the many. Sarah had learned a hard lesson about meddling in situations she wasn't equipped to handle, though. She put Mr. Quiffen as far out of her mind as she could, and concentrated on the tasks that lay at hand.

With not one but two new lodgers to welcome, Monday night's dinner had to be a gala occasion. It certainly was. Mrs. Sorpende wore her emerald green aigrette. Miss LaValliere, having evidently realized her jersey stovepipe wasn't going to get her anywhere, blossomed out in a confection of pink ruffles that blended charmingly with Mr. Porter-Smith's wine-colored dress suit, enhanced tonight by an extra-narrow bow tie and an extra wide cummerbund in a swashbuckling blue-and-burgundy plaid.

Mr. Hartler bustled in all smiles and enthusiasm, wearing the ancient and baggy black tie that was evening uniform among men of his generation and background. He'd hardly been introduced to the company when he made a beeline for Mrs. Sorpende's aigrette and proceeded to enthrall the lady under it with a description of the blue velvet gown trimmed with peacock feathers that Queen Kapiolani had commissioned from B. Altman's for her state visit to Queen Victoria. Professor Ormsby stood silently by wearing a black turtleneck instead of a brown one as his concession to the festivities, either lost in altitudinous abstrusions or wondering how Mrs. Sorpende would look in blue velvet and peacock feathers.

Charles was almost ready to announce dinner and Mr. Bittersohn had not yet appeared in the library. Sarah was wondering nervously whether he was going to show up when she heard Jennifer LaValliere breathe, "Oh, wow!"

As far as Sarah could recall, Max Bittersohn was dressed exactly as he had been the night Harry Lackridge introduced them, in a dark gray worsted suit, a plain white shirt, and a heavy silk four-in-hand tie of sober pattern. He wore no ornament of any kind, not even cuff links or a tie clasp, and he made everybody else in the room look like the leftovers from a rather tacky masquerade party.

It had been the same that time at the Lackridges: Harry in his silly old maroon velvet smoking jacket so disturbingly like Mr. Porter-Smith's getup, Bob Dee wearing a turtleneck jersey and sports jacket, Alexander with his aged dress suit that, like Mr. Hartler, he was determined to get the good out of. For a moment she could see nothing but a blur of tears.

However, landladies do not break down in front of their paying guests. In a moment, Sarah was collectedly performing introductions and Miss LaValliere was gurgling fab, or neat, or whatever the catchword of the moment happened to be. Mrs. Sorpende, though gracious as ever, was less effusive. In fact Sarah had an odd feeling the woman might even feel a trifle wary, though she couldn't for the life of her understand why.

To be sure, Mrs. Sorpende was much the elder of the two. Bittersohn couldn't be more than ten years older than Sarah herself, while Mrs. Sorpende must be a well-preserved fifty-five or more and Sarah, though she had no cash to spare, would have been willing to place a small wager on the "more." Did Mrs. Sorpende think Bittersohn too attractive a man for a young widow to take into her home? Was she afraid he might seduce Miss LaValliere, or vice versa?

Or did she fear he might be impervious to her own more mature charms? Why should she care, with Professor Ormsby panting into her aigrette and Mr. Hartler hurling himself into her silken net before she'd even had time to get it spread, as Cousin Dolph, Uncle Jem, and who knew how many other well-heeled bachelors of suitable age had already shown a disposition to do?

Perhaps Sarah was imagining things. At any rate, Mr. Bittersohn didn't appear to notice any coolness in the atmosphere. They'd agreed in advance that she was to present him simply as a consultant on art objects and paintings, and let the others interpret the description any way they chose. Mr. Porter-Smith evidently took it to mean appraiser and began airing his own knowledge of finance in the art world, which he made to sound far too intricate for any but the keenest minds such as Eugene Porter-Smith's.

Mr. Bittersohn listened with every appearance of respect. Mr. Hartler managed to tear himself away from Mrs. Sorpende long enough to interject a word about the Iolani Palace and was overjoyed to learn that Mr. Bittersohn had been there. The lady ought not to have been bothered by his defection, as Professor Ormsby at once closed in and began expounding some fascinating nugget of aerodynamical lore to the green chiffon scarf that only half screened her magnificent ramparts.

The dinner was excellent, the conversation much improved by the removal of Mr. Quiffen and the addition of jolly, voluble Mr. Hartler and quiet but impressive Mr. Bittersohn. Charles passed the sauceboat and refilled the wineglasses with even more lofty dignity than was his wont. This, his demeanor made clear, was a real jazzy turnout.

Sarah was in the habit of rotating her boarders at the table so that nobody could complain of feeling slighted. Tonight she'd put Mr. Hartler and Mr. Bittersohn beside her. After Charles had cleared away the main course and was having a gorgeous time setting fire to a chafing dish full of canned peaches that Sarah had found on sale and turned into a modified version of *pêches flambées*, Bittersohn surprised her by saying in a somewhat louder tone than he'd been using, "About those illustrations you promised to do for me, Mrs. Kelling. I hope it's not uncouth to mention business at the table, but my publisher's pressing me for a delivery date. Do you think we could discuss them sometime soon?"

"Why, of course." Sarah was surprised. She'd thought his idea about a book on antique jewelry had been dropped. Did he really mean to go ahead with it, or was this an excuse to talk with her about something else, such as Mary Smith and Mr. Quiffen? Anyway, she'd better play along.

"I'm so sorry. I did promise to get back to you ages ago, didn't I?"

As the rest of the boarders looked puzzled, she explained to the table at large, "My husband and I used to do a good deal of book illustrating. He was a marvelous photographer. That's some of his work on the walls."

She'd finally got to hang some of Alexander's framed prints in the dining room where she'd always wanted to put them but had never been allowed to while her mother-in-law was alive. Everybody admired the exquisitely sensitive photography for a moment in respectful silence, then Miss LaValliere burbled, "Can't we see some of yours?"

"If you like. There are several books in the library that

we worked on. My contributions are mostly just little line sketches. That's how Mr. Bittersohn and I happened to become acquainted. We were introduced by his publisher, who recommended me for a book he's doing. But then I —well, you all know what happened so we shan't go into that. I do still have those photographs I'm supposed to be working from upstairs in my studio, Mr. Bittersohn. Perhaps you and I might have our discussion there later this evening instead of boring everybody else with it now."

"I don't want to push you," he protested quite convincingly.

"But I need to be pushed. I knew I should be getting back to the job and I simply couldn't make myself get started."

"Creative work must be terribly difficult," said Mrs. Sorpende. She was looking politely unconvinced, Sarah thought. Either they weren't acting as well as Sarah had thought, or else Mrs. Sorpende was a remarkably perspicacious woman.

"I'll bring down some of the photographs to show you, if Mr. Bittersohn doesn't mind." Maybe that would wipe the skepticism off that Mona Lisa face. "They're quite breathtaking. This book is about antique jewelry, a subject on which Mr. Bittersohn is quite expert, though he's too modest to say so himself."

"How can I be modest, since I'm writing a book about it?" the man replied.

"I thought you'd been dragooned into doing it by the Jewelers' Guild or whatever they call it. Didn't you say you'd been given a grant?"

"I didn't, but apparently our mutual whatever-you-call-him did."

"Oh, dear, wasn't I supposed to tell?"

"It doesn't matter. In any event, I expect all these people are mainly interested in the fact that I'll be downstairs instead of up so they won't have to listen to me pounding a typewriter over their heads."

Or not pounding one, as the case might be. As for Mariposa and Charles, they were too racket prone themselves in their leisure time to hear or care, and too decent to snitch on the man in any case.

Sarah established her *bona fides* as an illustrator by displaying four books she and Alexander had worked on together and one she'd done alone. Then she went to get

Bittersohn's photographs from the studio she'd created by selling everything out of what Aunt Caroline had called her boudoir and moving in a banged-up chest, table, and chair. As the room was on the front, she'd added plain white curtains for respectability. It was a pleasant enough place now, she thought as she scrabbled in the drawers. And how very nice she hadn't remembered to throw out these supposedly useless photographs when she changed rooms. At least they could serve to convince Mrs. Sorpende of what might possibly even be the truth.

The buxom beauty did show a polite interest in the jewelry. Mr. Hartler did a quick run-through to see if the Hawaiian diamonds were represented, found none, and went back to talking about King Kalakaua's custom-gilded showcases. Miss LaValliere gushed without even bothering to look, and asked Mr. Bittersohn how one went about choosing the right engagement ring and had he happened to give anybody one recently? When the ritual half-hour was up, he sprang from her side like a startled chamois and leaped to follow Mrs. Kelling up the stairs.

Chapter 9

"Now," said Sarah when she'd brought an extra chair from her bedroom and got them seated in the studio, "what do you want to talk about? I'm sure it's not neck-lace clasps."

"No, but you may have to draw some," said Bittersohn. "La Belle Dame Sans Merci wasn't buying, did you no-tice?"

"Of course I noticed. Why do you think I made all that fuss about the photographs? You mustn't call her merci-less, though. At least she had the grace not to say what she thought."

"It's probably not the done thing to call your landlady a liar."

"Never mind her. Have you found out something?"

"Sort of. Look, how well did you know this Quiffen be-fore you took him on?"

"Not well enough, obviously, or I shouldn't have done it. I'd seen him a few times at the Protheroes' but never paid much attention to him, or he to me. There was al-ways a crowd around because George can't stay awake for more than ten minutes at a stretch and it does get dull for Anora. He was just one of those people you think you know and then find out you don't."

"Wouldn't your Mr. Hartler fall into the same cate-gory?"

"Yes, I suppose so, but don't you think he's a dear?"

"I'd just like to get a look at some of those royal Ha-waiian art treasures he's collecting," said Bittersohn cau-tiously.

"Why? Do you think he's being swindled? What could that have to do with Mr. Quiffen?"

"I haven't the remotest idea if he's being swindled, nor do I see any connection with Quiffen. Put it down to professional curiosity. What I want to talk about is your cousin."

"Which cousin? I have thousands."

"Adolphus Kelling. Didn't I hear you mention him in connection with your Great-uncle Frederick?"

"Cousin Dolph? Of course. His own parents died young and he was brought up by Great-uncle Fred and Great-aunt Matilda more or less as their own son. He's going to inherit their estate. What about him?"

"Hasn't he also been managing the funds or something?"

"Dolph was legally appointed conservator after Aunt Matilda died because by then Great-uncle Frederick had lost quite a few of his marbles and couldn't be trusted two inches with a checkbook. He'd always fancied himself as a Great Public Benefactor, you know, and Dolph had been his aide-de-camp or something of the sort for years. Dolph's still fighting the good fight in Uncle Fred's name and I expect he always will. It keeps him occupied and makes him feel important, and I daresay they have accomplished a certain amount of good in a half-baked way. What's Dolph up to now?"

"That's a good question. To put it in a nutshell, this Barnwell Quiffen had hired a private investigator to look into the way your cousin has been administering his uncle's estate."

"Whatever for?" gasped Sarah. "Do you mean Mr. Quiffen thought Dolph has been—what do they call it—cooking the books?"

"Diverting funds to his own pocket was the expression Quiffen used to the detective."

"But that's absurd. Why should he? Dolph got all his parents' money to begin with and I can assure you he's not one to fling it about, though he does take me to a nice restaurant about once a year so I can't exactly call him a cheapskate. But he always adds up the bill at least three times before he pays it. And Uncle Fred's money was coming to him in any case, so he'd just be stealing from himself if that's possible."

"Did he know he was due to inherit?"

"Heavens, yes. Everybody did. Every time the family got together Uncle Fred used to stalk around like General Pershing declaiming, 'To you from failing hands I throw the torch. Be yours to hold it high.' And Dolph would swell up like a blowfish and bug out his eyes and say in that pompous way of his, 'I shan't let you down, Uncle Fred.' And he wouldn't. I know Dolph very well. He's pigheaded and slow-thinking and has a low boiling point and can be the most awful bore, but he's so honest it's a downright pitiful, and he does have a sense of duty to the family. He used to get a bit testy with Uncle Frederick, as who didn't, but he never balked at doing whatever Uncle Frederick wanted, even when he should have."

"Such as when?"

"One sterling example was the frogs. You know how somebody's always making noises about there being no frogs in the Frog Pond? Of course it's impossible now that the pond's all concreted and dry half the time, but Great-uncle Frederick decided Boston must have its frogs regardless. So he made Dolph bring a great, dripping sackful into town on the subway, all croaking like mad. Then Great-uncle Frederick made a speech and dumped them in. Needless to say, the frogs weren't having any of this. They hopped straight over to the pond in the Public Gardens. Those that didn't get squashed crossing Charles Street hung around making a ghastly racket till another public-spirited soul went over and collected himself a frogs' legs dinner and that was the end of that.

"But none of Great-uncle Frederick's money was squandered on that episode. Dolph wouldn't go out and *buy* frogs. He spent a whole day wallowing around in a swamp with an old minnow net he'd had as a boy, catching wild ones. Furthermore, the swamp was on a piece of property his parents had left him so they were his frogs in the first place, if one can be said to own a frog. And that's more or less typical of how Dolph operates. Mr. Quiffen must have been imagining things. Only—"

"Only Quiffen's dead, isn't he?" Bittersohn reminded her gently. "And we've both decided Miss Smith was telling the truth about having seen somebody push him under the subway train. And this cousin of yours must spend a fair amount of time down around Government Center and City Hall on his civic business, mustn't he? Would he be apt to go over near Haymarket?"

"Oh yes, all the time. They have some excellent restaurants in the area and Dolph's always having working luncheons, as he calls them, with somebody or other, which are apt to stretch on for hours. As I mentioned, Dolph doesn't stint when it comes to food."

"Does he ever ride the T?"

"Always. He lives not too far from Chestnut Hill Station, so he walks down and comes in on the Riverside line. Anybody'd be crazy to bring a car into the city. Anybody save thee and me, of course." Sarah laughed nervously, remembering the elegant automobile Bittersohn kept parked in the Under-Common Garage.

He smiled too, perhaps glad of an excuse to get off this awkward subject for a moment. "Still got the old Studebaker?"

"Yes, but I'll have to give it up by the end of the year. It costs so much to insure and garage, and I don't have Alexander anymore to do the mechanics. It tears me to pieces to think of letting it go. Do you think there's any hope of finding a buyer?"

"A 1950 Studebaker in mint condition? I'd say you may be able to ease the pain of parting by a considerable amount. Want me to ask my brother-in-law what the prospects are?"

"I'd love it. I could use a little easing of pain about now. Mr. Bittersohn, did that detective find out anything about Dolph?"

"All I know so far is that Quiffen had launched an investigation. What he planned to do with the information if he got any, I have no idea."

"I have," said Sarah. "He'd have written to the papers about it. That's what he always did. And they'd have pounced on the story because of all the publicity Great-uncle Frederick's funeral has already stirred up. Look at the to-do they made about me this past week, just because Mr. Quiffen happened to have been living in my house. I've already had two poison-pen letters accusing me of having been his mistress and driving him to suicide."

"My God!" Bittersohn looked appalled.

"Oh, I don't care. By now I've been slammed around so much that I'm used to that sort of thing, but it would kill Dolph to be plastered all over the front pages as a suspected embezzler. Will this never end?"

"Hey, don't look like that! Put your head down. I'll get some brandy."

"No, please." Sarah fought to get herself together. "We're supposed to be having a quiet little business conference, remember? You might just get me a glass of water from the bathroom if you don't mind. I'm not going to faint, don't worry. It's only that—things keep coming."

"I know. Believe me, I didn't want to tell you this. I wouldn't have, but I was afraid Quiffen might already have started dropping hints about the investigation around town, maybe even here in the house, I thought you'd be less shocked by hearing it privately from me, and perhaps be able to alert your cousin to squash any rumors before they get out of hand. I'm sorry, Mrs. Kelling."

"You're not half so sorry as I am." Sarah took the glass he handed her, and drank from it. "That sounds nastier than I meant it to. I did ask for your help, didn't I? If you find out my boarder was killed by the cousin who wangled me a boardinghouse license, that's simply my tough luck, isn't it?"

"Want some more water?"

"Oh, stop being kind! You're making me ashamed of myself. Seriously, Mr. Bittersohn, I cannot picture Dolph sneaking up and shoving an old man in front of a train. I don't say he wouldn't be vindictive if he found out what was going on because he certainly would, but that's just not the way he operates. His idea of revenge would be to arrange a public meeting in Faneuil Hall, drag Mr. Quiffen up to the podium, and denounce him in front of the audience as a cur and a rotter. He'd then demand a complete audit of his handling of Great-uncle Frederick's funds from time immemorial."

"Including the frogs?"

"I shouldn't be surprised if someone brought that up, plus a few of their more spectacular lunacies, like the time Great-uncle Frederick overheard some boy teasing a girl about going down to the Esplanade that night to watch the submarine races. He at once got it into his head that the Russian Navy was doing subversive activities up and down the Charles River. He fumed around and got Dolph believing it, too. Finally the pair of them went storming into the National Guard Armory, demanding that troops be sent to guard the Hatch Memorial Shell so that Arthur Fiedler wouldn't get bombed."

"I'm surprised I missed that one."

"Well, you can believe a lot of other people didn't. Anyway, by the time the meeting was over, everybody would have come to the conclusion that Dolph wasn't fit to handle cookie money for a Girl Scout, and the family would have to appoint a conservator for him, too. Actually Dolph is sound enough on the fiscal end. His lawyers handle all the complicated parts, and he has a firm of certified public accountants to check on the lawyers, so unless a great many reputable people are in cahoots together, I cannot believe there's anything behind this investigation of Mr. Quiffen's except his usual nastiness. But the fact remains that Mr. Quiffen's been killed. If we go stirring up trouble for the murderer, he or she would be awfully stupid not to bring out this story about the detective trailing Dolph. It would make a perfect red herring, wouldn't it?"

"I'm afraid it would," Bittersohn agreed. "That's another reason why I thought we might as well face the issue now instead of later."

"And naturally you wanted to see how I reacted to the idea that Dolph might be guilty. I don't blame you, Mr. Bittersohn. But I just can't go along with it because it doesn't fit in with all the things I know and feel about Dolph. One does have to reply on one's instincts about people to some extent, doesn't one? You did. And you were right, weren't you?"

"For what that's worth."

"It was worth everything to me. All right, Mr. Bittersohn, suppose we do this: if you can get Miss Smith to be somewhere nearby, I'll get Dolph to take a walk with me. I don't know that you've ever met him but he's a tall, rather stout man; large enough to be noticeable in a crowd. Knowing me, Miss Smith could identify him and perhaps recall if she'd seen him on the platform that night, or at least tell you whether his gloves and coat sleeves are the right color."

"Would he be wearing the same ones, though?"

"Of course. Dolph is no fashion plate. He had to buy a new topcoat last year when he got so fat his old one wouldn't button and he's so afraid he won't get his investment back that he practically wears it to bed. And Aunt

Emma gave him a nice pair of gloves to go with the coat, so he wears them, too."

"It's a thought. How would you get him to go with you?"

"Easily enough, I should think. Dolph has been helping me with some of this legal rigmarole I've had to go through. I can ask him to go to the lawyer's with me, then pretend I've mixed up the appointments or something."

"Won't he be furious?"

"Not really. Dolph loves to rant at people for wasting his precious time. It tickles his ego. Before we get there, I can casually ask him if he happened to be in Haymarket Station around the time Mr. Quiffen was killed. That would be natural enough. They'd known each other from the Protheroes' and he had dinner with us one night while Mr. Quiffen was living here. I can say one of my other boarders was there and thought he caught a glimpse of Mr. Kelling standing head and shoulders above the hoi polloi."

"And shoving Quiffen onto the track? What sort of answer do you expect to get?"

"Oh, Dolph would tell me the truth, one way or another. Subterfuge isn't his strong suit. I've sometimes wondered if Dolph's such a rotten liar because he's so fanatically honest or if it's the other way around. If you don't think my idea would work, I can invite him to dinner again and let you pump him yourself."

"No, it would be far better for Miss Smith to get a look at him. Could we arrange it for tomorrow, do you think?"

"I can try. Dolph should be home by now, unless he's gone to a banquet at the Home for Retired Woolgatherers or some other of Great-uncle Frederick's philanthropies. But how can we reach Miss Smith?"

"We shan't have to. She has a regular daily route. Very organized lady. I got her schedule in case we needed her for any reason, such as this, and also because I thought we should keep an eye on her. She and I had lunch together this noon, as a matter of fact."

"You didn't!"

"We certainly did. She was down at Quincy Market and a guy came along with a hot dog wagon, so I stood treat. Diamond Jim Bittersohn they call me down among the pushcarts."

"That sounds like fun," Sarah said wistfully. "Miss

Smith is a marvelous woman. I do wish I could get to
know her better. Would it be safe, do you think, for me to
at least smile and nod if we should chance to meet?"

"I don't see why you mightn't stop and give her a quarter or something."

Sarah flushed. "You mean the lady of the manor condescending to notice the poor beggar woman? That's not
what I meant at all."

"I know that," said Bittersohn, "but it's a way to make
contact, isn't it? Somebody sees you fishing in your purse
and handing this down-and-outer a coin, they assume
you're performing an impulsive act of charity. If you stop
to pass the time of day, you're just being good-natured.
Furthermore, the old sport could use the dough."

"So could the young one. Miss Smith and I have a good
deal more in common than meets the eye. But she did say
people offer her money and she always takes it, so I daresay that would be the best plan. What's her schedule for
tomorrow?"

"Boston Common, which should be an easy one. Look
for her somewhere near the information booth about
eleven o'clock."

"Perfect. I'll phone Dolph right away. Thank you, Mr.
Bittersohn."

"What for?"

"I'm not quite sure at this point. But thank you anyway."

Chapter 10

Dolph was at home and not unwilling to be pressed into service on an errand Sarah had managed to think up, though he did make a long business of consulting his engagement book and holding a one-man debate as to whether he could postpone a vitally important meeting with somebody or other for half an hour.

"How long is this going to take, Sarah?"

"Not more than a few minutes, I shouldn't think."

That was the absolute truth, as all she had to do was hand over to the secretary a filled-out form she could perfectly well have dropped into the mail and didn't have to deliver for another six weeks in any case.

"It's just that I'd feel more confident if you were with me," she added, "in case any questions come up." Such as "Do you think we'll have snow for Christmas?" or some other burning issue.

Punctual to the dot, Dolph arrived at the house on Tulip Street, wearing his dark brown overcoat as expected, along with the nice brown leather gloves Aunt Emma had picked out for him and a natty brown Homburg which Uncle Fred had regretfully set aside during the Hoover campaign of 1928 because it was too reminiscent of Al Smith's brown derby, a Democratic symbol; but had prudently saved against a time when, as now, it might come in handy again. The hat alone should have been enough to catch Miss Smith's eye.

As they crossed the plaza by the fountain, which had been turned off for the winter, Sarah spied Miss Mary Smith diligently combing through a trash container. As Dolph turned to howl fulminations after a child on a skateboard, Sarah managed to pass her a quarter and a brisk nod. Miss Smith said, "Thanks, miss. Much obliged, I'm sure," and went on stuffing papers into her shopping bags.

She hadn't betrayed by the slightest flicker of an eyelash whether or not either Sarah or Dolph was known to her. Mr. Bittersohn must have briefed her well, or else Miss Smith was a very clever lady. If only nothing awful happened to her!

Dolph continued his oration on the perfidy of skateboarders all the way to Mr. Redfern's office, then engaged Miss Tremblay, the lawyer's long-suffering secretary, in an unnecessary catechism about the innocuous form they'd brought in. It wasn't until they were back outside the building and ready to go their separate ways that Sarah managed to ask the question she'd been working up to ever since her cousin's arrival.

"By the way, Dolph, I meant to ask you. I wonder if you happened to be at Haymarket Station the night Mr. Quiffen was killed."

"How the hell do you expect me to remember that?" he snorted. "I have important matters on my mind, Sarah, as you sometimes appear not to realize."

"I do realize, Dolph, and I'm truly grateful to you for giving up so much of your valuable time to my personal affairs," Sarah replied humbly as she was expected to do. "It's just that one of my boarders happened to be strolling past the station on her way home to dinner that day, and she'd noticed a tall, distinguished-looking man in an awfully smart overcoat going in. She thought it might have been you, and was concerned that you might have been unfortunate enough to get involved with the—the accident."

"Oh. M'er, dammit, Sarah, I just can't remember. Haven't got my engagement book with me."

"But surely you'd recall all that commotion, with policemen and ambulances and whatnot, and the trains being held up."

"Damn trains are always getting held up. Fires, rowdyism, accidents, mismanagement, damned bureaucratic incompetence." Dolph shot out his cuff and glared at his wristwatch. "Got to run. Best regards to the good lady. Kind of her to be concerned. Find your way back all right?"

"Of course. Have a good lunch."

Sarah had no intention of going straight back to Tulip Street. After that frustrating excursion she felt the need of a little extra exercise. Besides, it wouldn't hurt to pick up a fresh bottle of India ink and some drawing paper. Mrs. Sorpende was sure to ask before long how the artwork for Mr. Bittersohn's book was coming along.

She wasn't far from an art shop, though it lay all too near the bank that was holding so tenaciously to those either valid or fraudulent mortgages. It might be years before she learned whether she or they owned the properties; in the meantime she must keep on paying the interest and the taxes, and perhaps take a few lessons in recycling from Miss Mary Smith.

At the moment, what the court would decide was the least of her worries. Her biggest concern was, had Dolph been evading any straight answer about being in the subway on that fatal evening, or was he simply being Dolph? And what sort of verdict would Mr. Bittersohn be getting from Miss Mary Smith?

Were they sharing another pushcart lunch today, maybe eating some of those enormous hot pretzels Sarah had often longed for as a child and washing them down with bottles of poisonous-looking orange soda, the kind she'd never been allowed to buy because it had chemicals in it? What must it be like to do exactly as one pleased?

At least she'd bought roasted chestnuts from the chestnut man's pushcart in the wintertime, she and Alexander, and popcorn in the summer to feed the ducks from the swanboats on the pond in the Garden where Uncle Fred's frogs had gone, back when she was a child and Alexander a young man who hadn't yet started to count the pennies. That was something, she supposed, though it didn't seem to be much help to her now. Sarah forced herself, as she often had to do these days, to get her mind off her dead husband and on current subjects such as whether the skimpy leftovers from last night's dinner could possibly be turned into something interesting for tomorrow's breakfast.

By devious routes she wound her way back to the house, feeling a little better for the exercise, and was fishing in her purse for the door key when a man came out carrying a large package wrapped in brown paper. He paid her no attention whatever, a fact that took her somewhat aback. Sarah wasn't used to being ignored on her own doorstep.

Once she got inside, however, all was explained. Mr. Hartler came bouncing out of his room, insisted on taking her coat, and hung it up for her.

"Did you meet that chap going out? Thought he had one of the palace treasures. I had to tell him it was nothing of the sort. We get them all the time, you know. They come rushing in all fired up and saddle me with something or other. I go through the fuss and bother of trying to get the piece authenticated, then finally have to write the poor chaps to come and take it away because some great-aunt has been dreaming up family fairy tales. They don't mean to cheat, you know, it's just the romantic notion of owning something they can associate with royalty."

"But surely some of the things must be genuine," said Sarah. "Otherwise, why should you bother?"

"Oh yes, once in a while I strike a real treasure, like this little beauty."

He darted back into the former drawing room and reappeared holding a delightful Victorian trinket box in chased silver and enamel. "See, here's your royal coat of arms, a shield with red and blue stripes and the three white circles, and the two spear-carrying warriors guarding it. Beautiful workmanship, isn't it?"

"Lovely," Sarah agreed. "The same crest was on that fan I told you about. I always thought those circles with the stems must represent the different islands joining together as one kingdom."

"You're very acute, Mrs. Kelling."

Mr. Hartler didn't say she was very correct, but neither would he have been likely to tell her she was talking nonsense. Mr. Quiffen would have, at the slightest excuse, with that sharp little nose of his dipping and twitching like a parrot's beak, his voice grating and squealing till one felt like stuffing a napkin into his mouth to shut him up.

That was the awful part. Sarah could understand only too well how somebody might have murdered Barnwell Augustus Quiffen simply to stop his wrangling for a change. Somebody who liked to hold the floor himself, perhaps. Somebody who could explode like a charge of dynamite at the slightest annoyance, the way Dolph had carried on about that child on the skateboard who'd skidded too close to his precious overcoat. She'd been awfully positive to Mr. Bittersohn about Dolph's being a yeller instead of a hitter. Was she really all that sure?

When would Mr. Bittersohn be coming home? Sarah was beset by such a seething mixture of impatience and dread that she rushed to the kitchen, began chopping carrots at a furious rate, and almost lost her left forefinger under the cleaver.

The near-accident sobered her down. It was foolish to think of Dolph as a prime suspect just because Mr. Quiffen had got some paranoid notion about him and was rich enough to follow it up in a particularly nasty, underhanded way. After all, the old man had managed to antagonize her and everybody else in the house on a very short-term intimacy. He must have acquired a long list of enemies with grudges stretching back years and years.

And why should she have expected Mr. Bittersohn to drop his own work and rush to the rescue of a woman who couldn't even afford to pay? With art thefts becoming more fashionable every day, he must already have plenty of profitable cases on his hands. She'd meant to deal with her own problems. Only she hadn't expected to have to cope with anything like Miss Mary Smith.

Sarah stared down at the small mountain of raw carrot she'd accumulated. "What on earth am I going to do with all this?" she wondered. Put the surplus to soak in cold salt water and pray for guidance, perhaps.

Or make a carrot pudding. Anora Protheroe's cook and her now deceased but still lovingly remembered cat Percival had been particular friends of Sarah's ever since the little Kelling girl used to be sent out to pet the nice kitty while the grownups visited. Cook had taught her the recipe ages ago. This elegant but economical dessert, so like plum pudding but so much lighter and more digestible, was always hailed with delight at Anora's dinner parties. Sarah had made it for her father a few times, quite successfully. The one time she'd tried it here, Aunt Caroline had snapped, "Much too spicy," and laid down her dessert fork and spoon with disdain.

Perhaps her boarders would be less critical. Anyway, it was something to do with all these carrots and a good excuse to use the old tin pudding mold that had hardly ever been taken down from the top pantry shelf after

Uncle Gilbert died and the cook was let go. Edith had foisted the cooking off on Sarah by the simple expedient of never producing an eatable meal. The young bride had often found it excellent therapy during her difficult marriage. Now in her sudden widowhood she turned to her pots and pans even more eagerly.

After the pudding was mixed and set to steam Sarah still had some minced carrot left so she hunted out a recipe for carrot bread that could be baked and kept until needed in the secondhand freezer her henchman Mr. Lomax had got for her at a pittance from some people who were moving out of state. In order not to waste the oven heat, she threw together a batch of muffins for breakfast and an apple cobbler from the fruit she and Mr. Lomax had salvaged. She'd serve the cobbler tonight and save the pudding for tomorrow, she decided. Cook always said it tasted better after standing a day.

All in all, Sarah passed a far more productive afternoon than she'd expected to, forgot about Mr. Quiffen in her anxiety over the pudding, and was unmolding her creation with total success and immense relief when Max Bittersohn entered the kitchen.

"Wow, what are we celebrating? Do you do this every day?"

"No, I was just trying to get ahead of the baking for a change. The pudding's for tomorrow, but you may have a muffin if you like."

"You mean a muffie. That's what my mother calls them. She makes a batch now and then to relieve the monogamy."

"Does it?"

"Who knows? My mother tends to invent her English as she goes along."

"She sounds delightful. Why don't you invite her and your father in to dinner sometime?"

"They don't go out much."

Of course, they probably kept a kosher home. Sarah mentally kicked herself. Well, no doubt it would have been a mistake to have them anyway. One oughtn't get on family visiting terms with one's boarders, ought one? Only Mr. Bittersohn wasn't exactly in the same category as her other boarders, was he? If he wasn't, he'd better be. And she'd better get back to the business at hand.

"Did you have a chance to talk with Miss Smith?"

"I did."

"What did she say about Dolph?"

Bittersohn shrugged. "She was sure she'd seen him around, but she couldn't say just where or when. It might have been that day or it might not. It might have been Haymarket Station or someplace else. He looked too tall, but he might have been bending over. The overcoat might be the right color, but it was so hard to tell under those lights. The gloves were okay, but she wasn't sure about the size of the hands. It added up to what you might call a doubtful maybe. Did you get anything out of your cousin?"

"I flopped completely. In the first place, I couldn't manage to put a word in edgewise until the very last minute. When I made my little speech, Dolph just did a bit of snapping and snarling about rotten service on the T, then looked at his watch and rushed madly off toward the Parker House. I honestly can't say whether he was dodging my question or being his usual sweet self. You'd have to know Dolph to understand."

"Then maybe you'd better arrange for us to meet," said Bittersohn. "So that's all you have to report?"

"Not quite. I think you can stop worrying about Mr. Hartler's being taken in by swindlers. As I was coming in this noontime I met a man who'd just had his genuine Hawaiian art treasure rejected. He was going out with whatever it was, neatly wrapped in brown paper. Mr. Hartler came out and told me all about the agonies he goes through having to turn down most of the stuff people bring in because he can't get it authenticated.

"He says they don't mean to defraud him, it's just that families tend to attach romantic tales to their heirlooms. I could understand what he meant. Remember we were speaking the other day about that old campaign chair in the cellar?"

"The one I was sitting in when the mouse ran up my pant leg. There can't be much left of it now."

"There isn't, but I'd stuck the pieces in the broom closet and Uncle Jem found them while he was prowling around trying to find where I'd hidden the whiskey. He dragged them out to show the boarders, and to hear him tell the story you'd think Great-uncle Nathan rode that chair up San Juan Hill two lengths ahead of Teddy Roosevelt. Mr. Hartler did show me a sweet little trinket box that I know is authentic because it's got the same crest on it as the fan we turned in."

"Bully for him," said Bittersohn, reaching absentmindedly for another muffin. "Well, I'd better get out of here before my high-class landlady catches me hobnobbing with the cook. Am I supposed to dress for dinner, by the way, or do I maintain a discreet distance in rank from the upstairs gentlefolk?"

"You do whatever you feel comfortable doing," Sarah told him. "I hope you don't think Mr. Porter-Smith's cummerbund was my idea, but it seems to make him happy so I go along as best I can. Now, scat! I see Charles coming in through the alley gate and you're not supposed to know I do the cooking. Charles thinks it might lower the tone. Thank you again for your trouble today. I'm sorry it was such a complete bust."

Chapter 11

As Sarah had anticipated, Mrs. Sorpende did express a polite hope at dinner that Mrs. Kelling was making satisfactory progress with her artwork.

"I've progressed to the point of buying myself a new bottle of ink," Sarah replied. "My cousin and I had to go and do some legal business which rather took up my time. He sends you his particular regards, by the way."

"How kind of him."

Mrs. Sorpende smiled. Professor Ormsby made a low growling noise. Miss LaValliere and Mr. Porter-Smith exchanged knowing glances. Mr. Bittersohn went on eating his ham, a fact which Sarah noted with relief. She'd forgotten to ask whether he observed Orthodox dietary restrictions, but she might have known there'd be nothing orthodox about Mr. Bittersohn.

After dinner, Miss LaValliere suggested going over to the Common to see if the Christmas lights were still up, but found no takers. Mrs. Sorpende had letters to write and so did Mr. Hartler. Professor Ormsby had to give a paper over at MIT, and Miss LaValliere could walk over with him if she wanted to, but Miss LaValliere didn't want to. What she wanted was Mr. Bittersohn, but Mr. Bittersohn had unspecified business elsewhere. When Mr. Porter-Smith, who preferred to go someplace where he could show off his new cummerbund, suggested the alternative of dropping down to a coffee house on Charles Street, Miss LaValliere faced reality and accepted.

Sarah left Mariposa and Charles to practice togetherness in the kitchen and went upstairs to grind out an illustration or two. She picked one of the photographs at random, and began making a detailed sketch of the clasp. Trying to make out its intricacies tired her eyes, so she began inventing them as she went along, as Mr. Bittersohn claimed his mother did with the English language. What difference did it make? The sketch was only for window-dressing, anyway.

Sarah hadn't drawn anything since she'd made that fatal sketch of the family vault. She'd had to screw up her courage even to pick up a pencil. Once she got into it, however, she began taking some of the old pleasure in what she was doing. Before she quite realized, the clasp had turned into a design for earrings to go with Granny Kay's bluebird.

What a charming idea! She'd never have them, probably, but it was fun making believe. She'd turned on the FM radio that she'd brought up from the library when she was setting up her private lair and found WXHR was playing César Franck's *Symphony in D Minor,* which she loved and hadn't heard in ages. All at once Sarah realized she was, for the first time since the day Alexander died, quite happy.

Her first reaction was guilt. How could she know any joy, with another murder on her hands and Dolph perhaps involved? Then she got angry. Why shouldn't she? Barnwell Quiffen's nastiness and Dolph's temper weren't her fault, were they? Anyway, how could she be a hundred per cent sure Miss Mary Smith hadn't been building an amusing little fantasy, just as she herself had been doing with the earring design?

But the pleasure was gone. The sketch was finished, the concert was over. Sarah switched off the radio and got ready for bed. She took two aspirin and tried to read Schopenhauer. Even his dreary prose took a long time to put her to sleep.

She woke feeling strangely confused, but this was no time for confusion. Because of her boarders' varying time schedules, Sarah had elected to serve breakfast English-style from assorted dishes on the sideboard, with herself presiding over the coffee urn and Mariposa fluttering decoratively about in her orange ribbons to poke more bread into the pop-up toaster or take away used plates and cups.

Professor Ormsby was always the first one down, and Mrs. Sorpende most often the last. After the queenly matron had eaten her way through whatever was left from previous depredations, Sarah and Mariposa would retire to the kitchen to wash dishes together and talk business.

Because both of them were always so busy keeping the house in order and the lodgers happy, this was about the only chance they ever had for real conversation. Though they kept up the pretense of an employer-employee relationship in front of the others, the pair of them had become real partners in their private war on poverty. Mariposa served as acting general as often as Sarah took her turn at the dishpan. She was a great deal the more knowledgeable of the two in many ways, had an original turn of mind and an often hilarious way of expressing her ideas.

Today, however, Mariposa was in no mood to be funny. As Sarah was scrubbing egg off forks, she said, "I got to talk to you about something."

"Then spill it. Hand me that silver polish, will you? What's the big problem?"

"It's Mrs. Sorpende. I'm worried about her."

"After the breakfast she just ate? Surely it's not her health? I cannot imagine how that woman manages to keep her weight under any sort of control."

"She skips lunch," said Mariposa.

"How do you know?"

"Simple logic, as Charles would say. If she had the dough for a sandwich, she'd spend it on something else. You know she washes out her underwear in the bathroom?"

"Actually I didn't, but what if she does? Unless she leaves it hanging where it will drip all over Miss LaValliere."

"Uh-uh! She'd never leave it where anybody could see it. You know why?"

"She's too modest?"

Considering the amount of frontage Mrs. Sorpende exposed to public view every evening, Sarah didn't think that could be the right answer, and it wasn't. Mariposa sniffed in contempt.

"Because it's in rags, that's way."

"So is mine."

"Yeah, we got to get you something decent. It's bad for the image, you sitting in front of that silver urn with holes in your underpants. What if there was an earthquake or something? But anyway, yours was good quality to start

with. Hers is nothing but junk. And how many dresses
you ever see her wear?"

"Why, I haven't the faintest idea. I never kept track.
She seems to have a different outfit about one night in
three."

"Seems to, right. But you take away all them scarves
and flowers and beads and stuff, and what would you
have?"

"A plain black dress, I suppose. She always wears
black."

"You said it, honey. One plain black long dress for
evening and if that didn't come from Filene's Basement
then I'm Queen Liliuokawhoozis. And one plain black
short dress for daytimes and one plain black coat and one
pair of plain black leather pumps and one pair of black
vinyl boots and a drawer full of fake flowers and cheap
scarves and five-and-ten jewelry, and one pair of nylons
and some knee-highs that have been darned real nice, and
anybody that takes the trouble to sew up a run in a pair
of forty-nine-cent knee-highs—"

"Mariposa, you've been snooping through her dresser
drawers!"

"Honey, you got class. Charles has got class. We get
too much class around here, this place is going to fold up
flatter than a four-flusher's wallet. Me, I got no class. I
never could afford it. And believe me, honey, that lady
can't afford none, either. She's not behind in her rent, I
hope?"

"Why, no. She pays right on the dot, like everybody
else."

"How?"

"Hands it to me in a little envelope. Oh, you mean
does she pay by check or whatever? Actually she always
pays cash. Come to think of it, she's the only one who
does. Everyone else writes me a check. Is that supposed
to mean something?"

"It sure does to me," said Mariposa. "You start a
checking account, you need money to start it with, right?
You don't keep a big enough balance, you pay a service
charge for every check, right? You add up a few service
charges, you got the price of another pair of them forty-
nine-cent knee-highs you can wear under that jazzy black
dinner dress nobody's going to know the difference,
right?"

"But, Mariposa—"

"Don't go buttin' me, honey. I figure she's got a little savings account someplace. That way she gets maybe a buck or two interest on her money instead of paying out. She takes out a week's rent, she hands it to you, she eats what you give her, she doesn't spend a cent more than she has to anyplace else. She keeps on doing her dance of the seven veils, maybe she can kid you along for a few more weeks she's the society dame she makes herself out to be. But anytime she don't come across with the rent on time, you better have a sick aunt who needs that room in a hurry."

"Really, Mariposa! I'd hardly make a sick aunt climb two flights of stairs."

"Then you got a well aunt. Look, maybe what you better do is come down with a sore throat and let Charles handle it. I guess you never had much experience at giving anybody the bum's rush, huh?"

"But I like Mrs. Sorpende," wailed Sarah. "I like her the best of the lot, except—well, of course I'd known Mr. Bittersohn before."

"You'd known Mr. Quiffen before, too, honey. I haven't noticed you hanging out any black crape for him."

"Maybe you don't see as much as you think," Sarah snapped back. That was as close as she'd ever got to being cross with Mariposa. "If you have all that surplus energy to work off, I wish you'd do something about that front hallway instead of counting the holes in people's underwear. It's always a mess these days, I can't think why. We've never had this problem till the past day or so."

"It's all them visitors Mr. Hartler has sashaying in and out all the time. Don't even wipe their feet and act like they done you a favor letting you open the door for them. Mr. Hartler may be one of your fine old Boston gentlemen but he's sure got some mighty peculiar friends."

"They're not his friends," Sarah corrected. "They're just people trying to sell him things that are supposed to have come from that Iolani Palace he's always talking about."

"Then how come they all come in empty-handed and go out carrying bundles?"

"Because they've left their pieces to be authenticated

and he's had to let them know they're not what he's looking for and would they please come back and take them
away. I suppose they're all cross and disappointed, and
that's why they don't bother to be polite."

"That's no excuse for bad manners." said Mariposa
huffily. "Specially not in a high-class joint like this.
Charles says inability to cope with frustration is a sign of
immaturity. How does that grab you? Anyway, I guess
that's why Mr. Hartler told me not to bother cleaning his
room. He's afraid I'll pinch some of those genuine fake
antiques, I bet."

"I'm sure he thinks nothing of the sort. It's just that
he's so wrapped up in this business about the Iolani Palace that nothing else seems important to him. If Mr.
Hartler doesn't want us dusting things that don't belong
to him, that's understandable, but we're certainly going
to keep the room clean. Otherwise we might start having
earwigs and cockroaches and heaven knows what. I think
I'd better have a little chat with him about that. I'm also
going to tell him to make sure his callers wipe their feet.
After all, this is a private house. Semi-private, anyway.
Now I have to go to the bank and deposit the rent checks,
and pick up Aunt Emma's order at Boston Music Company, which I forgot to do yesterday, and buy whipping
cream for that pudding we're going to serve tonight. Anything else?"

They did their heavy marketing on Saturdays when
Charles was available to carry the bags, trundling off in
the Studebaker to a run-down neighborhood store Mariposa knew of where the food was a lot cheaper. However, there was always something to be got at the last
minute so the neighborhood grocers got their share of the
Kelling business as they always had. Mariposa mentioned
one or two items, Sarah put on her coat and left the
house.

She crossed Beacon and cut through the Common to
the handsome building that had housed Boston Music
Company years before either she or her parents had been
born. She was walking slowly, keeping an eye peeled for
a possible glimpse of Miss Mary Smith, when she spied a
commanding figure in a black coat, a plum-colored velvet
turban and scarf, and plain black boots strolling some
distance ahead of her. Sarah had no conscious intention
of shadowing her boarder, but she found herself altering

her path slightly to keep Mrs. Sorpende in view. It soon became obvious that she was making a beeline for the women's public rest room.

That was odd. No, perhaps it wasn't. Mrs. Sorpende was, after all, a middle-aged woman who had drunk three cups of coffee with her breakfast. But she'd only just left the house. Sarah had heard her go out while she herself was collecting her purse and gloves. Might Mrs. Sorpende have been taken with sudden cramps or something? What was a landlady's responsibility in such a circumstance?

One couldn't very well enter the rest room, too, and catch so dignified a person in what was more than likely to be an undignified situation. On the other hand, one didn't like to go away and leave her in possible distress. Maybe one should simply hover at a discreet distance and wait to see how Mrs. Sorpende looked when she came out. Sarah stationed herself behind a convenient Ulmus procera (Boston Common trees wear erudite name tags) and lurked.

Chapter 12

Mrs. Sorpende did not come out. One or two others did. Sarah saw a child of fourteen or so, who ought to be in school at this hour, slouching from the building in a pair of too-tight blue jeans, a fuzzy fake fur jacket so short that it might indeed lead to severe kidney disturbances, and backless mules with fantastically high heels she didn't have the remotest idea how to manage. The girl was puffing inexpertly at a cigarette and made Sarah want to cry out of pity for her.

There was a tweedy woman who tied two afghan hounds to the doorknob by their leashes and made a fast trip in and out. Right behind her Sarah caught sight of a black coat emerging and sighed with relief for her own feet were getting cold with standing. However, it was on a stooped old woman who had a ratty scarf tied over her head and a pair of broken-out red sneakers on her feet. She was carrying a large plastic trick-or-treat bag that must date from many Halloweens ago. Another amateur ecologist, no doubt.

And still there was no sign of Mrs. Sorpende. By now Sarah felt she had good reason to be concerned. Indelicate though she might be, she walked over and went in.

The place was surprisingly clean, and totally devoid of life.

"Well, you idiot!" she said aloud.

Had she really seen Mrs. Sorpende come in here? Of course she had, she wasn't blind. Had the woman left by another entrance? No, there wasn't one. Then Mrs. Sorpende must simply have come out and slipped quickly around to the other side while Sarah's attention was mo-

mentarily diverted by that pathetic child in the fuzzy
jacket or the old woman who might have been Miss
Smith but wasn't. God willing, the boarder hadn't happened to notice young Mrs. Kelling making a fool of herself behind that elm tree.

Feeling very cross with herself, Sarah went along about
her business. It was one of those days when nothing goes
right. She had a long wait at the music store while some
odd mix-up about Aunt Emma's order for the parts to
Cosi Fan Tutti was straightened out. She got into the
wrong line at the bank as one always does, and after
having stood on one aching foot then the other for some
while, found she'd been blessed with a trainee teller who
could not cope with the complexities of depositing five
rent checks and one trust fund allowance and handing
Sarah back the little extra cash sum she allowed herself
for emergencies.

The store she usually went to for cream was out of it,
for some unexplained reason, so she had to go elsewhere
and pay a good deal more. All in all she got back to the
house far later than she'd meant to, and her temper was
not sweetened by finding that she hadn't brought her door
key with her. She poked the bell, dropping Aunt Emma's
package in the process and scattering Mozart all over the
vestibule. At last Mariposa came downstairs from the
third floor where she'd been mopping bedrooms, and let
her in.

"I thought you were going to clean up this hall," was
Sarah's ungracious greeting.

"I did," Mariposa protested. "I mopped and dusted
and vacuumed as soon as you left."

"Then somebody's messed it up again in a big hurry.
We simply can't let this sort of thing go on. Is Mr. Hartler
in his room now, do you know?"

"Yes, but he's got somebody with him."

"Somebody with muddy feet, no doubt. Stand guard
here, will you, and let me know the second he's free. I'll
be in the kitchen."

However, Sarah never got to the kitchen. As she was
going down the long hallway that led past the dining
room, she happened to look in. A woman she'd never
seen before was coolly opening the china cupboard and
taking out one of Great-grandmother Kelling's Coalport
vases.

All the resentments of that frustrating day, all the anger Sarah had been so carefully brought up to suppress, came surging out. She charged at that woman with a ferocity she'd never realized she could show, and snatched the vase from her hand.

"How dare you?"

The woman was not the least bit intimidated. "How dare I what? Look, I didn't come here to be insulted. That's not a bad piece. Reproduction, of course, but not bad. Tell you what, I'll give you fifty dollars for the pair. What do you say?"

What Sarah said was, "Mariposa!" and she said it in a shriek.

The maid came running. "What's the matter— madam?" she added hastily, seeing the stranger.

"Go put the night latch on the door," Sarah ordered, "then come straight back here and help me count the silver."

"Hey, just a minute," yelled the strange woman. "You can't hold me here against my will."

"Can't I?" Sarah was a trifle more collected now. "You entered this house against mine. How did you get in?"

"He opened the door for me, naturally. Your boss."

"My what?"

Mr. Hartler must have heard the commotion, for he popped into the dining room, beaming as usual. His irate landlady wheeled to attack.

"Mr. Hartler, can you explain why I found this—this person rifling my china cabinet? She claims you let her in. Is that true?"

"Why, I suppose I must have, if she says so," he replied. "Yes, I believe I do recall going to the door. But you see, I happened to have someone else with me at the time, so I—dear me, what did I do? I'm so excited, you see. This chap I have in my room now—"

"Mr. Hartler, I'm not interested in your excitement. I am demanding to know why you're turning my house into a pigsty and letting strangers roam freely where they have no business to be."

"Just a second," interrupted the strange woman. "Whose place is this, anyway? Is she crazy, or what?"

Sarah got her answer in first. "I am Mrs. Alexander Kelling. This is my house and Mr. Hartler is my boarder. I've allowed him to carry on his—"

"Yes, yes," the old man bubbled. "Mrs. Kelling has been most kind, most kind indeed. I'm afraid she finds me a dreadful old nuisance. Now, Mrs.—I'm sorry, but I'm afraid I didn't quite catch your name—perhaps it might be better if you came some other time when we're not quite so—er—preoccupied."

"I should prefer that she not come at all," said Sarah coldly. "She's just offered me fifty dollars for a pair of my great-grandmother's Coalport vases."

"Oh, dear! Oh, dear! What a pickle. Mrs. Kelling, I do apologize most humbly. Most humbly indeed. Here, Mrs.—er—I'll just show you to the door."

"Hold it!" barked Mariposa. "We didn't count the silver yet."

"But surely—that is—"

"Mr. Hartler, take your visitor to the front hall and stay there with her until we finish here," Sarah ordered. "As soon as we've made sure nothing is missing, we'll come and release the night latch so she can leave. In the future, you must schedule your appointments far enough apart so that this sort of thing never happens again. You must also instruct your callers to leave their boots outside and quit using my oriental rug for an ashtray. I don't know what sort of people you're entertaining here, but if they can't behave in a civilized manner, you'll have to see them somewhere else. Have I made myself clear?"

"Yes, yes. I'm a dreadful old man and I do apologize, Mrs. Kelling. I give you too much trouble, too much trouble. Please come this way, Mrs.—er—"

The woman was sputtering, "Well, I must say!" and Mr. Hartler was soothing her with, "Yes, yes, all my fault. Terrible misunderstanding," as he led her into the hall and courteously shut the door behind them.

Counting the family treasures was no doubt a hollow gesture at this point, but Sarah and Mariposa did it anyway. Nothing appeared to be missing, but it was clear that the Coalport vase wasn't the only thing Mr. Hartler's errant visitor had handled. Sarah worked as fast as she could, not being at all sure whether she was in fact within her rights in keeping the woman locked in the hall, and having no desire to find herself in the papers again, this time charged with kidnapping. It wasn't more than fifteen minutes before she went out and released the lock.

"Well," snapped the woman as she flounced out, "I'm certainly never coming here again!"

"Splendid," Sarah replied. "I shall look forward to not seeing you."

That was about the rudest she'd ever been in her life. She'd thought an explosion might relieve her feelings, but it didn't. By six o'clock she had a raging headache. When Max Bittersohn phoned to say he wouldn't be in to dinner, she almost burst into tears.

"But I was going to give you the carrot pudding," she wailed, then realized what a fool she was making of herself and felt even worse.

"Save me a piece," he replied. "I'll be in sometime or other. I wish I could have given you more notice, but I just checked with my answering service and they tell me I've got to see a man about a Matisse."

"That's quite all right."

It wasn't all right. Sarah was appalled to realize how much she'd been counting on Mr. Bittersohn for moral support. Now what was she going to do?

Chapter 13

It was a mercy she'd done all that cooking the previous afternoon. Otherwise, Sarah might never have got through dinner. She set things in motion as best she could, then went upstairs for a couple of aspirin and half an hour's rest before having to begin the evening performance. The prospect of having to make polite conversation in particular with Mr. Hartler after the dressing-down she'd had to give him was almost more than she could face.

Maybe she ought to have gone in and apologized after his obstreperous visitor was gone; but, damn it, why should she? This was her house, not his.

With the help of Uncle Jem, Sarah had drawn up a tough, practical set of house rules. Mr. Hartler had got a copy as had everybody else. Guests were to be received publicly in the library or privately in the tenants' own rooms. They were to come and go at reasonable hours, and to behave in a seemly enough fashion so that they wouldn't be a nuisance to anybody else. They were to enter the dining room only if proper arrangements had been made and the extra fee had been paid.

Under no circumstances whatever did any outsider have the right to wander unescorted through the house handling the landlady's personal possessions as if they were trinkets in a gift shop. If Mr. Hartler couldn't abide by the rules, then Mr. Hartler would have to leave. And if Mrs. Sorpende had to be ejected for nonpayment of rent, then she could go and housekeep for him and he could buy her some new underwear.

Feeling a trifle better for her rest, Sarah took a shower, put on more make-up than she was accustomed to and a

gray satin dress Aunt Emma had owned in younger, slim-
mer days, and went downstairs to be gracious if it killed
her.

As she was crossing the hall into the library, Mr.
Hartler burst through the front door, still in his daytime
outerwear: tweed hat askew on his tumble of white hair,
tweed-lined poplin storm coat buttoned awry, arms laden
with bundles. "For you, Mrs. Kelling," he panted. "Apologies. Horrible old man. Now I'm late. Must change at
once. Shopping impossible this time of day. Should have
realized. Wicked old man. Happy old man!"

He bounded into his room, leaving Sarah to open her
presents. There were a dozen voluptuous white roses, a
lavish flask of benedictine, a three-pound box of expensive chocolates. As an apology, she had to admit, this was
no mean effort.

Once he'd rejoined the company in his usual evening
attire, though, self-abasement was forgotten. His afternoon caller—not that unfortunate woman who had, as he
put it, behaved so naughtily, but the other one—had
brought in photographs of what purported to be no fewer
than seven out of a set of sixty-two dining room chairs
King Kalakaua had commissioned from a Boston firm in
1882 and never collected. Paeans of joy, Mr. Hartler was
going to see them that very evening! He was so excited he
didn't think he'd be able to eat his dinner and he fer-
vently hoped Mrs. Kelling would forgive him if he didn't.

Before they'd even got to the table, Sarah's head was
throbbing. Everybody was thoroughly fed up with Mr.
Hartler and his sixty-two chairs. Miss LaValliere, who'd
got her hair done that afternoon in an even more gro-
tesque fashion than usual, went into sulks when she
learned Mr. Bittersohn wasn't there to be impressed. Mr.
Porter-Smith became morose in consequence since he
was, after all, a good deal closer to Jennifer's age than
Bittersohn was and besides, he'd seen her first.

Since Professor Ormsby never bothered to talk anyway,
dinner could have become a total disaster were it not for
the consummate tact and skill of the puzzling Mrs.
Sorpende. She complimented Miss LaValliere on her coif-
fure and Mr. Porter-Smith on his erudition until she got
them both to act civil. She jollied Professor Ormsby into
telling a genuinely funny anecdote about something that
had happened at a faculty meeting. She couldn't get Mr.

Hartler out of the clouds long enough to eat his dinner, but she did manage to tone down his raptures to endurable level.

By the time they got back to the library they were all in reasonably good humor with themselves and each other. Charles had presence of mind enough to serve the benedictine with the coffee even though Sarah forgot to tell him. That reminded her to open her opulent box of candy and pass it around. Bonhomie was restored, at least on the surface, and that was enough for her.

Nevertheless, Sarah made her escape as soon as she decently could, and the party broke up with her. Professor Ormsby had another paper to read. Mr. Hartler got Charles to call him a taxi and charged off in hot pursuit of King Kalakaua's chairs. Mr. Porter-Smith failed to interest Miss LaValliere in scaling the outside of the Bunker Hill Monument by moonlight, but she consented to display her new hairdo at the coffee house. Mrs. Sorpende was the only one not going anywhere, so Sarah left the chocolates conveniently close to her on the coffee table, as a tacit acknowledgment of her magnificent performance.

Either the sweets were too tempting, though, or not tempting enough. Sarah had barely got into a robe and done her face when she heard deliberate, stately footsteps on the stairs. Though she couldn't have been less in the mood for company, she was impelled to open her bedroom door.

"Mrs. Sorpende, would you mind coming in for a moment?"

"Why, certainly." With her usual serene courtesy but a tiny pucker between her well-plucked eyebrows, the older woman stepped into the room. "Was there something—"

"I simply wanted to thank you for taking over so marvelously this evening. I'm sure none of the others noticed because you did it so gracefully, but I can't tell you what it meant to me."

The tears Sarah had felt like shedding ever since Max Bittersohn's anxiety-provoking phone call spilled over at last. She groped on her dressing table for a tissue and tried to stem the flow.

"I'm sorry," she sniffled. "I didn't mean to do this. It's just that ever since I lost my husband—"

"Dear Mrs. Kelling, I do understand. Only I did most

of my crying before mine went," said Mrs. Sorpende in an unusual burst of self-revelation. "Believe me, if I was of any help to you at all this evening, I can only say that I'm grateful for the opportunity."

What a darling she was! "Do sit down a moment if you have nothing better to do," Sarah urged. "This slipper chair is quite comfortable, unless you think it's too low. My mother-in-law often used it, and she was even taller than you."

"That beautiful, tragic woman," said Mrs. Sorpende. "It's strange to realize that I'm sitting where she sat. When I read in the papers—but I'm sure you'd rather talk of something else. Mr. Hartler's new chairs, for instance?" She laughed in her gentle, pleasant way. "He is a real enthusiast, isn't he? Though one does sometimes get the impression that his enthusiasm isn't universally shared."

"It certainly isn't by me! As you may have gathered from all that largesse he was showering on me tonight, we had a bit of a set-to this afternoon. I had to straighten him out in no uncertain terms about the string of visitors he's been having. They've been creating such a nuisance that I completely lost my temper. Now, of course, I wish I hadn't."

"I expect we all wish that sort of thing now and then, but think what a dull world this would be if everyone were perfect. You must find it difficult, having your lovely home filled with a motley collection of strangers like us."

"Once in a while I do," Sarah admitted, "but on the whole it's far less difficult than trying to stay here by myself. I'd be lonely and worried about how to manage, and nervous about being alone in this big place. Now I'm so busy all the time that I don't have a spare moment to worry in. Anyway, this was never my home."

"But I was under the impression—" Mrs. Sorpende caught herself. She'd almost fallen prey to vulgar curiosity.

"Oh, I've lived here ever since I was married, if that's what you mean, but this had been my mother-in-law's home for a great many years by then. Since she was both blind and deaf, we had to keep everything exactly as she herself had arranged it, so that she could find her way around. It's hard to feel you really belong in a place when you don't feel free to so much as pull a chair out of line. If you'll forgive my mentioning chairs again."

They both had a little laugh over that, then Sarah had a bright idea. "Would you excuse me for one second? I'm just going to run into the studio. It used to be Aunt Caroline's—that is, my mother-in-law's boudoir."

She came back with a huge armload of lace, georgette, and crepe de Chine. "Would you be terribly offended if I were to offer you a few of her things? You've been so sweet and I—it would please me if you were to have something that belonged to the house. She was a famous beauty in her day, you know, and when her husband was alive she always dressed in the most exquisite clothes. You wouldn't believe what I found when I cleaned out her closets. Everything was far too big for me, of course, so I passed most of it out among her friends and relatives."

Cousin Mabel had managed to wind up with the lion's share as always, and what she intended to do with all those beaded chiffon evening gowns, only the Lord in His infinite wisdom knew.

"But there are still some negligees and nightgowns and undies, camisoles and those floppy-legged step-ins and so forth, that are quite lovely. You have such a charmingly imaginative way of dressing that I've been thinking you might find them rather fun to play around with."

In fact, Sarah had thought no such thing until a moment ago. It was just that she'd happened to find the garments in the basement room where they'd been stuck and forgotten after Aunt Caroline's death. Rushing to get the room ready for Mr. Bittersohn, she'd thrust them back upstairs in the former boudoir because she couldn't think offhand what else to do with them. Now, watching Mrs. Sorpende's face aglow at sight of the soft colors and rich fabrics, she was grateful for her oversight.

"Oh, Mrs. Kelling! I'm simply overwhelmed. Are you sure you care to part with these wonderful things?"

"Quite sure. I'd never use them myself, and they're not the sort of stuff one cares to pass on to outsiders. I only hope some of them fit."

"They will, I can assure you, one way or another. I'm very clever with my needle. Such lovely, lovely materials! I feel like the Queen of Sheba just touching them. Or should I say Queen Liliuokalani?"

"No, don't. I used to think that was such a lovely name, but if Mr. Hartler says it one more time, I'm planning to throw a full-scale tantrum."

They giggled again like two well-brought-up little girls who knew perfectly well they shouldn't be making fun of nice, nutty old Mr. Hartler. Then Mrs. Sorpende said she must go along upstairs and let Mrs. Kelling get some rest. Knowing what she really meant was that she couldn't wait to try on her new hole-free underwear, Sarah let her go.

Surprisingly, the headache was almost gone, too. Sarah finished her preparations for the night, got into bed, and had read less than a paragraph of Schopenhauer before she switched off the light and drifted into sleep.

Chapter 14

Sarah was having a lovely dream of being in a public restaurant with Queen Elizabeth and Prince Philip. The Prince was singing along with the orchestra in an extempore serenade to the Queen, who was wearing a lovely frock and matching hat in moss green and looking quite lovely, terribly embarrassed, and tremendously gratified as who wouldn't. Then Sarah realized the drumming noise she was hearing didn't come from the orchestra accompanying His Royal Highness but from somebody's loud tapping at her bedroom door.

She sat up, switched on the bed lamp, and snatched for her robe. The time, according to her alarm clock, was twenty-seven minutes past one.

"Who's there? What's the matter?"

"It's me." Charles must be badly shaken. "You better come. We got the fuzz downstairs."

"The what? Oh, my God!"

Sarah couldn't find the sleeves of her bathrobe, got her slippers on the wrong feet and had to change them, made an ineffectual sweep at her hair with a brush, then rushed downstairs. Police at this hour weren't selling tickets to the Policemen's Ball. Was it Uncle Jem? One of the boarders? Was he, or she, in jail, in the hospital, at the morgue?

By now Sarah was practically on first-name terms with everybody in the division. "Hello, Sergeant McNaughton," she sighed. "What's the matter now?"

"Hi, Mrs. Kelling. Sorry to keep bothering you. You got an elderly gentleman named—uh—Hartler living here?"

"Yes, I have. What's he done now?"

"Would he be a little guy maybe five feet four or five, good head of hair for a man his age. Wearing sort of old-fashioned evening clothes with a black cashmere overcoat and black patent leather elevator shoes."

"Is that what they are? I've always thought he had bunions or hammer toes or something and needed those orthopedic ones you have to have made specially. Yes, that's Mr. Hartler, at least it sounds like him. I'm reasonably sure he didn't stop to change after dinner. He was in a mad rush to get out."

"Where was he going, Mrs. Kelling?"

"To look at some chairs that are alleged to belong at the Iolani Palace in Hawaii. Mr. Hartler's been trying to collect furniture and whatnot for the restoration. Sergeant McNaughton, what's this all about? Have you caught him trying to buy stolen property? Is he in jail?"

She ought to have remembered Sergeant McNaughton was too experienced a law enforcement officer to let himself get switched off from what he was doing. He waited politely until she'd finished talking, then asked, "Where were these chairs supposed to be?"

"He didn't say, at least not to me. Mr. Hartler and I aren't on the chummiest of terms at the moment. He's had swarms of people in and out of here about this Iolani Palace business of his, and they've been making a nuisance of themselves. I got fed up this afternoon and pinned his ears back in no uncertain terms. He apologized and we more or less smoothed things over for the moment, but when he got going on those chairs, I was in no mood to ask politely interested questions. Charles, you got him a taxi and put him into it, didn't you? Do you recall his giving the driver an address?"

"He did not do so in my presence, madam. Mr. Hartler was still thanking me in a profuse, not to say fulsome manner when the vehicle departed."

Sergeant McNaughton didn't bother to ask in which direction. Tulip Street, like so many others on the Hill, was one way and barely passable at that. The cabbie would have headed straight for Beacon Street because there was nowhere else he could go. Mr. Hartler needn't have given him any direction until they were in a position to change course.

"If he was only going a short distance, like say over to Arlington Street, would he have bothered with a cab?"

"In this case, I should think he might," Sarah replied. "He was all of a twitter to get at those chairs, and riding was faster than walking. And it was dark and raw, and though he's lively enough for his years, he does have a heart condition."

"How's the condition of his bankbook?"

"Fine, as far as I know. I believe Mr. Hartler is quite well-off."

"In the habit of carrying a wad of cash around with him?"

"I couldn't say. He spent a fair amount of money on me this evening. After that blasting I gave him, he rushed out and bought me a big bunch of roses, and some expensive chocolates, and a bottle of benedictine. He probably paid cash, because he hasn't been living back in Boston long enough to have charge accounts around the Hill, I shouldn't think. What's the matter? Has he been robbed?"

"I shouldn't be surprised," said Sergeant McNaughton. "We found nothing in his wallet except some personal papers and an I.D. giving this address. Loose change in the pockets, that's all."

"You mean you had to search him? Then he's—"

"Afraid so, Mrs. Kelling. Hey, somebody catch her!"

After that, things became fuzzy. Sarah had a dim awareness that Mr. Bittersohn had somehow manifested himself in a maroon bathrobe and was yelling at the policeman. "Why didn't you hit her over the head and be done with it? How much do you think she can take?"

Mariposa was being rude in Spanish. Charles was trying to get the madam to drink something that unfortunately turned out to be the benedictine Mr. Hartler had brought. Sarah got sick to her stomach just smelling it. Poor Sergeant McNaughton was trying to apologize. Sarah didn't want any more apologies. She'd had one too many tonight already. She sat up, noting with surprise that she was on the library couch although she had no idea how she'd got there, and shouted, "Shut up, all of you!"

They were so astonished that they did.

"Charles, give that stuff to Sergeant McNaughton. He needs a drink more than I do. Mariposa, go make some

coffee. And put some more clothes on before you freeze
to death. And straighten your cap!"

Mariposa must have become suddenly aware that a
sheer black nylon peignoir set and her ruffled cap worn
backward with the orange ribbons dangling down over
her nose did not constitute an adequate uniform, for she
bolted toward the kitchen. Charles, with a low bow, presented the liqueur to the policeman. Sergeant Mc-
Naughton, having given it a suspicious sniff, drained the
tiny glass.

At that point Mrs. Sorpende joined the party wearing
a sumptuous ecru satin negligee that Sarah thought
looked vaguely familiar although she couldn't recall ever
having seen the lady *en déshabillé* before. The other
lodgers must still be asleep. With any luck, they'd stay
that way.

"Now," said Sarah, "would you all please quit dithering and sit down? You're making me dizzy. Mr. Bittersohn, what are you doing with that whatever-it-is?"

"Covering you up," he said, suiting the deed to the
word. "You've got to be kept warm. You're in shock."

"I daresay I am and I'm sure I have every right to be,
but isn't that your good overcoat?"

"It's the first thing I could find. Lean back."

Sarah did, and found a nest of pillows had been prepared for her. They felt extremely comfortable. She was
tempted to close her eyes and drift back to wherever she'd
been a moment ago. Perhaps she did, because after a
while she heard whispering and rustling and scraping of
chairs to which she did not deem it necessary to pay attention. Then she smelled coffee and somebody said, "Do
you think we should wake her?" and somebody else said,
"No, let her sleep," and she sat up again.

"Set the tray here, Mariposa. Mrs. Sorpende, will you
take sugar?"

"I'll take the pot. You lie still and let me pour. Here,
drink this. Mr. Bittersohn, would you be good enough to
steady the cup for her?"

Mr. Bittersohn would be good enough. Sarah sipped,
made a face though she knew landladies weren't supposed
to make faces, and said she didn't care for sugar, thank
you. Mr. Bittersohn and Mrs. Sorpende both told her to
drink it anyway because sugar was good for shock.

Perhaps it was. At any rate, the room came slowly back

into focus. Sarah made sure everybody else had coffee, too, especially Mariposa, who might have taken a chill, although Mariposa was now engulfed in a large and lurid robe that must date from Charles's pre-Hudsonian period. Then she called the meeting to order.

"Now, Sergeant McNaughton, if you're quite sure you feel up to talking, would you kindly tell us what this is all about? Where did you find Mr. Hartler?"

Sergeant McNaughton uncrooked his little finger, set down his empty cup, cleared his throat, and became official again. "I must remind you, Mrs. Kelling, that no formal identification has as yet been made. However, considering that the victim answers your description, has his name on identification papers, stamped inside a hat that was found nearby, embroidered inside his overcoat and suit coat, and printed in indelible ink on his underwear—"

"And he's not here and his bed hasn't been slept in," Charles prompted *sotto voce*. "We looked, remember?"

"Oh yeah, thanks. Anyway, we can assume for purposes of investigation that he's the guy. The body was found in the Public Garden right beside that fancy birdhouse down by the pond on the Arlington side before you get to the bridge. The foot patrolman who discovered the body deduced from the evidence that the victim had been mugged and robbed. Acting on approved police procedure, he then—do you want the whole report?"

"No," said Sarah. "Just give us the gist. Was Mr. Hartler—had he already—"

"We don't get 'em much deader, Mrs. Kelling. He'd been dealt a number of blows on both the front and the back of the skull with a heavy instrument. There's no way we can see that it might have been anything other than deliberate homicide. The medical examiner's report isn't in yet, but we think he was knocked out from behind and then—well, you said to skip the details."

"When did it happen?" asked Bittersohn.

"Sometime close to midnight, probably. Not long before he was found, anyway."

"Then I expect he'd have been on his way back here," said Sarah.

"Walking? But you say he had a bad heart. Why didn't he call another cab?"

"Sergeant, how do I know? Maybe there wasn't a

phone where he was. Maybe he just decided to walk. Mr. Hartler was—unpredictable. Wouldn't you say so, Mrs. Sorpende?"

"Totally, I should say, although I'd only known him a few days," the older woman agreed in her deliberate, well-bred voice. "Mr. Hartler appeared absorbed in this project of his almost to the point of monomania. If those chairs did in fact prove to be what he was looking for, I'd think he'd have been so excited he wouldn't know whether he was walking or flying. I must admit I amused myself this evening wondering what he'd be like when he came back. I pictured him rushing through the house waking us all up to spread the good tidings, and I was thinking what various people's reactions would be if he did. Then of course I realized our excellent Charles would hardly permit such a disruption to occur."

The excellent Charles allowed the merest ghost of a gratified expression to flit across his handsomely composed features. Mariposa said, "Damn right he wouldn't." Mrs. Sorpende kindly pretended she hadn't heard.

McNaughton nodded to Mrs. Sorpende, then turned to Sarah. "This lady says she hadn't known him long. What about you, Mrs. Kelling?"

"I'd met him a few times over the years at my Aunt Marguerite's. Actually she's only an aunt-in-law, but I'm sure you don't care about that. Anyway, Mr. Hartler had heard, I suppose from her, that I was opening my house to lodgers and got in touch with me. At that time I'd already rented the room he wanted to Mr. Quiffen. Then when Mr. Quiffen was killed—would you all mind if I were to faint again?"

"Don't be funny," snarled Bittersohn. "Charlie, can't you find something to give her besides that goddamn benedictine? McNaughton, do you think there's any chance you can keep this away from the papers?"

"Jeez, I don't know, Max. You mean this old Mr. Hartler had the same room Quiffen did, the guy that got hit by the train? Boy, that ought to be good for a few more headlines."

"Remind me to recommend you for the tact medal, Mac. Why don't you get out of here and go see if you can lose yourself somewhere?"

"Okay, Max, if that's how you feel. Mrs. Kelling, I

hate to keep pestering you like this, but do you know of any relatives we could notify?"

"Mr. Hartler had a sister, but he told us she'd gone to stay with a friend in Rome. No doubt he'd have her address in his room. Charles, did you lock his door after you looked in to see if he was there? If you did, go get the key."

"Stay where you are, Mrs. Kelling," said Bittersohn. "You're not up to this."

"I know, but it's my responsibility, isn't it?" Sarah untangled herself from the overcoat and stood up, Mrs. Sorpende assisting her on one side and Mr. Bittersohn on the other. "You might as well join the party, Sergeant McNaughton. It's just across the hall."

Sarah herself had been making a point of staying out of the lodgers' rooms herself and leaving the cleaning to Mariposa, in order to avoid being tagged a snoopy landlady. She hadn't set foot in the erstwhile drawing room since they'd got rid of Mr. Quiffen's things and spruced it up for Mr. Hartler. It was going to need resprucing. During his so-short stay, the old man had contrived to make an unholy mess of the place.

Uncle Gilbert's beautiful desk was heaped with papers. The file drawers that had been installed to hold Mr. Quiffen's vituperative but neatly organized correspondence hung half open, revealing a welter of newspaper clippings, travel folders, plastic leis, and, for some reason, a tattered felt pennant bearing the slogan, "Let's Hear It for Hawaii!"

Vases, cardboard cartons, trinkets, jardinieres, bits and pieces of antique or semi-antique furniture were crammed everywhere. The somewhat threadbare but still precious oriental carpet that Sarah had paid to get professionally cleaned before she started renting her rooms now looked as though it would have to be sand-blasted.

"He wouldn't let me clean," said Mariposa defensively. "I told you so yesterday."

"I know you did," Sarah answered. "That's another thing I meant to scold him about. Ridiculous, isn't it? I suppose we might as well tackle that beastly desk first."

The task that had looked impossible turned out to be a cinch. Almost on top of the heap lay a letter on flimsy air-mail stationery from an Italian hotel.

"Dear Wumps," it began. "You were right as usual!!!

I was a fool to have come and, as you see from this heading, I've had to move out. It wasn't so much Dorothea's
DRINKING that I found impossible to cope with, though
you know my views on EXCESS, but there were OTHER
problems I cannot bring myself to put on paper, EVEN
TO YOU!!! I refuse to remain in such an ATMOS-
PHERE and have already started haunting the airline
offices. I can't tell you what flight I'll be on because I intend to take the FIRST CANCELLATION THAT
COMES UP!!

"So glad to hear you are comfortably settled with dear
little Sarah Kelling, though that leaves ME out in the
cold! Anyway, perhaps she will have a SPARE CORNER
I can crawl into until I can find a place to stay. I will
come DIRECTLY THERE from the airport so that we
can talk over what to do. Sarah will pardon the liberty,
I'm sure. Such a sweetly pretty little thing, I always
thought, and such NICE MANNERS. Give her my best
regards. Hope to see you SOON!!!! Hastily, Bumps."

"Well, that's better news than we'd bargained for,"
said Sarah. "It's dated over a week ago so she may even
be on her way here by now. Poor soul, it's going to be a
dreadful homecoming for her. They always appeared to
be so very devoted."

"Bumps and Wumps," mused the sergeant. "Were they
twins?"

"I don't believe so," Sarah replied. "I'm quite sure
Miss Hartler is several years the younger. I don't honestly
remember her very well."

"Here's a picture," said Mariposa, who'd been running
a stern housewifely eye over the dresser. "Maybe it's her."

Sarah took the pretty silver frame out of Mariposa's
hand. "Oh yes, now I recall the hat. She always wore
the same one, or else she kept buying them all alike. Apparently she still does, because this picture must have
been taken quite recently. That reminds me, Mariposa,
we'd better get in some cranberry juice. That's all she
ever drinks, because it's good for the kidneys, or the liver,
or something. She got me off in a corner once and told
me all about it, but I'm afraid I wasn't paying much attention. She really is the mousiest creature! I can't imagine why this Dorothea person invited her in the first
place."

"There doesn't seem to be a picture of the brother," said McNaughton. "Would you say they looked alike?"

"But you saw his face."

"Well, no. You see——"

"Shut up, Mac," snapped Bittersohn. He took a firm grip on Sarah's arm, and she was grateful for his support.

They searched among the rubble awhile longer, but found no address book, and nothing to indicate the presence of a more accessible relative. It appeared they would have to wait for Bumps to make the formal identification of Wumps.

Chapter 15

"There's something I have to tell you."

Sarah was in her place behind the coffee urn, trying to be poised and collected although her hands were rattling every cup she touched. Professor Ormsby, Miss La-Valliere, and Mr. Porter-Smith were in their places. Mr. Bittersohn and Mrs. Sorpende had not appeared. That was not surprising, considering what time they'd got back to bed. Sarah herself would rather have kept on sleeping forever, but that ingrained sense of duty had compelled her to come and break the news before her boarders got it somewhere else.

"Tell us what?" yawned Miss LaValliere. Then she smirked. "I know. Mr. Hartler's eloped with Mrs. Sorpende. That's why he's not here."

"I wish you were right," Sarah answered. "Last night, we had the police in. They'd found a man we're quite sure was Mr. Hartler near the birdhouse in the Public Garden. He'd evidently been beaten and robbed on his way back from seeing those chairs he was so thrilled—"

Sarah steadied herself with a sip of hot coffee. "The last I knew, he hadn't been officially identified, but since they found his name on his clothes and in his wallet—"

"Great Scott!" gasped Mr. Porter-Smith. "You mean he was killed?"

"I'm afraid I do."

"But that's awful! I mean, two in a row! I mean—" Miss LaValliere didn't seem to know quite what she did mean, but there was nothing affected about her agitation.

"I know how you feel," said Sarah. "Considering what's happened during the very short time you people have been living here, I shouldn't blame you one bit if you packed your bags and left this instant. I must have some magnetic attraction for disaster."

110

"Garbage!" roared Professor Ormsby. "Unscientific swill! What time did this alleged assault take place?"

"Sometime close to midnight, the police said it must have been."

"In the Public Garden? Still wearing his tuxedo?"

"Yes."

"Well, there you are, aren't you? Who wears tuxedos these days? Rich old men and waiters. Waiters go off duty with their pockets full of tips. Rich men have gold cuff links, studs, collar buttons, whatnot. Gold worth five hundred dollars an ounce or some such monstrous price. Don't keep track myself. Don't walk through the Garden alone at night, either. Perverts. Dope addicts. Hartler was an old fool. Quiffen was a worse fool. Trouble you for the marmalade."

"Of course." Sarah passed the cut-glass jar in its little silver basket. Professor Ormsby was right. Mr. Hartler should have known better than to be wandering around alone at that hour, practically asking to be mugged. Mr. Quiffen should have kept his nose out of other people's business. Neither death had anything to do with her. If only she were sure of that!

"I quite agree with Professor Ormsby," Mr. Porter-Smith pontificated. "Mr. Hartler, having lived away from Boston for a number of years, may not have been aware that an area where he had perhaps been accustomed to wander freely as a younger man was now unsafe for our senior citizens late at night. Mr. Quiffen was an elderly person who indulged, if I may say so, rather freely in the pleasures of the table, and was of an unusually choleric disposition. Therefore, he almost certainly suffered from an elevated blood pressure that might well subject him to occasional fits of dizziness. That both should have met their demise—I mean demises—"

"How about demeese?" Professor Ormsby suggested helpfully.

Mr. Porter-Smith flushed, but stuck to his guns. "As I was saying, this is a most unfortunate coincidence, but surely nothing more than that. Professor Ormsby, if you happen to have left any marmalade in the jar, I believe I shall also partake."

Miss LaValliere wasn't quite ready to buy the mere coincidence theory, but neither did she wish to move in with her grandmother, which would be the only way her parents would continue her allowance if she left Mrs. Kelling's. When Mr. Porter-Smith passed her the marmalade, she took it.

However, she was almost as silent as Professor Ormsby for the rest of the meal. When Mr. Porter-Smith realized he had the floor to himself, he took full advantage of the circumstance, while Sarah sat and wondered what time they'd all three got in last night and where they'd gone beforehand. And what about Cousin Dolph?

That was what Professor Ormsby would doubtless call a damn fool question. Dolph hadn't even met Mr. Hartler yet.

But he had. The very expression, "damn fool," brought back a far too distinct memory of one of Aunt Marguerite's more disastrous parties. Aunt Caroline had dragooned Dolph into going with them, and he'd ranted all the way home about which was a bigger damn fool, that babbling jumping-jack Hartler or his damn fool of a cranberry-swilling sister.

That had been six years ago or more. Sarah couldn't remember what had set Dolph off about the Hartlers, but she knew from experience that it seldom took much. Furthermore, since the Hartlers were so chummy with Aunt Marguerite, they were more apt than not to have met the Protheroes and therefore to have had at least a passing acquaintance with George's old buddy Barnwell Quiffen.

Suppose for instance that Dolph had happened to run into Mr. Hartler last night during their respective wanderings. Considering the circles they both moved in, such a meeting was by no means impossible. The man who owned King Kalakaua's chairs, assuming they were indeed genuine, might well have been one of the old guard and a friend of Dolph's. Or both might have taken the same notion to stop in at the Harvard Club or the Ritz for a nightcap. The club was on Commonwealth Avenue, only a few blocks from where the body had been found, and the hotel was on the corner of Arlington and Newbury, directly across the street from the Garden.

No matter what he thought of the Hartlers, Dolph wouldn't snub a man he'd met in the home of a family member, especially if Mr. Hartler offered to pay for the drinks. Suppose he misunderstood something the older man said. That wouldn't be unlikely. Mr. Hartler's speech had been so rapid and so prolix that he'd often been hard to follow, and Dolph's was not the swiftest brain in town. What if Dolph had jumped to the conclusion that in taking over Mr. Quiffen's room, Mr. Hartler had got hold of some evidence that private detective had turned up? What if he'd thought Mr. Hartler was seeing himself as the man to whom from failing hands Mr. Quiffen had thrown the torch?

Well, what if he had? Sarah could see Dolph yelling the place down and maybe getting them both thrown out. She could not see him deliberately beating an older, smaller man's face to an unrecognizable pulp. Could she?

If Dolph had deliberately shoved Barnwell Quiffen under a moving subway train, then Dolph was a homicidal maniac and there was no telling what he might do. But surely that was ridiculous. Anyway, Dolph wouldn't have faked a robbery. He couldn't think that fast, for one thing.

He could very quickly have made himself scarce, however. The Arlington Street subway entrance was only a short sprint from where the body had been found, and who was to say more than one person hadn't been involved in the crime? Suppose that after he'd been killed, one of those drug addicts or perverts Professor Ormsby was so vehement about might have come along, taken advantage of the chance to rob a prosperous-looking corpse, and kicked Mr. Hartler's face in just for the fun of it. That was sickening even to think of, but such things did happen.

Sarah didn't think she could sit there any longer watching Professor Ormsby mop up egg yolk with his toast. She was trying to think of a plausible reason to leave the table, when Mariposa handed her the most cogent one possible.

"Mrs. Kelling, she's here!"

Sarah blinked. "Who's here?"

"She says she's Mr. Hartler's sister and she wants to know if her brother's up yet."

"Show her into the library. Excuse me, please, everyone."

Sarah remembered Miss Hartler the moment she laid eyes on her. As far as she could recall, the woman was wearing the identical outfit in which she'd appeared some four years ago at Aunt Marguerite's, totally without style or color interest. The same might have been said of the

wearer. Miss Hartler bore a family resemblance of sorts to
her brother and had his abundant white hair, which could
have been her redeeming feature if she hadn't got it
cropped far too short by some dropout from barber college and hidden most of what was left under a truly awful
hat. At the moment, she was showing an unaccustomed
spark of something that could almost be taken for anima-
tion.

"Dear little Sarah!"

To Sarah's secret horror, Miss Hartler insisted on planting a dry-lipped kiss on her cheek. "I was so sorry to hear
of the terrible, terrible deaths of your dear Aunt Caroline
and her *devoted* son! And of course Mr. Frederick Kelling, too. Such a tragic loss to the city! I hope you got my
little note?"

"Why, I—yes, of course. You were so kind to write."

Sarah hadn't the slightest recollection as to whether
she'd heard from the Hartlers or not, there had been so
many condolences. But she'd diligently acknowledged
them all, or thought she had, with Aunt Emma's help.
"I'm sure I sent a reply. But if you were in the process of
going abroad—"

"Oh, I expect William opened the envelope and tossed
away your message without bothering to show me. That
would be just like him. Big brother still doesn't quite believe little sister's learned to read yet, you know. Where is
old Wumps? I can't wait to surprise him! He'll never
dream I could be here so soon, but I simply *camped* at
that airport until they found me a seat. Did he tell you I
was coming?"

"He told me how much he missed you," Sarah tempo-
rized.

"I can well imagine! Wumps and I have always been
very close, you know. It was quite an adventure for me to
leave him as I did, and as things turned out, a dreadful,
dreadful mistake. But I shan't bore you with my sordid
history! Which is Wump's room? Isn't he up yet, the lazy
thing? Perhaps I might just tiptoe in. I can't wait another
second to see him!"

She rose and started for the door. Sarah took her arm.

"Miss Hartler, you—you'd better sit down again.
There's something I have to tell you."

"About Wumps? What is it? Is he ill? In the hospital?"

Sarah shook her head. "I'm afraid it's a great deal worse than that, Miss Hartler. He was—assaulted last night in the Public Garden."

"Oh no! Not Wumps!" Miss Hartler stared at Sarah, then buried her face in the dun-colored silk scarf she had twisted around her wizened throat.

"No positive identification has been made yet, but his name was on his things, and he never came back last night. We found your letter on his desk, and I'm supposed to let the police know when you arrive so that you can—I'd better get you some brandy."

"No, please, I couldn't touch it. Just—just let me be alone in his room for a little while. Wumps dead? You do mean dead, Sarah?"

"I'm afraid I do. Here, let me help you."

Miss Hartler sorely needed help. Her legs could barely support her. She wobbled across the hall and collapsed on the bed, her face pressed into the clean sheet Charles had so neatly turned down for the old man who'd never come back. Sarah decided the kindest thing was to slip out and leave her there by herself until those thin old shoulders stopped heaving so convulsively.

Mariposa met her when she stepped back out into the hall. "Did you tell her?"

"I had to, didn't I? She wants to be alone in his room, so I came away. I didn't know what else to do. She looks so frail, and she's taking it awfully hard, as I knew she would. We ought to call a doctor, but we'd never get one to come."

"You go on back and have yourself a cup of hot coffee, honey. She'll get over it pretty soon. Old folks don't mind death the way young ones do. That's what my grandma says, and she ought to know by now. Come on, honey, you got to take care of yourself first, else you'll be no good to nobody."

"I know. Thank goodness one of us manages to stay sane around here."

Sarah gave Mariposa a hug and kiss, greatly shocking Mr. Porter-Smith, who was emerging from the dining room correct in what the well-dressed accountant's assistant should wear and making a beeline for the gold-initialed attaché case he had left prominently displayed in the front hall.

By now Professor Ormsby had finished ravening over

the eggs and gone off to his classes. Miss LaValliere was
still at the table nibbling at a piece of toast and mutter-
ing over a book she ought no doubt to have stayed home
and studied the night before. Sarah took some scrambled
eggs she didn't particularly want, and sat down to eat.
When she and Miss LaValliere had finished and the two
remaining boarders showed no sign of appearing, Sarah
took the used dishes out to the kitchen, where Mariposa
was already busy at the dishpan.

"I wonder if I should take Miss Hartler in a cup of tea
or something?" she remarked. "She's just off the plane
from Italy and goodness knows how long it's been since
she had anything to eat. That reminds me, there's a stack
of her luggage in the vestibule we'll have to do something
about."

"No sense bringing it in, till we find out where she in-
tends to go," said Mariposa. "Only have to lug it out
again."

"That's true, and it'll be safe enough with the outer
door locked. At least we shan't be getting any more of
King Kalakaua's whatnots dragged through the hall. That's
not very kind of me, is it? Poor old Wumps, what an awful way to go!"

"Oh, I don't know." Mariposa lifted a soap bubble on
her shapely fingers, and blew it away. "He was prob'ly
dancing along like he always did, thinking about them
chairs, and then, whammo! Quick and easy. I wouldn't
mind something like that for myself. Live it up till I'm
ninety-five, then get shot by a jealous wife."

Sarah wouldn't have believed she could laugh that
morning, but she did. By the time they'd finished the
dishes, she felt up to facing Miss Hartler again. She went
and tapped on the drawing room door.

"Miss Hartler? It's Sarah. May I come in?"

"Yes, dear." The voice seemed to come from very far
away.

"I was wondering if I might get you something? Tea
and toast, perhaps?"

Miss Hartler struggled to raise herself from the pillows
into which she'd been weeping. Her eyes were red, her
hair disheveled, her clothes a mess. She wiped a sodden
handkerchief across her blotched, terribly aged face.

"Thank you, dear. Perhaps a cup of very weak tea? I

never touch stimulants as a rule, but this—this—I knew I should never have left him. It's all my fault!"

Her shoulders began to heave again. Sarah said, "I'll get the tea," and fled.

As she was fixing a tray, Mr. Bittersohn came up the stairs from the basement. "What's happening?" was his greeting.

"The sister has arrived," Sarah told him. "She's in his room crying her eyes out, poor soul. I'm trying to get her to drink a cup of tea. Would you mind terribly just going into the dining room and helping yourself? There's coffee in the urn and things on the sideboard. Mrs. Sorpende should be down soon."

"So?"

"Oh, don't argue!" Sarah picked up the tray and left. He wasn't arguing, but she had to take it out on somebody. Strange that she should pick Mr. Bittersohn.

Miss Hartler was up off the bed, at any rate. She'd evidently been to the bathroom and tried to do something about her face and hair. Though her eyes were still very red, she was a little more composed. She seated herself at the desk and pushed some of the litter aside.

"Dear Sarah, how kind! But really I don't think I—"

"Now, Miss Hartler, you mustn't give way. Your brother wouldn't have wanted that." Sarah was dragging out all the clichés she could recall that had been visited upon her during her own recent bereavement. "He was such a cheerful person. We must try to remember him as we knew him."

"Ah, but nobody knew Wumps as I did."

Miss Hartler poured an inch or so of tea from the pot and added a great deal of milk. She peered at the arrowroot biscuits Sarah had put on the tray, then slowly picked one up and took an apologetic nibble. "We were so close, you know, so very close. Not that we lived in each other's pockets, of course. I had my church work, and Wumps had his own enthusiasms."

"The Iolani Palace," said Sarah.

"Ah, yes, that famous Iolani Palace! Wumps was a zealot, you know, Sarah. A genuine zealot. I see he's been collecting again." She waved the arrowroot biscuit at the bibelots that covered every available space.

"I'm not too sure how much he'd actually collected,"

Sarah replied. "He said most of the things he'd got proved not to be genuine and had to be given back. We've had people in and out of here—"

"Don't tell me! I've been through it all. Tracking up the rugs and letting their wet umbrellas drip on the floor. And the reason Wumps wanted to move back here was that we weren't getting enough of them. He thought Boston would be his Happy Hunting Ground. I must confess, Sarah dear, that I positively *quailed* at the mere thought. That was why, when I got this invitation from an old schoolmate to join her in Rome, I packed my bags and *fled*. But Dorothea has changed. Sadly, sadly changed. I suppose I have, too. Ah, me, time flies."

Making a pathetic attempt to put on a brave face, Miss Hartler picked up her teacup. "Sarah, I've been trying to think what to do, and it seems the sensible thing—I'm trying so hard to be sensible, you see. Wumps was always the strong one, but I don't have him to lean on anymore so I must manage as best I can alone. I thought if you'd let me stay here for just a few days, until we can get the dreadful, dreadful funeral over with—our plot is in Mount Auburn, you know, like yours—perhaps you'd know how to go about making the arrangements—I've never had to —when dear Mother and Father—"

She mopped her eyes and took an infinitesimal sip of the cooling tea. "That will give me a chance to find out how I stand and do something about all this stuff Wumps had left. Dear Sarah, you won't mind, will you? I have nobody else to turn to! If you could just have your man bring in my bags—"

"He's—not here just now," Sarah answered, rather stunned by this sudden turn of affairs.

Of course it made sense for Miss Hartler to use her brother's room. His rent was paid till the end of the week, and she had nowhere else to go, except a hotel or the YWCA. Somebody had to sift through this welter and decide what to do with it, and who could be better qualified than his own sister? But to have Miss Hartler around oozing gloom and respectability on top of everything else was going to be plain ghastly.

Well, it wouldn't be for long. If Mr. Porter-Smith's dinner jacket and Miss LaValliere's hairdo didn't drive the woman out, Mariposa and Charles, in their own adroit ways, would manage.

Chapter 16

Nevertheless, Sarah didn't give in without a struggle. "But —but we'd have to clean the room first. I couldn't let you move in here with the place in such a state."

"Oh, I can do that. Please let me. I'm so used to cleaning up after Wumps, you see. It would be like having him back, just for a little, little, precious while. Just have your maid bring in the vacuum cleaner and a duster, and I'll have everything spotless in no time. This will be the last chance I'll ever—" Her voice quavered and she hid her face again.

What could one say to that? Anyway, there were all those breakable objects belonging to heaven only knew whom, and it would be better for Miss Hartler to undertake the responsibility. Sarah went and got the cleaning materials, and left Miss Hartler to it.

Or thought she did. Miss Hartler couldn't figure out how to turn on the vacuum cleaner. Miss Hartler needed a sponge, a scrubbing brush, disinfectant, fresh linens, glass polish, brass polish, silver polish, a mop, a wall brush, a reviving glass of cranberry juice. Miss Hartler, in one way or another, took up Sarah's entire day.

There was the dreadful trip to the morgue to make her formal identification of darling Wumps. Luckily he'd had an old triangular scar on his right wrist that made the experience a degree less harrowing than it might have been but still bad enough for Miss Hartler to need another glass of cranberry juice before she felt up to facing the vicar concerning dead Wump's last rites. She was astonished to learn Sarah wasn't personally acquainted with the dear

vicar. Sarah was rude enough to reply that she at least
knew the undertaker.

"Yes, yes, we must see the undertaker. How terrible!
But dear Wumps wouldn't want old Bumps to let him
down, would he? I always called him Wumps because
when I was a baby I couldn't say William. And he re-
taliated by calling me Bumps because I kept falling down
when I tried to walk. I'm afraid a lot of the bumps were
Wump's own doing. He had such an impish sense of humor, even as a little boy. You must have adored having
him here."

"He was with us such a short time," Sarah murmured.
It wasn't pleasant to recall the blasting-out she'd given
him so soon before he'd gone out to his death, even more
painful to think that if she'd kept her mouth shut he might
have had the chairs brought to him and still be alive.
Nevertheless, Sarah couldn't be hypocritical enough to
pretend Mr. Hartler had been an unmixed blessing, and
she couldn't really believe his sister had always found
him so, either.

But she herself had got furious with Alexander sometimes, and that didn't make the hurt any less when she
lost him. She hadn't ducked the fact that he'd been murdered, though, as Miss Hartler was doing. The police
were naturally pressing her to search among the papers
for anything that might reveal if he had an enemy, an
article of exceptional value, and particularly if there was
any information as to whom the man with the chairs had
been, if in fact such a person existed. The sister was putting all that out of her mind, not reading the papers but
just stacking them neatly and waxing the desk; fussing
about the stately high-church service, about whether
Wumps would have preferred a gray or a mahogany
casket, about what music he would have preferred and
what flowers to choose. Sarah thought of suggesting they
fly in a ukulele band and a hibiscus lei from Honolulu because by that time she was getting thoroughly fed up with
Miss Hartler, but she couldn't because she was cursed
with too decent a nature.

Late in the afternoon she managed to get Miss Hartler
back into the fresh-cleaned drawing room for a rest and
herself rushed to the kitchen, trying to cram a day's work
into two hours. Uncle Jem phoned to ask if she wanted
him to rally around and she yelped back, "No, for God's

sake, don't!" Dolph didn't bother to call, he just came, taking it for granted that his presence would be required on so grave an occasion.

For that, Sarah was grateful. Miss Hartler knew Dolph, and his pompous solemnity struck just the right note with her when she emerged from her seclusion in a high-necked, long-sleeved gown of some lank material and some dark color, smelling faintly of mold and moth balls. As Dolph mouthed the correct phrases, Sarah couldn't help thinking that if he had by some wild chance been the instrument of William Hartler's demise, he was showing either remarkable self-possession or a degree of loopiness to which not even Great-uncle Frederick had ever attained. She found herself eying him as a mouse might watch a crouching cat. Was he dangerous, or was he only asleep. What would she do if she found out her familiar bumbler of a cousin had become a criminal lunatic? Go stark raving herself, most likely.

The lodgers were gathering. Mrs. Sorpende was first down, and Sarah was interested to see that she had, in respect to the demised, filled in her low-cut dinner gown with an elegant jabot of rich ivory-colored satin that just might, not long before, have been the legs of a pair of Aunt Caroline's step-ins. However it had been achieved, the effect was so flattering that Dolph suddenly ran out of platitudes on the subject of family bereavement and sidled over toward the sofa on which Mrs. Sorpende liked best to sit.

Miss Hartler then settled into an attitude of gentle melancholy. Sarah presented each of the others as he or she arrived, each offered condolences, then each settled down to enjoy the customary period of relaxation before dinner. However, it was not so easy to enjoy an innocent glass of preprandial sherry with Miss Hartler recoiling from the tray as from a striking cobra every time Charles passed within recoiling distance.

Mr. Porter-Smith's well-meant urging that she take a glass with him as medical studies had proven that moderate amounts of alcohol taken before a meal could be a valuable aid to general health and well-being earned him nothing but a stiff-lipped, "Thank you, I never touch spirits."

Miss LaValliere's attempts to cheer Miss Hartler up with an account of the senior Mrs. LaValliere's most re-

cent attack of shingles did strike a responsive chord since
Miss Hartler had once served on the altar guild with Miss
LaValliere's grandmother; but both the granddaughter
and her topic were soon exhausted.

Professor Ormsby didn't even try. Once he'd been
coerced into shaking hands and grunting some obligatory
word of sympathy, he took the other end of Mrs. Sorpende's sofa and glowered across her jabot at Dolph. Mr.
Bittersohn, again the last to arrive, was more compassion-
ate. He drew a chair close to Miss Hartler's, shook his
head when Charles offered him a drink, and began talking to her in a low, concerned voice.

At first, Miss Hartler appeared to respond. Then for
no reason that Sarah could see, she became monosyllabic
and at last so totally withdrawn that it was a relief when
Charles announced dinner and she said piteously that she
really didn't think she could face it and mightn't she
please just have a little something on a tray in her room?

That meant extra work for the staff and a quick re-
shuffling of the table, but Sarah couldn't have cared less.
She was so relieved to get out from under this wet blanket
that she didn't even try to change the subject when Mr.
Porter-Smith began explaining what the capital gains tax
meant to her, although in fact it meant nothing at all
since she wasn't having any gains these days, only losses.

By degrees, the group relaxed. With Dolph present the
atmosphere was bound to be a trifle on the stuffy side
anyway; but he, with his duty to Miss Hartler behind him,
Mrs. Sorpende beside him, and a good dinner in front of
him, waxed as genial as Dolph knew how to wax.

Mr. Bittersohn's thoughts seemed to be elsewhere.
Surely he couldn't have taken offense at Miss Hartler's
sudden cooling-off in the library. An elderly woman
who'd come straight from an overseas flight to find her
beloved brother murdered and herself at the morgue having to identify his battered corpse could hardly be expected to keep a stiff upper lip for any extended length
of time. Sarah dropped a gentle hint to that effect, and
Bittersohn gave her a look that puzzled her a good deal.

After dinner, she told Charles to serve the rest of Mr.
Hartler's benedictine. She wasn't sure why. Was the gesture in tribute to his memory, or was it an expression of
a wish to get rid of everything pertaining to the Hartlers
as quickly as possible? Anyway, they all had some; then

Dolph announced with blowing of horns and fanfare of trumpets that he was late for an important meeting, and took his departure. Mrs. Sorpende went upstairs, perhaps to remodel another item of lingerie. Professor Ormsby had papers to correct. Mr. Bittersohn said he had to work on his book, which was surely a lie. Miss LaValliere, in desperation, asked Mr. Porter-Smith to help her with her bookkeeping homework.

Sarah watched Charles collect the empty liqueur glasses, then decided she'd better check in on Miss Hartler. She found the sister in her nightgown, which was not to say scantily clad, since Miss Hartler wore the sort of garment R. H. Stearns used to carry for Boston ladies who went in for modesty. Nevertheless, Miss Hartler made a point of covering her yards of cotton with several more yards of flannel wrapper as she came to open the door.

"I know you're exhausted," Sarah told her, "so I shan't stay. I just wanted to make sure you have everything you need for the night."

"Dear little Sarah! You grow more like your Aunt Marguerite every day."

Sarah winced. One Marguerite in the world was already one too many for her. However, since there was no blood relationship there was little likelihood of resemblance. Miss Hartler must either be hallucinating or trying to pay a compliment. One might as well take the more charitable view.

"Do sit down and talk to me a moment," the woman went on. "I feel so—so terribly alone."

"Of course you do," said Sarah. "That's only natural. One gets over it sooner or later, or so they tell me."

"Ah, yes. We must comfort and support one another in our bereavement. I can see how valiantly you're trying to cope, and I admire your strength. But, Sarah dear, I can't help wondering—of course it's not my place to say anything, but—well, quite frankly, dear, I really don't think that if I'd been in your place I'd have been quite so quick to fill my home with a somewhat peculiar assortment of strangers. I only say this because I'm so much older. We old folks can't resist spreading our wisdom around where I'm sure it's not wanted. Personally, I'd be the last to inferfere—"

"And there's no earthly reason why you should feel any

need to do so," Sarah interrupted, a good deal more briskly than she'd meant to. "I get all the advice I can handle from Cousin Dolph and my uncle, who lives a few streets over, and the rest of my relatives. As to my boarders, I'm chiefly concerned that they pay their rent on time and obey the house rules, of which I'll give you a copy first thing in the morning. So far the only one who's given me any serious trouble was your brother. If I'd known what a dreadful nuisance that Iolani Palace project of his would turn out to be, I doubt if I'd have taken him on. However, he was always pleasant in other respects and got along with the rest of the group even though he did manage to keep us in an uproar a good deal of the time."

"Oh, Sarah!" Miss Hartler shook her white head sweetly and sadly. "I know Wumps was just a prankish schoolboy at heart and sometimes got a bit overexuberant, but at least he was our own sort. What do you know about those others? Little Jennifer LaValliere is all right, I suppose. Flighty and silly, but I've met her grandmother. This Porter-Smith, as he calls himself—"

"Came highly recommended by my Cousin Percy."

"Oh. And that man Ormsby—"

"Professor Ormsby is a distinguished member of the faculty at MIT."

"Ah, these mad scientists! Inventing those dreadful clones and goodness knows what else. Still, I suppose MIT is respectable enough as colleges go these days. However, that rather dangerous-looking young man who runs an art gallery or whatever it is. Bittersohn, he calls himself."

Miss Hartler inched closer and lowered her voice to a shocked murmur. "I was trying to make conversation with him before dinner, as one does, and since little Jennifer and I had been talking about her grandmother's work on the altar guild, I happened to ask if his own mother was involved in any such thing. He made the most incredible reply. He said, 'No, she doesn't even get to sit downstairs.' Now, Sarah dear, of course you're a young thing and you wouldn't know, but I'm very much afraid that man is a *Jew*."

For a moment, Sarah was so furious and disgusted she couldn't even speak. Then she managed to say through stiff lips, "I am perfectly well aware that Mr. Bittersohn is a Jew. His people are neighbors of ours at Ireson's Landing."

"Good heavens! Did your dear Aunt Caroline know his mother?"

"Mrs. Bittersohn is very selective in the people she chooses to know." Sarah could be bitchy, too, given the kind of provocation she was getting now. "However, as you learned this evening, the son is not the least bit snobbish, provided one doesn't try to overstep the line. And he doesn't run an art gallery, he's an internationally known art expert. His work requires a great deal of travel, so he finds it convenient to have a pied-à-terre here, and I must say I consider myself unusually fortunate to have him as a tenant."

"Dear me, I had no—I must—" Miss Hartler floundered a bit, then chose another victim. "Then this Mrs. Sorpende—this *femme fatale*, who is making such an obvious play for your cousin's fortune—what's she an international expert in, or would it be indelicate to ask? May one know where on earth you managed to become associated with a woman like that?"

Sarah played her trump card. "Through Aunt Marguerite."

"Marguerite? But she's never once mentioned—we were always such great friends—how could I have missed—"

"I believe Mrs. Sorpende is not personally acquainted with Aunt Marguerite." Few people would be, if they knew what they were getting into when they accepted the introduction, in Sarah's opinion. "She heard about my venture from a mutual acquaintance of theirs."

"Oh? Then I must know that person, at any rate. Who was it?"

The only way to end this distasteful conversation, Sarah supposed, was to satisfy this nasty old creature's curiosity once and for all. She racked her brain for the name Mrs. Sorpende had given. "Something with a B, I think. Brown? Baxter? Burns? No, Bodkin, that was it. Mrs. G. Thackford Bodkin."

Miss Hartler emitted an odd little whinny. "But, my dear Sarah, how could she? Vangie Bodkin has been dead for two years. I've never been to a lovelier funeral."

Chapter 17

Sarah passed another terrible night. After she'd got Miss Hartler quieted down, she'd taken the almost unprecedented step of phoning Aunt Marguerite on her own initiative. Her ostensible reason was to pass the word about Mr. William Hartler's impending funeral. In fact, she wanted to make sure Vangie Bodkin's had already taken place.

Yes, Mrs. Bodkin was well and truly demised. Yes, Joanna Hartler had been her bosom friend and had wept copiously at the interment. No, Marguerite had never happened to run into a Theonia Sorpende. What was she like, and why didn't Sarah bring her down sometime?

That was what had upset Sarah so dreadfully. Aunt Marguerite was not one to forget a name or deny an acquaintance, however slight. She liked to pass herself off as the most sought-after hostess in Newport. Since she was far from being that, she had to do a good deal of seeking on her own hook. If the late Vangie Bodkin had ever so much as mentioned Theonia Sorpende in her hearing, she'd have insisted on Vangie's bringing the woman to one of her teas, cocktail parties, luncheons, dinners, charity balls, and certainly to what she called her Sunday afternoon salons.

Even if Mrs. Sorpende had turned out to be Mrs. Bodkin's poor relation or favorite manicurist or the lady who took up her hems, she'd probably still have got invited. Aunt Marguerite would have managed somehow to check out her appearance and conversation, found her more than presentable, and at least put her on what Sarah and Alexander used privately to call the desperate list: reasonably well-mannered nobodies who could be called upon to fill in the gaps when too many somebodies fought shy of being salonized. If Mrs. Sorpende had been involved in a scandal, that would make her even more desirable because then she could be pointed out and whispered about behind her back. Aunt Marguerite had aped a famous Washington hostess by embroidering herself a sofa pillow with the message, "If you can't think of anything nice to say about anybody, come and sit next to me," and she practiced what she preached.

So unless Mrs. Sorpende was an adept with the oiuja board, she must have learned from somebody other than Vangie Bodkin that Sarah Kelling was renting rooms. Then why hadn't she given that person's name as a reference, instead of telling a lie that could so easily get found out? There was no second Mrs. G. Thackford Bodkin; the widower was still a widower and living, so far as Miss Hartler knew, in semi-seclusion.

But exactly how secluded was Mr. Bodkin? If he was acquainted with Aunt Marguerite, and now in the position of being an available extra man, she must be pestering him with invitations right and left. Surely he must have to respond sometimes, if only to decline, unless he'd gone senile or something. Miss Hartler had no information on that point. She'd merely described him as a quiet sort of man and gone on exclaiming over the perfidy of Mrs. Sorpende's having taken Vangie Bodkin's name in vain while Sarah tried to make believe she herself must have got the name wrong.

G. Thackford Bodkin was not the sort of name one got wrong. Mrs. Sorpende must have heard it somewhere, somehow, and who was to say that even if she didn't know the wife, she hadn't been acquainted with the husband? Her own marriage had not been happy, Sarah deduced that from her one little confidence over the lingerie. If Vangie Bodkin was an intimate of Joanna Hartler, she couldn't have been any Cleopatra, either. Perhaps the two disappointed spouses had become clandestine lovers, and perhaps Mr. Bodkin had mentioned Sarah Kelling's lodging house venture to Mrs. Sorpende after he'd got the news from Marguerite.

Maybe that was why she'd come up here to Boston. After a decent interval, Mr. Bodkin would follow, pretend to strike up an acquaintance with an attractive stranger, and marry her.

But if the two years that had already passed since Vangie's death wasn't a decent enough interval, then what was? Mrs. Sorpende was no chicken and Mr. Bodkin probably well into his seventies. More likely, she'd decided she'd better get on a streetcar that was moving.

Everybody knew Sarah Kelling was broke, but everyone also knew Sarah had rich relatives, that some of them were bachelors, and that one of those bachelors was about to become a great deal richer than he was already. And Mrs. Sorpende had already met him and been a smash from the start, but Dolph was a fusty old prig and if he found out she'd been carrying on with one of Marguerite's neighbors on the sly, he'd back off in a hurry. And if Mrs. Sorpende did have a scandal in her past, either Mr. Bodkin or any other person or circumstance, who'd have been likeliest to know and most eager to use it against her if he got the chance?

She must have sized up Mr. Quiffen right away as a troublemaker of the first water. She might also have known he was having Dolph shadowed. Who knew what her sources of information might be? If Mrs. Sorpende did want to find out anything about anyone, the odds were there'd be some man ready and willing to tell her. And if she saw her way clear to snaring the heir to Great-uncle Frederick's fame and fortune, and if nasty old Barnwell Quiffen posed a present threat to either Dolph's or her own prospects, might not a big, hefty woman without a decent shred of underwear to her name take drastic steps to remove that threat?

Suppose Mrs. Sorpende had got rid of Mr. Quiffen with a minimum of fuss and bother? Suppose that by a hellish coincidence she'd found his room taken over almost at once by a man from Newport; a man whose sister had been the bosom buddy of the woman she'd falsely named as a reference; a garrulous indiscreet old man who of course knew Vangie Bodkin was dead and might know a good many other things she wouldn't care to have him blurt out at some inconvenient time. Mightn't she be tempted to try her luck again?

Mrs. Sorpende had gone straight up to her room after he'd left the house on the night he died, but Sarah knew how easy it would have been for her to sneak down the back stairs again. By then, the rest would have gone their various ways, Sarah would be on the second floor, Mariposa and Charles in the kitchen or the basement. Mrs. Sorpende's coat was in the front hall closet, she'd simply have to put it on and go out. If anybody did happen to see her, she could have pretended she needed something at the drugstore or wanted a breath of air or had decided to drop in on a sick friend. Sarah had known better than to give her boarders door keys, but Mrs. Sorpende had only to snap the latch back so that she could return without having to ring the bell, provided she made it before Charles put on the night lock sometime around midnight.

Mr. Hartler might very well have told her where he was going about those chairs. Mrs. Sorpende had that pleasant, gracious way of chatting at least a few minutes with everyone in the company. It would have been natural enough for her to observe, "I hope you're not going far on such a cold night," or something of the sort. He'd almost certainly have replied, "Oh no, just over to Fairfield Street," or wherever it happened to be.

She'd then have known just how and where to arrange a supposedly accidental meeting, and suggest a cozy stroll through the Garden on their way back. It really was lovely with the lights in the trees and the golden dome of the State House in the background. He'd have accepted, either to oblige a lady or because he was happy the chairs were authentic or down in the dumps because they weren't. Bashing him over the head would have been an extremely unladylike thing for her to do, but it was the most plausible way for him to die there and she could have managed easily enough, being so much larger, younger, and stronger. With his bad heart, he might have died from the shock of the blow alone.

And she could have rushed back to the house, up the rear staircase, and been ready to put on Aunt Caroline's elegant negligee and do her act of kindness when Sarah collapsed after hearing the news. How did she happen to be awake when everyone else on the upper floors slept through the disturbance?

Mr. Bittersohn had been awake, too. He'd also been out for the evening, and he'd never said where. Maybe he himself wouldn't mind getting his whack at those seven chairs, if they were worth as much as Mr. Hartler had seemed to think. But Mr. Bittersohn would never do a thing like that!

Anyway, what about the rest of them? How did Sarah know Professor Ormsby was really giving a paper at MIT? Or that Mr. Porter-Smith and Miss LaValliere had been together at that coffee house the whole evening? Or that some totally unknown person hadn't come along and committed a haphazard murder for no reason other than to get at the money that was missing from Mr. Hartler's wallet? Why should she get so wrought up just because Mrs. Sorpende had happened to drop a little white lie about her social connections?

That was no little white lie. It might have started out as one but it wouldn't be for long. If Sarah was any judge of character, Joanna Hartler was cast in the same mold as Cousin Mabel. Cousin Mabel would never have drawn a peaceful breath, notwithstanding the death of a beloved brother or of the whole vast Kelling tribe, until she'd got in touch with Aunt Marguerite and everybody else who'd ever known Vangie Bodkin and found out precisely what connection she'd had with Theonia Sorpende and if she'd had none, why hadn't she? Mrs. Sorpende might have been wicked or foolish or just plain unlucky, but she was going to be the target for a great many wagging tongues in any case. And those tongues could wag Sarah right out of business if she didn't find a way to shut them up very, very soon.

Exhausted as she was, Sarah appeared at the breakfast table before anybody else. She poured coffee. She agreed with Mr. Porter-Smith's observation that the barometric high moving rapidly eastward from the Great Lakes meeting the barometric low moving rapidly northward from Cape Hatteras might well result in precipitation which could take the form of rain, sleet, snow, or a mixture of all three at the same time, Boston's weather being what it is.

She listened to Miss LaValliere's plaints and Professor Ormsby's grunts. She thanked Mr. Bittersohn politely when he told her she looked like hell. She waited until Mrs. Sorpende had finished a late and leisurely breakfast as usual. Then she put on a coat she hadn't worn for years, tied a scarf down over her head and face as far as it would go, and lurked.

Sure enough, it wasn't long before Mrs. Sorpende

came out the front door in her black coat, plum-colored turban and matching scarf, and that large black handbag that looked like leather but on close inspection was not. Sarah let her get a good start, then followed.

She'd somehow expected Mrs. Sorpende to take the same route across the Common that she'd followed before, and that was exactly what happened. Again her quarry made a beeline for the public convenience.

Now what? Did she make a fool of herself as she had the other day? No, luck was with her. Not far away stood a familiar shopping bag, and beside it the bundle of garments that could only be Miss Mary Smith, industriously sorting through one of those concrete trash containers that are supposed to look like tree stumps.

Pretending to be cleaning out her handbag, Sarah sauntered up to the stump. "Miss Smith," she murmured, "did you happen to notice a large woman in a black coat and purple turban go into the lavatory a moment ago?"

She dropped a clean tissue, last week's shopping list, and a dollar bill she could ill spare into the stump. Miss Smith deftly retrieved the right scrap.

"Yes, she comes every day."

"Where does she go when she comes out?"

"She never comes out."

"What?" Sarah forgot she was acting. It was a good thing nobody happened to be within earshot at the moment.

"Keep your voice down," said Miss Smith primly. "Just watch. In a minute or so you'll see an old scavenger like me wearing red sneakers and carrying a Gilchrist's bag. She'll cross the street and head for Temple Place. Go hide in a doorway and wait."

So that was it. Why hadn't she guessed the first time? She'd seen Mrs. Sorpende ring enough changes on that one black dress. The coat didn't look shabby with its elegantly co-ordinated accessories. But unwind that velvet turban, take off the matching scarf and gloves, pull an old paper shopping bag, a pair of sneakers, and a ratty scarf out of that oversized pocketbook, take off your high-heeled boots and walk with a stoop to reduce your height, use the scarf to hide your face and the bag with a few newspapers on top to conceal your other belongings, and a well-dressed matron could become a shuffling bag-woman quickly enough. But why?

Sarah followed Miss Smith's advice and slipped across Tremont Street when the lights changed. Pretending to be enthralled by a display of rock-and-roll records, she waited with her back to the street. Sure enough, just as the proprietor inside was beginning to look hopeful, a pair of red sneakers and a bag from a store that had gone out of business were reflected in the glass. Sarah waited three seconds, then followed.

Most of the façades along Tremont Street have been remodeled out of all resemblance to their original concepts, but some of the buildings behind those tatted-up fronts have changed hardly at all. Tucked in among the showy display windows are modest doorways leading to tiny lobbies with self-service elevators and bulletin boards oddly assorted names: optometrists, furriers, toupee makers, dental laboratories, embroiderers, jewelers, hairdressers; some of them so eminent they had no need for more pretentious quarters, some who could afford no better, some who just needed a place to work and liked the convenient location and the view over the Common. It was into one of these doorways that Mrs. Sorpende ducked.

Sarah's heart sank. She'd go up in the elevator, and that would be that. But she did not go up in the elevator. As Sarah recklessly opened the door, she glimpsed the red sneakers disappearing up a filigreed wrought-iron staircase that must antedate the elevator by many years.

Having come this far, Sarah was not about to quit. She tagged after the sneakers, expecting them to stop at the second floor. But they didn't. The staircase was sturdily built in late Victorian style, and the sneakers made no noise on its worn marble treads. However, the paper shopping bag, bumping and crackling against the railings, gave her sounds to follow without letting herself be seen. She was on the third landing when she heard a door immediately overhead being unlocked, opened, then locked again.

Sarah turned and went back the way she'd come, feeling somewhat winded. If this was part of Mrs. Sorpende's daily routine, no wonder she bounced up and down those stairs to the third-floor bedroom so nimbly.

In the lobby, Sarah studied the bulletin board. There didn't seem to be much on the fourth floor except a dental laboratory, a china-painting shop, and—aha!—a tearoom that gave readings. Sarah knew about tearooms. Cousin

Mabel adored them. Some were cozy, and had been around the downtown area so long they were practically Boston landmarks. Others were not, and folded so quickly that one wondered why the proprietors, so glib at foretelling their patrons' futures, hadn't checked on their own before they laid out the rent money. This place was strange to Sarah, but she could guess what she might find there: shabby plastic-covered chairs and tables, a minuscule sandwich, a cup of bitter tea half full of leaves, and three dollars' worth of chat from some earnest soul who had shown remarkable psychic powers since earliest childhood. Maybe Mrs. Sorpende was an addict like Cousin Mabel, but why should she put on such an elaborately unbecoming disguise just to get her tea leaves read?

Sarah poked the "up" button, got into the elevator, and stepped off at the fourth floor. It was obvious to her at a glance that Mrs. Sorpende's secret life was not involved with china painting, at any rate. Nobody was in that tiny shop except a youngish woman in a paint-streaked smock. She came eagerly forward.

"Can I help you?"

"I was—just interested," Sarah stammered. "I'm an artist of sorts myself, and one always wonders about chances to make a little extra money, doesn't one?"

"One sure does," replied the proprietress with feeling. "I honestly don't know what to tell you about the commercial possibilities. It would depend on how good you were and how much you know about marketing, I suppose. I do some restoration, myself. Most of my customers are antique dealers and hobbyists."

They got into talking shop, and Sarah was so delighted to find someone she could chat with about art that she spent more time than she'd meant to. She also blew some of her grocery money on china-painting supplies. She'd been wondering what she could possibly give as thankyou presents to Aunt Emma, Anora Protheroe, and some of the others who'd been particularly kind during her recent ordeal. Plates and cups of her own design would be both appropriate and affordable, and would give her a chance to learn a new skill that could perhaps be utilized to some profit.

Well, at least she'd accomplished something, but not what she'd come for. Mrs. Sorpende wasn't getting her dentures repaired, either. The laboratory doors were ajar and Sarah could see five or six earnest men bending over plaster casts of people's jaws but no middle-aged, stoutish woman with black hair and red sneakers.

So it had to be the tearoom, as she'd known all along it would be. The time she'd spent with her new chum in the china shop turned out to have been a fortunate delay, as they were just opening for business. A middle-aged woman wearing a voluminous gypsy costume and talking with a nasal down-Maine twang came forward, beads and bracelets clanking in merry greeting.

"Well, our first customer of the day! You've got a lucky face, dear. I can tell that just by one look at you."

Then she'd better take a second look, Sarah thought, sitting down in the rickety chair that was pulled out for her and depositing her fragile bundle of blank china on the chair closest by.

The proprietress offered a mimeographed menu that offered a meager choice of sandwiches and Peach Delite Salad, which Sarah knew from her experiences with Cousin Mabel would most likely be a dab of cottage cheese and half a canned peach. People didn't come to such places for the food. She ordered a cheese sandwich she didn't want. The tea came as a matter of course. The hostess said briskly, "Now, since you're the first, our readers happen to be all unoccupied at present. Take your pick."

The pick was not large. Two other women dressed like the hostess in floppy blouses, wide skirts, and a great deal of costume jewelry were sitting at the table in the corner nearest the kitchen. The one facing Sarah was tiny and wizened. The one with her face turned away was large and stately, with exquisite hands and a long black braid hanging down below her flowered kerchief. Sarah said with her heart in her mouth, "I'll take the black-haired lady, please."

Whatever else she might be, Mrs. Sorpende was a trouper. She brought in the skimpy lunch with the aplomb of a high priestess, took the chair opposite Sarah, and waited in an attitude of serene contemplation until the sandwich was eaten and the tea drunk. Then she picked up the cup, spilled the dregs into the saucer, went through the usual routine of poking among the wet leaves, and said with a rueful smile, "I see you are about to part with one of your third-floor tenants."

"Surely you've picked the wrong leaf," Sarah replied. "If you mean what I think you do, then please be assured that what my tenants do outside the house is no business of mine provided, as Mrs. Pat Campbell once remarked, they don't do it in the street and scare the horses. One tenant in particular must have led an exceptionally blameless life. Otherwise she'd know that the police might take a dim view of any landlady who'd evict one of her boarders while they're investigating the murder of another. Therefore I can't do anything but apologize for any awkwardness the present situation may have created and continue to muddle through as best I can. Is there any sign the tenant will co-operate?"

"I am sure you can count on the tenant's fullest co-operation," said Mrs. Sorpende, her regal manner belied by the tears in her eyes.

"Good. And the tenant can count on mine. I realize how annoying it could be for a professional person to be pestered by her housemates for free advice at odd hours."

"Speaking of professionals . . ." As the proprietress happened to be passing the table on her way to greet an elderly man who must be a favored regular customer, Mrs. Sorpende picked up the cup again and poked at the soggy residue. "Are you aware that you may have somebody in the house whose profession is quite different from what he says it is?"

"Who, for instance?"

"Offhand, I'd say your handsome author is a plain-clothes policeman."

Sarah's heart skipped a beat. "Why do you say that?"

"Because I can smell them in the dark. My life has not been wholly blameless and my experience has been vast. Since you're paying for advice, here's mine: don't waste too much of your time on illustrations that will probably never get printed or paid for."

"Thank you for telling me," said Sarah with perhaps a shade less gratitude than Mrs. Sorpende might have felt entitled to expect. "I hope you'll keep your suspicions to yourself, though, until I've had a chance to do some checking. If this man is putting on an act he may have a perfectly valid and possibly important reason for doing so. On the other hand he may be what he represents himself to be and I shall get paid for my work. And quite frankly, I could use any spare cash that's coming just now."

"Who couldn't?" The strain Mrs. Sorpende must have been under exploded into a nervous little giggle. "Please don't think I'm hinting for a tip. I shouldn't accept one if you offered."

"Good, because I don't think I have any extra money left anyway." Sarah laid her last three dollars on the table, pulled on her gloves, picked up her china, and walked out.

As she left, the proprietress gave her a toothy smile and said, "Come again." Sarah smiled back automatically but she wouldn't be returning. She'd already got what she came for, and a little more besides.

Chapter 18

As Sarah came over the hill, she found a station wagon blocking Tulip Street and somebody loading the last of several items into the back. None of them, she was relieved to see, had ever belonged to the Kellings. Miss Hartler must be getting rid of the stuff Wumps had amassed, and the sooner the better for both her and her unhappy landlady.

It would be lovely if Miss Hartler decided of her own volition to go back to Rhode Island where her friends and her church work were. If she didn't, Sarah was quite prepared to do the deciding for her. One couldn't go on ladling cranberry juice over a wet blanket forever.

At least Miss Hartler must be up and functioning, if she'd bestirred herself to make people come and get their spurious artifacts. In fact, when Sarah entered the front hall, the woman came popping out of the drawing room much as her late brother would have done.

"Oh, Sarah, there you are. That maid of yours didn't seem to know where you'd gone or when you'd be back. I don't think she even understands what I'm saying half the time."

"I'm sure Mariposa understands perfectly well," Sarah answered. "However, if you've read that list of house rules I put on your tray, you must have learned that the staff are responsible only to me."

"Yes, dear, and I was trying to obey. I knew I mustn't go interfering in the kitchen, but I did think somebody ought to let your cook know as early as possible about putting dinner forward."

"Putting dinner forward? Whatever for?"

137

"Why, my dear, you know we're to have the—the viewing this evening. Only of course there can't be one because dear Wumps—but naturally people will wish to pay their respects—and I naturally assumed—"

"The visiting hours are to be at the funeral parlor, aren't they? You don't mean to tell me you've invited anybody here?"

"Well, no, not tonight. But we're supposed to be there from half-past seven until ten o'clock. That means we shall have to serve dinner an hour early in order to—"

To her credit, Sarah managed to reply in a calm, level voice. "Miss Hartler, if you'd like a tray in your room at six, I'll be glad to see that you get it. Afterward, Charles can call a taxi for you. The household will stick to its usual schedule. No doubt some of us will go to the undertaker's this evening, but we'll have plenty of time after dinner."

"But, Sarah, I was counting on your support!"

This was a bit much. "Then you weren't thinking very realistically, were you? I'm sure you have plenty of old friends who'll be only too willing to help you get through the funeral. You also have the undertaker and his assistants whose job it is to manage everything for you. As for myself, I have this big house to run and six people paying me a good deal of money to stay in it. My boarders work hard all day, they come here afterward expecting a period of relaxation and a leisurely home-cooked meal. If I were to disappoint them, I'd be liable for a breach of contract. Anyway, I don't intend to."

"Surely, in a house of mourning—"

"I'm sorry, but this is not a house of mourning. It's a boardinghouse, and your brother was one of the boarders. I know that sounds cruel, but it's something you absolutely must understand. Mr. Hartler may have meant the world to you, but to me he was no more than a casual acquaintance and the others had never even met him until last Monday. Of course we all feel dreadful about what happened to him, but you can't expect us to heap ashes on our heads for a man we hardly knew."

The sister's blue lips quivered. "Everybody loved Wumps."

"I'm sure his friends loved him," said Sarah as gently as she could. "Would you like me to call any of them? I do understand how painful all this must be for you, and

I'm quite willing to do anything I reasonably can. Have you eaten lunch? How about a grilled cheese sandwich and a glass of cranberry juice?"

"Oh no, thank you. I shouldn't dream of putting you to the trouble. As to the telephoning, I've already got in touch with dear Marguerite and one or two others. They've promised to spread the word around. By the way, Marguerite will be driving up later this afternoon with Iris Pendragon and she wasn't sure who else. Perhaps you might care to call her back, and explain about dinner. She naturally assumed you'd be putting them up."

"Then she'd better change her mind in a hurry. I haven't a spare bed in the house, and we don't take extra guests at dinner without at least a day's advance notice. They're all rich as Croesus, they can go to the Copley Plaza or somewhere. And pay for it themselves."

"Sarah, your own aunt!"

"She's only my aunt by marriage and I'm no longer married, so that doesn't count anymore. We'll invite her and the rest of her crew back here for a glass of sherry or something after the funeral, if you want."

"Oh, as to that—well, dear, there was nothing else I could do, was there? One has to make a gesture, and this is the only home I have now."

"How many gestures did you make?" Sarah asked with a sinking feeling in her stomach.

"My dear, how can I possibly know? I did explain, didn't I, that I'd only spoken to a couple of the people personally. The matter is quite out of my hands by now. Friends will surely rally around. Dear Wumps was so very popular. Marguerite may have some idea of how many to expect."

By this time, Marguerite was no doubt chartering a plane to fly dear Wumps's old buddies in from Honolulu. Sarah groaned.

"I don't know where you thought I was going to put them all. I don't even have a drawing room anymore. We'll have to stuff those vases and whatnot under the bed and open up the room you're sleeping in."

"No, please! We can't let anybody in there."

"Suit yourself. Then they'll just have to stand out on the sidewalk and you can hand their refreshments through the library window."

"Sarah, I must say I did expect a little co-operation from you, considering what I'm paying for this room."

"So far you're not paying anything, Miss Hartler. You're simply using up the week's rent your brother had already paid."

"Well, naturally I intend—"

"We'll talk about that when the time comes, shall we?" Sarah had already made up her mind what she was going to say. "What you don't appear to realize is that you've put me in an impossible position. If there were any way to get in touch with all those people who have no doubt by now been invited to come here after the funeral, I'd insist that you tell them you've arranged for a little reception at a hotel or somewhere, as you should have done in the first place. Perhaps you could have the vicar make an announcement after the service."

"Sarah! That would be unthinkable."

"And probably useless because there are sure to be a bunch who'll dodge the ceremonies but show up for the free drinks. There always are. All right, you've stuck me with it and I'll have to make the best of it. But we'll have to use that room whether you like it or not, so you'd better start putting things away and at least give people a place to stand."

"I can't. I'm simply not up to it."

"You were energetic enough yesterday. Thank goodness it's clean, at least. Come on, I'll help you."

"No!" Miss Hartler threw herself across the doorway in a dramatic gesture quite out of keeping with her usual mousiness. "If my brother's last haven is to be invaded, then I will make it ready as best I can. This is a cruel, cruel imposition!"

"It certainly is." Sarah gave up trying to be considerate. "And you'll have to give me the money for whatever you intend to serve."

"But can't you simply give me the bills after this is," Miss Hartler choked, "all over?"

Jeremy Kelling had drawn up one inviolable rule that was not on the list. "When it comes to money, don't trust 'em one cent's worth. Get everything in advance, cash on the button." It was a good rule, and Sarah was not about to break it.

"No, I'm sorry but I can't. Surely Aunt Marguerite's

told you how desperately hard-up I am? What were you planning to offer them?"

"Oh, dear, I hadn't—you're being so very—I suppose I mustn't—couldn't your cook just make some little sandwiches, and perhaps petits fours? And a nonalcoholic fruit punch for those who don't want sherry, though I suppose some will expect cocktails—and tea and coffee for those who insist on—"

"Nobody's going to want fruit punch but you," said Sarah. "We'll stick to sherry and biscuits and a few spreads or dips or something. Unless you want to hire a caterer, though I can't imagine you'd be able to find one at the last minute willing to take on an unspecified number of people. Give me fifty dollars and I'll do the best I can. If there's any left over I'll return it to you with an itemized statement of what I spent."

"But, Sarah, Wumps would have hated such a meager—"

"We're not going to argue about this, Miss Hartler. We can't put on a big spread because we haven't the room. Anyway, I don't want them hanging around. You'll have to get them all out of here by five o'clock so that we can scramble the place together and have things presentable for my boarders. By then you'll be exhausted and glad to see them go, anyway. Believe me, I know. Now would you please give me the money?"

Tight-lipped, Miss Hartler went and got fifty dollars out of her handbag, then shut herself in the drawing room and began banging things around. At last Sarah was free to get rid of her coat and her china and find herself a bite to eat.

It was no doubt rotten of her to be treating an old woman this way, but it had been pretty scaly of Miss Hartler to pull such a trick on her, too. She and her brother had been peas in a pod, no doubt about that, both thinking they could do as they pleased in somebody else's house.

Sarah tried several times to reach Aunt Marguerite and straighten her out on the entertainment situation, but the line was always busy. When she at last did get through, she was informed that the mistress had already left for Boston in the limousine with several friends. The mistress and her coterie didn't know it yet, but they were in for a cool reception if they came here with any great expectations.

They did, of course. Marguerite swooped in dripping mink and gush, wanting to know where the chauffeur should put up the car.

"Tell him to drive around the block and pick you up in half an hour," Sarah told her before Miss Hartler could get a word in. "They're holding a couple of rooms for you at the Copley."

"But I thought we'd be staying here!"

"I could put you up at Ireson's Landing if you want to rough it by yourselves. There's no heat or light and the water isn't turned on, but you could use oil lamps and camp around the fireplace. That's absolutely the only scrap of extra room I have, Aunt Marguerite. I've even got tenants in the attic and the basement. I thought you understood."

"Well, apparently I didn't. I must say, Sarah—"

"Must you?" said her former niece-in-law wearily. "I did try to get you on the phone to make the position clear, but first your line was busy and then you'd already left. Bring your friends in for a cup of tea if you want. You can have a little visit with Miss Hartler, but you'll have to sit in the library. She's sleeping in what used to be the drawing room."

"Good heavens! Poor Caroline must be positively spinning in her grave."

Even Marguerite realized that was not a tactful remark. She went back to the front door and called in her friends. "This way for tea, girls. The loo's down the hall, Iris, since you were about to ask. Show her, Sarah."

"It's only reachable through the front bedroom now. I've had some remodeling done. You can use mine, Mrs. Pendragon. First door to your left at the head of the stairs. Miss Hartler, please make your guests comfortable while I get the tea."

It was jolly well going to be tea, too, although Sarah knew perfectly well that when Marguerite and her crowd said tea they meant something else. Not being served cocktails would get them out of here faster than hints, snubs, or even threats of bodily harm.

No doubt, she mused as she warmed the pot and set out the tray, Miss Hartler was in there now telling them how unutterably horrid Sarah was being about Darling

Wumps's terrible, terrible tragedy. Granted, it was a terrible tragedy and granted Sarah was being horrid. However, she had every intention of being even horrider if Miss Hartler showed any sign of wishing to linger on here once darling Wumps was safely underground.

She lugged in the tray, noted the expressions of shocked disappointment with sardonic satisfaction, left Aunt Marguerite to pour, and went back to the kitchen for more hot water. As she was refilling the kettle, Mr. Bittersohn came in through the back alley door.

"Hi, Mrs. Kelling. What's new?"

"Don't ask," she snarled. "I'm in the midst of a full-scale snit."

"Any special reason?"

"Go open that back hall door for a moment."

He obeyed. The blast of gabble from the library hit like a sonic boom.

"My God! Have you started a turkey farm?"

"Oh, no, that's just Aunt Marguerite and a few of her friends from Newport who breezed in here a few minutes ago expecting me to give them dinner and put them up for the night. And if you think that's a racket, wait till tomorrow afternoon. Miss Hartler very sweetly invited all dear Wumps's old friends back here after the funeral."

"What the hell did you let her do that for?"

"I didn't let her, she simply went ahead and did it. And we can't call it off because everybody's been calling everybody else and nobody has the remotest idea who's been notified and who hasn't. I've told that crowd in there they can either freeze to death in the dark at Ireson's Landing or go to a hotel at their own expense. A moment ago I actually found myself wishing I had Mr. Quiffen back. He was the nastiest person I've ever come across, but you knew he was going to be awful, so you could plan your strategy accordingly. The Hartlers have both been angels by comparison, and they've driven me to screaming frenzy. Don't bother trying to explain it, I have to go and pour some boiling water down Aunt Marguerite's back."

"Sounds like a great idea to me."

Bittersohn held the door and she went on down the hall with her hot water. When she returned with a tray-load of used cups, he was still in the kitchen, munching on one of the Ireson's Landing apples.

"Did you?" he asked.

"Did I what?" said Sarah abstractedly, fishing under the sink for the dishwashing liquid.

"Pour boiling water down Aunt Marguerite's back."

"Oh, that. No, I'm sorry to report that my loftier nature prevailed. I did give them lapsang souchong instead of martinis, though, and I quite pointedly refrained from inviting them all to dinner. I hope I was inhospitable enough so that they won't show up tomorrow, either, but no doubt they'll have forgotten by then. They haven't an ounce of gray matter among them. Here, if you intend to hang around the kitchen, you might as well grab a dish towel. There's no room for drones in this hive. Why aren't you out detecting something, anyway?"

"It's my afternoon off.'"

"Oh, good heavens!" Sarah almost let a Spode saucer get away. "I quite forgot tomorrow is Mariposa's afternoon off, and her niece is in a play at school and she's promised faithfully to be there. And Charles can't possibly take another day off from the factory because he's already missed once this week and they'll dock him if he takes another, and he can't afford that because he's saving up to buy a new tooth."

"What for? He's already got a tooth, hasn't he?"

"Yes, lots of them, but he broke one off playing soccer and he thinks it's hampering his stage career so he wants to get it capped. Mariposa and I keep telling him it looks —what's that ridiculous word—macho, because we're scared to death he may be right. If he gets a good role, we're up the creek, but of course I can't deliberately stand in his way."

"So you plan to face the screaming mob alone tomorrow?"

"Actually I was planning to see if I could borrow Egbert from Uncle Jem."

"Why don't you ask Mrs. Sorpende to pitch in? She likes to be helpful, doesn't she?"

"Yes, but she's got a job already."

"Doing what?"

"Telling fortunes in a *soi-disant* gypsy tearoom. And if you ever breathe a word about that to one living soul, I'll put my own personal hex on you, and if you think I don't mean it, go ask Miss Hartler. I've really been treating her miserably today and I suppose I ought to hate myself for it, but, honestly! Asking thousands and thousands of people to my house without so much as breathing a hint to me first, and then throwing a kitten fit because I told her she'd have to let us use the drawing room."

"Did she, now?"

"She certainly did! And she was going on about fancy sandwiches and little frosted cakes as if— Oh, don't mind me! They'll get cheap sherry and crackers out of a box and if they don't like it that's just too bad."

"Maybe nobody will come."

"You know better than that. They'll flock in droves because he got his poor old face bashed in. People are such ghouls! And I'll be rushing back and forth trying to wash enough glasses and make sure nobody puts lighted cigarettes down on the furniture, and you simply have no idea what it's going to be like. Consider yourself lucky that you won't have to find out."

"Mrs. Kelling, do you think I'd fink out on a pal in a crunch? Sorry, I forgot this is going to be an upper-crust brawl. I will abide by thy right side and keep the bridge with thee, or at least I'll send a trusted member of my investigative staff to keep an eagle eye on the furniture."

Bittersohn dried a final saucer and hung the damp towel neatly on the rack, as Alexander might have done. "Now, if we're quite through here I'll just step down the hall and see if Miss Hartler would like some help juggling the Iolani Palace around. I assume the tumult and the shouting have temporarily died?"

"Oh yes, they cleared out as soon as they saw I really meant tea. It would be awfully nice of you to help Miss Hartler, if she'll let you. I offered and she did a Sarah Bernhardt about handling dear Wump's precious relics, but perhaps she'll be more receptive with you."

"Why should she be?"

"Elderly maiden ladies are apt to be more gracious with kind young men, aren't they? Besides, she started grilling me about my tenants yesterday, and I explained that your people are neighbors of ours at Ireson's Landing, and that your mother doesn't call but you yourself aren't a bit snobbish. Could you try to combine a pose imperious with a demeanor nobly bland?"

"You can bet I shan't be too deucedly condescending to that old bat, anyway." And with that gracious promise, Bittersohn was gone.

Chapter 19

In less than three minutes, Bittersohn was back in the kitchen. "Miss Hartler does not require any help, thank you. She wonders if it would be too much of an imposition to remind Mrs. Kelling that she was promised a tray in her room before she goes to fulfill her sad duty. A glass of cranberry juice and a poached egg on toast will do nicely. It will be unnecessary for your butler to call a cab as dear Marguerite has kindly offered to send the limousine. She would find it a great comfort if any of dear William's former housemates would care to pay a brief visit to the undertaker's this evening although she realizes that is rather too much to hope for since, as dear Mrs. Kelling took the trouble to point out, we knew him for so short a time. I expect that means show up or else, eh?"

"It means do as you please, as far as I'm concerned," Sarah replied. "I'll go myself, of course, and I daresay Mrs. Sorpende won't mind going with me. And it wouldn't kill Jennifer LaValliere to put in an appearance because Miss Hartler knows her grandmother, who'll no doubt be there, too. And if she goes, Mr. Porter-Smith might tag along for the ride. I'm sure Professor Ormsby won't. I rather doubt if he ever happened to notice Mr. Hartler's existence, much less his demise."

"Ormsby does tend to have a single-track mind," Bittersohn agreed. "Or would you call it double-track? Sorry, that was rude and uncouth. Do you mean that's what she does for a living? Read tea leaves, I mean."

"I don't know whether she earns a living by it, but that's what she was doing this morning, and that's what

146

she's been doing for some while, according to what Miss Smith told me. We had a little tête-à-tête over one of the trash cans on the Common."

Sarah gave him a brief rundown of her morning's adventure and its strange outcome. "Would you have believed such a thing possible?"

"No. I naturally assumed she modeled corsets for stylish stouts," Bittersohn replied. "It doesn't make sense. She's intelligent, good-looking, well dressed. Nice appearance, anyway. Has a pleasant personality and talks like a duchess. Surely a woman like Mrs. Sorpende could find a better job than that, unless she's just doing it for kicks."

"She can't be. She's desperately hard-up. At least Mariposa thinks she is, and Mariposa's an expert on poverty. And a teashop wouldn't pay much, would it? Besides, it was so—so out of character for her to be there. I'd begun to think she and I were getting to be perhaps not quite friends, but certainly something in that general direction. And now I realize I don't know her at all. Excuse me, I have to get at the toaster."

Sarah fussed over the tray she was preparing for Miss Hartler. "Mr. Bittersohn, do you think I did the right thing in telling her she oughtn't to move out while the police are hunting for whoever killed Mr. Hartler? You see, I can't help wondering."

She told him what she'd been thinking about Mrs. Sorpende and Dolph. "That's ridiculous, isn't it? I'd have been doing her a terrible injustice if I'd asked her to move, wouldn't I?"

"Not only her. What about Ormsby? You want a blighted romance on your hands on top of everything else? All I can say is, you did just about what I'd have done, Mrs. Kelling, if that makes you feel any better."

"Oh, it does! Would you hand me that tiniest frying pan? Murders come and murders go, but trays go on forever, it seems. What on earth is keeping Mariposa? She ought to be setting the table by now."

As Sarah was lifting Miss Hartler's poached egg out of the frying pan, Mariposa rushed up the back stairs, wearing a brand-new uniform of royal purple with fuchsia trimmings.

"Sorry I'm late, but I went shopping. How does this grab you?" Hands on hips, she twirled in a very good imitation of a professional model. "Charles said I better get something less jazzy than that orange job I been wearing, because we've got to act dignified at a time like this. I blew thirty bucks of the tooth money."

"It was worth every nickel," Bittersohn assured her solemnly. "Don't you think so, Mrs. Kelling?"

"I only wish you'd been here this afternoon to serve tea to my aunt-in-law and her friends," said Sarah. "You'd have knocked them dead."

"Invite 'em back," said Mariposa.

"I would if I thought it would really work. Here, you can take Miss Hartler's tray to her instead. She'll be impressed, I'm sure."

"Though I hope not favorably," Sarah added after Mariposa had got through the swinging door. "Oh, dear, I do wish I didn't have to go through this business tonight. The mere thought of it makes me sick to my stomach."

"I tell you what," said Bittersohn, "after we finish eating, I'll bring my car around and drive you over, along with anybody else who wants to go."

"That's awfully kind, but why should you get stuck with a miserable evening? I could get the Studebaker."

"Mrs. Kelling, you wouldn't take that precious antique out in the cold night air? It might catch cold in its plugs. Besides, I think my brother-in-law has a customer for you, so you'd better not risk scraping a fender."

"Has he really? How much did he say—"

Bittersohn named a figure and Sarah gasped.

"As much as that? But this person's never even seen the car."

"Actually, I believe he did go over it when they had it at the station last month. He was ready to make an offer then, but Ira and Mike didn't think you'd want to hear about it. This is a serious collector, and he knows what a 1950 Starlite Coupe in top condition should be worth. Ira says it's a fair price. You might get more if you held off, but since you're planning to take the car off the road pretty soon anyway there doesn't seem to be a great deal of point in letting a bona fide buyer slip out of your hands."

"No, I don't suppose there are all that many, are there? And I'd have to pay storage. I'd never dare leave the Studebaker out at Ireson's after what happened to the Milburn."

Bittersohn studied her face. "You'd rather refuse, wouldn't you?"

"Naturally I would, but I'm not stupid enough to do it. Please tell your brother-in-law that I shall be happy to accept whatever offer he thinks reasonable, and that I shall expect him to deduct the usual agent's fee with my sincere thanks."

"Ira wouldn't take a fee from you."

"Why not? Most other people would, like a shot, if they ever got a chance. I must say your family isn't much like mine. You're tremendously kind to take so much trouble over my affairs, and I'd be delighted to ride with you this evening if you're sure you want to go."

"I want to go. I'm studying the tribal customs of the Wasps. Miss Hartler will be there before us, I gather."

"Oh yes, ages before. She did suggest omitting our little happy hour and having dinner early so that we could all go together, but I did not take kindly to the suggestion. You know, I think that's what's been giving me fits about the Hartlers. Poor old William was sweet in his way, but he was so utterly wrapped up in his own quirks and quiddities that he couldn't imagine everyone else might not want to share his enthusiasms. The sister's just like him, only without charm. At least Mr. Quiffen was willing to loathe you on your individual merits. Now do me one more favor, since you're in such a generous mood, and go nobble Mr. Porter-Smith and Mrs. Sorpende as they come in. Tell them I shan't be dressing for dinner tonight since I and anybody else who wants to will be going over to the undertaker's, and there won't be time to change."

"It's not the done thing to show up in your cummerbund?"

"Nor your rhinestone tiara with the green chicken feathers. Mariposa's new uniform has no doubt strained Miss Hartler's nerves to the breaking point already. I have enough ado to cope with my own hysterics, let alone hers as well. If we can just get through tomorrow!"

"We shall overcome."

Bittersohn vanished. Mariposa reappeared. Charles burst forth in white-gloved effulgence to escort Miss Hartler out to the waiting limousine. Sarah cooked like mad, then whisked off her apron and dashed to the library to dispense sherry and small talk.

She was at least as nervous at having to face Mrs. Sor-

pende after that bizarre encounter in the teashop as the
fortuneteller herself must be about what sort of reception
she'd get tonight. Mrs. Sorpende was no coward, though.
She was already in the library when Sarah entered. Sarah
solved the problem in the only way she knew, by tackling
it head-on.

"Oh, Mrs. Sorpende, I'm so glad of the chance to have
a word with you. It looks as if this may turn into a rather
sticky evening. Miss Hartler is expecting us all to troop
over in a body to pay our respects to her brother's remains, and I'm sure not everyone will want to go. Is there
any hope of your helping me carry the torch? Mr. Bittersohn has offered to drive us there and back."

"How kind of him," Mrs. Sorpende replied warily. "Will
it be just the three of us?"

She knows Mr. Bittersohn's a detective, Sarah thought.
She told me so. She thinks he and I plan to get her alone
somewhere and give her the third degree. Oh, God, do I
have another Aunt Caroline on my hands?

"I hope not," she said aloud. "I'm particularly determined to push Jennifer LaValliere into going if I can. Her
people were acquainted with the Hartlers when they lived
in Boston, and it wouldn't hurt her to show a little character for once, do you think?"

"Why not? She's already shown just about everything
else she owns," the woman answered with a flash of her
usual calm amusement. "I've reached an age where I can't
boast of any special rapport with the modern generation,
but I'll certainly do what I can to persuade her if you
want me to. And Mr. Porter-Smith is an amiable young
man, I'm sure he'd be willing. If you care for a professional character reading on Professor Ormsby, however,
I'd advise you not to waste your breath."

"That strikes me as very sound advice," said Sarah,
laughing with relief that the tension was broken. "Let me
give you some sherry."

One by one the others trickled in. Professor Ormsby, a
male chauvinist to his boot heels, showed obvious distress
at seeing Mrs. Sorpende in her high-necked daytime frock.
Mr. Porter-Smith was naturally chagrined at having to
keep on his mundane business suit. Miss LaValliere pouted
when Sarah made the observation that her grandmother
would be expecting to see her at the funeral parlor, but

brightened when she found out she'd get to ride in Mr. Bittersohn's car.

On the whole, they got through dinner comfortably enough. Professor Ormsby managed to content himself with noting how trimly Mrs. Sorpende's black dress accented the Rubenesque contours of her well-girdled figure. Jennifer LaValliere had the supreme and astounding tact to say to Mr. Porter-Smith, "Why, Gene, I didn't realize what broad shoulders you have." By the time they drank their coffee, the atmosphere was quite agreeable.

Then Mr. Bittersohn vanished to get the car. Sarah went through the routine of asking who wanted to go to the undertaker's. Professor Ormsby, in accordance with predictions, grunted and went upstairs. The rest got into their wraps and waited for Mr. Bittersohn out on the steps, since picking up passengers on Tulip Street invariably led to honking horns and bellowed insults from cars blocked in their efforts to get down the narrow, twisting lane.

"Mind sliding in under the wheel, Mrs. Kelling?"

Bittersohn had Sarah in the front seat before Jennifer LaValliere could get to it. She showed signs of wanting to sit in the middle, but Mr. Porter-Smith showed a burst of *machismo* by stuffing her in back beside Mrs. Sorpende and climbing in after her. She had to content herself with gurgling down the back of the driver's neck about what a fabulous car it was, and asking questions that Mr. Porter-Smith took it upon himself to answer at great length. All in all, Sarah enjoyed the short ride a good deal more than she'd thought she would.

They found Miss Hartler holding court in front of a mercifully closed casket surrounded by many expensive floral tributes which probably should have included one from the group at Tulip Street but didn't because Sarah simply hadn't thought of sending any. She and her entourage got what very nearly amounted to a brushoff from Aunt Marguerite and the Newport contingent, who'd appointed themselves ladies-in-waiting to the chief mourner. That was fair enough, since they'd got the same sort of treatment from her, but Sarah did feel a trifle embarrassed at having dragged her boarders over here for so little purpose.

Luckily Dolph was in the room feeling a bit out of things since he hadn't known Hartler or Hartler's friends

all that well, and bustled over to greet them. Anora
Protheroe, who never missed a funeral if she could help it,
was also ready to chat. The dowager Mrs. LaValliere
soon collared Jennifer and trotted her off to meet some
people. Mrs. Sorpende was taken over by Dolph and Mr.
Porter-Smith entertained Anora with an account of picturesque funeral customs among the ancient Franks and
Teutons.

Sarah looked around to make sure Mr. Bittersohn
wasn't being neglected, and found him in affable conversation with a well-dressed, attractive-looking couple in
their fifties.

"Mrs. Kelling, have you met the Saxes? They've been
active in the Iolani Palace project."

"Mrs. Kelling, this is a pleasure," said Mrs. Saxe, taking her hand cordially. "How could you ever bear to part
with that beautiful fan you and your husband sent us?"

"Don't suppose you have any more of Queen Kapiolani's house gifts kicking around?" asked Mr. Saxe.

"Not unless they're hidden under Miss Hartler's bed,"
Sarah told him. "I'm so sorry about those chairs that Mr.
Hartler thought he'd turned up. His sister can't seem to
find any information about who has them among his papers. I expect whoever it is will get in touch with you or
somebody else, though."

"I must confess I'm not exactly holding my breath in
expectation," Mr. Saxe admitted. "Hartler was a well-
meaning old chap, but to be quite candid with you, he
had more enthusiasm than expertise. I'm afraid he got
badly cheated a few times. We finally had to ask him not
to bring in any more of his great finds till he'd got them
authenticated. And even his authentications weren't always authentic, I'm afraid."

"Darling," said his wife, "I'm sure Mrs. Kelling doesn't
have to be told that poor Mr. Hartler was soft as a grape,
and getting softer by the minute, though he was a sweet
old thing in his way. I'd been wondering for some time
what was going to happen to that man, and I must say I
can't help being a little bit relieved that he went quickly,
though of course it's utterly ghastly that it happened as it
did. Still, I think I'd rather be knocked on the head myself than shut up in a high-class looney bin."

"I'll remember that when the time comes, dear."

"Thank you, darling. Mrs. Kelling, do have Max bring

you over to visit us soon. We're always at home on Sunday evenings and we have some marvelous things that will be going over with the next shipment. George would adore telling you all about them. Now don't you think we've done our duty here? There's such a mob we'll never be missed. Could we give you people a lift back to the Hill?"

"Thanks, but I have my own car and a load of passengers to round up," said Bittersohn somewhat abstractedly. "Good to see you both."

The Saxes smiled and faded through the crowd. Sarah turned to Mr. Bittersohn. "Then Mr. Hartler wasn't really a Friend of the Iolani Palace at all?"

"Sounds more like an enemy to me. I'm not sure what their membership setup is, but he obviously didn't hold any sort of official position."

"I can't believe it! Rather, I couldn't if I hadn't known Great-uncle Frederick. He's the only other person I've ever seen get totally involved in something that was none of his business. No wonder Mr. Hartler was so scatty about letting his visitors wander around loose and mess up the house. I should have realized from the beginning that he was missing on one or two cylinders, as Alexander would have said. Don't you think it's strange Miss Hartler would go tootling off to Rome and leave him on his own in a city he'd been out of touch with for so long? Of course she may not have realized because she adored him so and I'm not sure she isn't a bit shaky in the brain herself. Or perhaps she didn't feel able to cope so she blocked it out and tried to escape. People can be awfully blind about things they don't want to see."

"That's right," said Bittersohn. "How about introducing me to your ex-aunt-in-law?"

"Whatever for?" gasped Sarah.

"I just want to ask her something."

"And I'm sure she'll want to ask you something. Like are you married and can you play bridge and what are you doing for dinner tomorrow evening. You don't realize what you'd be getting into, Mr. Bittersohn. Meeting Aunt Marguerite is like getting a formal introduction to the giant squid in a horror movie."

"That's a risk I'll have to take."

"Then on your own head be it." Sarah wriggled back

through the mass of humanity with him and went through
the ceremony with what grace she could muster.

"This is Mr. Bittersohn, who has my downstairs room,
Aunt Marguerite. You didn't meet him before because he
was parking the car. He's an art expert."

That bit of information was, she knew, superfluous.
Aunt Marguerite wouldn't have cared if he was the window washer. Sarah got shunted to the periphery and
buttonholed by Iris Pendragon, who was so eager to know
how Sarah had ever managed to latch on to anything so
gorgeous that she couldn't hear a word of what he'd
wanted to ask Aunt Marguerite. Poor man, little did he
ken what a spate of invitations he was calling down on his
head from this gaggle of bored women. But perhaps he
met a great many bored women in his profession. Perhaps
he didn't find them all boring, either. Sarah rather wished
she hadn't thought of that.

In any event, he must have developed a knack for
dealing with them. In less time than she'd thought possible, he'd managed to break away and put a protective
wall of bodies between himself and her and the ladies
from Newport.

"Mrs. Kelling, could you help me round up our passengers? I've got to take you home and then get back to
work."

"Yes, of course. I didn't realize—"

But he was already gone from her side and heading
toward Miss LaValliere, who would need no coaxing.
Sarah, able to slip under people's arms and elbows because of her slender littleness, managed to reach Mrs.
Sorpende, who was better equipped than she to serve as
a battering-ram. This crowd was horrendous. What if
they all showed up at the house tomorrow?

They wouldn't, surely. Some, like the Saxes, must be
people who'd felt an obligation to put in an appearance
but would be unlikely even to attend the funeral. And no
doubt there were a number who'd never met Mr. Hartler
at all but merely wanted to be in on a sensation.

The papers had played up Mr. Hartler's gruesome
murder, but somehow the fact that he'd been Sarah Kelling's second boarder to die by violence had been kept
out. How Mr. Bittersohn and Sergeant McNaughton had
managed that she couldn't imagine, but she'd be grateful
to them both forevermore. No doubt she was being

pointed out right now as the dead man's landlady and the story would leak to the press sooner or later, but by then, God willing, the funeral would be over and Miss Hartler gone and she wouldn't have to call the police to control the hordes.

Between them, she and Mr. Bittersohn got the group herded out of the place and walked down to the elegant car that was parked around the corner. Miss LaValliere suggested dropping in somewhere for a drink, and was shattered to learn that she'd be driven straight back to Tulip Street and left standing on the sidewalk while Mr. Bittersohn drove off into the night alone. Sarah was none too happy about that, either, but right now she wasn't too happy about anything.

Chapter 20

Sarah stayed downstairs after they got home, not because she wanted to, not because she had to. Aunt Marguerite's chauffeur would drive Miss Hartler to Tulip Street after the visiting hours were over. Charles would be on the alert to meet the car and help the old woman into the house. Having her back would be no joy, and the sooner they could get her out of here, the better for everyone. Nevertheless, Sarah waited.

There were so many things that could happen to a person her age, especially if that person might not happen to have all her wits about her. Look what had happened to the brother.

But exactly what had happened to William Hartler? Was he robbed and killed by that still-unidentified man who'd lured him from the house with a beguiling story about King Kalakaua's dining room chairs? How did the man know the crime would be worth the effort? Most people with any sense at all didn't carry large sums of cash around in the city.

Maybe the man had insisted he must be paid in cash that same night and Mr. Hartler had withdrawn a large sum earlier in the day when the banks were open. No, that wasn't possible, because the man was still in Mr. Hartler's room when Sarah had returned to find that odious woman ransacking her china closet. That was his excuse for having left the woman where he couldn't keep an eye on her. Mr. Hartler hadn't gone anywhere afterward, except for his quick shopping spree on Charles Street just before dinner.

Sarah's impression was that Mr. Hartler had known

nothing of the chairs until the man with the photographs showed up. If he'd got wind of them earlier, he'd surely have been bending everyone's ear at breakfast, or shouting the glad tidings to Mariposa over the roar of the vacuum cleaner.

Miss Hartler had insisted to the police that dear Wumps was always careful about money, though she didn't seem to have the foggiest idea about the true state of his affairs. She'd also been unable to find any reference to the man with the chairs among his papers, but that didn't mean anything. There probably had been no letter, only the personal interview. Mr. Hartler would have made a note of the address and stuck it in his pocket for later reference. After he found the right place, he'd have thrown the note away, or lost it in his excitement, or had it taken from him either inadvertently or on purpose.

After what the Saxes had said, Sarah thought it quite possible someone had been setting the old man up for a swindel. If the chairs were authentic, the seller would have been more apt to get in touch with the curator or one of his approved agents, of whom Mr. Hartler had certainly not been one. That woman who'd given her such a hard time in the dining room might have been there for that specific purpose, to distract anybody else who might be in the house so that the man could dangle his bait before the gullible Mr. Hartler and get away without being seen.

If that was the case, she'd done her job well. She'd got both Sarah and Mariposa so busy counting the spoons that they hadn't given a thought to what was happening out front. The woman had been a stranger to Mr. Hartler. He couldn't even recall whatever name she'd given him. After the previous visitor had gone, she'd made no effort to accomplish what she'd supposedly come for, but cleared out as fast as she could. Whoever the woman was, she'd been no shrinking violet. If she'd left something of value for appraisal, wouldn't it have been more in character for her to insist on getting either her money or her property before she left?

Everything fitted in nicely, except the murder. Swindlers didn't usually kill their victims; Mr. Bittersohn had told her so. Why should they? It was easier and less risky to get the money and slip away before the purchaser realized he'd been stung.

What if Mr. Hartler had got there and realized he was dealing with the same person who'd tricked him in some previous deal? And why should he recognize the man on the second visit when he hadn't spotted him back in his own bedroom? Anyway, what if he had? Surely an expert confidence man could fast-talk someone so easily fooled into believing the previous episode was merely some dreadful misunderstanding, or that he himself had been taken in by a third party. Or he could have paid Mr. Hartler back with a rubber check and gone hunting for a new victim.

If anybody had tried such a stunt on Barnwell Quiffen instead of feckless old Wumps, murder might have been the only way out. Left alive, Mr. Quiffen would have called the police, filed a lawsuit, sent damning letters to every newspaper between Boston and Los Angeles, and put his own private eye on the trail. But Mr. Quiffen had been dead and buried a week ago. Why try to drag him into this just because he'd happened to occupy the same room for almost as short a time, and meet almost as violent an end?

Suppose more than one swindle was going on. If Mr. Hartler could let himself be gulled by a whole series of bogus antiquarians, mightn't he also be apt to fall for a scheme set forth by, say, a young man with an urge to rise in the world, an expert's knowledge of figures, and a gift for talking wisely on a wide range of subjects? Or an old friend's wide-eyed granddaughter with a thirst for adventure and a pair of strait-laced parents keeping her on a short leash and a tight allowance? Or a noted professor with some great scientific project to finance, or a lady with a handsome front and a murky past who was earning a hand-to-mouth existence reading tea leaves?

Or, she might as well face all the possibilities, an art expert who knew the Iolani Palace at least as well as William Hartler did? Or a frustrated actor who wanted his tooth capped, or the woman who was in love with him and had no money except what she got washing dishes and mopping floors for a hard-up widow with back taxes and interest on two mortgages to pay? Maybe if she'd happened to think of it in time, Sarah herself would have had a go. Well, she could rule herself out, but how did she really know what anybody else would do if the temptation was great and an easy mark available?

Sarah didn't want to dwell on such thoughts. She didn't want to think about Miss Hartler and what was to become of the old woman, either, but she couldn't help it. There weren't any relatives to look after her; that was why Bumps had stuck so close to Wumps all these years. Anyway, relatives didn't come with any guarantee. What about those two sharks who'd rushed over here as soon as they heard of Mr. Quiffen's death? What had they ever done for old Barnwell Augustus while he was alive, except perhaps to make sure he didn't stay that way?

Since she was making up a list of possible swindlers, why exclude either the nephew or the cousin? They both knew Mr. Hartler was going to take over the dead man's room because she'd told them so when she was urging them to get his stuff out quickly. They'd probably had some sort of casual acquaintance with Mr. Hartler, since he seemed to know everybody, and knew what a cinch he'd be to deal with. And, as Mr. Bittersohn would probably say, would she buy a used car from either of them?

But they had Mr. Quiffen's money now, or would have once the estate was settled. And what if one of them couldn't wait that long? And what if one, or both, might be in for a disappointment? She'd been so busy with her own concerns, she'd never checked back with George and Anora to find out who got how much. That cantankerous man might well have left a secret will cutting them both out and turning over the lot to some casual acquaintance out of pure cussedness. Somebody like William Hartler and his Iolani Palace project, for instance.

Oh, that was absurd! Why didn't she concentrate on the most immediate problem? Did Miss Hartler have anybody to protect her interests, or did she not? Precisely how dangerous would it be to tell her she had to move?

How many of that mob there tonight really cared about her and how many simply felt they ought to put in an appearance? Aunt Marguerite was putting on a great show of being Joanna's loyal friend, but Sarah knew how much that was worth. How many times had she herself entreated Aunt Marguerite to invite Aunt Caroline, her own and only sister, for a week or a few days or even overnight so that Sarah and Alexander could have a little time to themselves? How many times had Marguerite found urgent and pressing reasons why she didn't care to be bothered?

There were lots of delightful people in Newport. Sarah

had met quite a few of them at those many parties which had meant a long drive down and a long drive back and often stark boredom in between. But she'd never met anyone interesting at Aunt Marguerite's more than once or twice. The only acquaintances who stuck were the ones like Iris Pendragon, who hadn't the wit or the wisdom to find places in more discerning company. And William Hartler, who was quaint and fun in his way and didn't care whom he talked to so long as he got to talk, and his sister Joanna, who went wherever Wumps went.

After all, if the Hartlers had been particularly close to anybody in Newport, they'd have been reluctant to uproot themselves at their time of life and move back to Boston. If they'd had strong ties in Boston beforehand, they'd never have gone to Newport in the first place. That disappointing trip to Rome was an example of how they operated. Miss Joanna couldn't ever have taken the trouble to know this Dorothea, who turned out to be totally different from the classmate she'd thought she remembered. People didn't change a great deal as they aged, they only became more like whatever they'd started out to be in the first place.

Even Alexander must always have had that boy-stood-on-the-burning-deck streak in him, or he'd have found some way to break away from Aunt Caroline. Then he and Sarah would never have married, and his young widow wouldn't be sitting here wondering who was going to get murdered next. A footfall sounded in the hallway, and she jumped a foot.

It was Mrs. Sorpende. "I thought you might be down here, Mrs. Kelling, after I rapped at your door and got no answer. You're waiting for Miss Hartler, I expect."

"Yes, I felt I ought to. I don't know why, particularly, except that she's an old woman going through a dreadful experience, and I've got her on my conscience because I plan to get rid of her as fast as possible and I'm wondering what's going to happen to her after that."

"And what about me?"

Sarah blinked. "What do you mean?"

Mrs. Sorpende was standing square in front of her, those lovely, tapered hands twisted into an ugly, white-knuckled knot. "Please, Mrs. Kelling, don't try to spare my feelings. Just tell me. Do I stay or go?"

All Sarah could think of to say was, "It depends."

"On what?"

How did one answer that? On whether you happen to be the person who's killing off my boarders? Sarah hedged as best she could.

"Mrs. Sorpende, I can't tell you at this point because I don't know. I started this boardinghouse thing in the hope of helping myself out of a dreadful mess, as you know. So far all it's brought me is worse trouble. I may be able to carry on with it, or I may not. As for you personally, if you think I feel any more embarrassed by your job than I do about my Uncle Jem's pretensions to satyriasis or my Cousin Dolph's making a jackass of himself in public about once a week, forget it. I want Miss Hartler out because she's even more disruptive than her brother was and harder to get along with than Mr. Quiffen. You know I like you as a boarder because I've already told you so. That's as plain as I can put it."

"That's as plain as anyone could want it. You're a most unusual woman, Mrs. Kelling."

"Am I? Perhaps so. I never had a chance to be usual. I didn't even go to school. I learned from my parents and out of books. I've never been anywhere except to visit among the family. My husband was also my fifth cousin once removed, whom I'd known all my life. That's hardly a normal sort of existence, is it?"

"No, I don't suppose it would be, from your point of view. As it happens, I myself had much the same sort of upbringing. The main difference was that you lived comfortably in a stable environment, and I slept in the corners of empty stores, in whichever city we hadn't yet been driven out of."

"Your people were refugees?"

"No, they were gypsies. At least my mother was. My father, as far as I know, was a college student who happened to be doing research in sociology and got more closely involved with his subject than he meant to. I haven't the faintest idea what his name was. My mother hadn't got around to asking when the police came and moved her family on. She didn't even know she was pregnant until it was far too late to go back and try to find out. She was fourteen at the time, which didn't constitute an acceptable excuse for her behavior according to our rules."

"But she was only a child!"

"Gypsy girls aren't children at fourteen, Mrs. Kelling. Anyway, she never got a second chance to stray. From the time I can remember, my mother was worked like a dog and watched like a hawk. She'd managed to pick up a little schooling here and there. I myself was never allowed to attend school for fear I might pick up the sorts of ideas that were supposed to have led to my mother's downfall, but she taught me what she could.

"We read anything: scraps of newspaper we found in the gutter, billboards, cracker boxes, movie posters. One of my aunts, who was more sympathetic than the rest, used to shoplift a book for us now and then. It might be anything from *Peter Rabbit* to *How to Make Out Your Income Tax*, but we'd pore over it as if it were the world's greatest treasure."

"I've always been the same way," said Sarah, trying to establish some sort of rapport with this haunted creature. "I even read the labels on aspirin bottles. But do go on."

As if by some compulsion, Mrs. Sorpende kept pouring out her story. "I suppose I didn't have as bad a life as some. Gypsies are indulgent with their children as a rule. Even I, the little bastard, was never beaten or left to go hungry. I was often cold, but that was on account of the miserable places we lived in, and I was seldom clean because there'd be no hot water or soap. But I survived, and learned to *dukker*. Tell fortunes, that is. I did it rather well, perhaps because reading gave wider scope to my powers of invention, but I was hopeless at the little tricks that tend to go with the fortunes. Consequently I never made more than the legitimate fees, and that didn't boost my stock in the family much.

"To make a long story short, when I was about twelve or thirteen, my mother simply gave up and died. The night of the funeral, I ran away. I stole a dress off a clothesline, leaving my gypsy clothes in its place to persuade myself I wasn't really stealing, and lied about my age and got a job in a diner washing dishes. The pay wasn't much but the food was all right and I didn't mind sleeping on the floor behind the counter because that was the only sort of bed I knew.

"Then the counterman got funny. I broke a plate over his head and ran off again, and lied a little harder and got myself promoted to waitressing in a greasy spoon restaurant. I was on my way up. By the end of that year, I owned a good pair of shoes, a decent dress, and even a warm winter coat. I'd learned how to sleep in a bed and eat with a knife and fork. I even knew what a napkin was for. I'd discovered the public libraries where I could get all the books I wanted without paying a cent, and I'd settled on my life's ambition. I was going to be a lady."

She laughed at herself. "That sounds absurd to you, I'm sure, but it meant everything to me. Some day I'd live in a grand house and be waited on by a maid and a butler. I'd wear a long evening gown and jewels in my hair when I came down to dinner. That was the dream I sustained myself with while I was slinging hash and dodging grabby hands and fishing nickel tips out of the cigarette ashes and gravy. Some day they wouldn't be treating me like this. Some day they'd respect me. Some day I'd be somebody.

"Well, I shan't bore you with my whole life's history. I took lessons in elocution and deportment, once I'd found out what those words meant, from a drunk who'd played bit parts with Gloria Swanson and Theda Bara. That was as close as I ever got to greatness. I attracted the wrong sort of man and made a rotten marriage that lasted far too long. Now I'm back telling fortunes and clearing up dirty dishes. But I'm living in a beautiful house with a maid and a butler to wait on me, and I come sweeping down to dinner in a long evening dress with jewels in my hair. Your hard luck gave me the chance to fulfill my lifelong dream. If that's any consolation to you, take it and welcome."

"It is and thank you. But would you kindly tell me why, if it's been your lifelong dream to become a fine lady with jewels in your hair, you go slopping down Tremont Street in dirty sneakers and a frowsy kerchief? Surely that's not part of the dream, too?"

Mrs. Sorpende flushed. "No, that was an attempt to protect my position with you. Since the distance between here and the teashop is so short, I worried about being recognized. I know it's a dreadfully tacky disguise, but it's easy and didn't cost me anything. My means are a good deal more than straitened, as you must realize by now. I hoped that if I could manage to keep my two identities separate, I might squeak through a few more weeks here. No doubt you find the whole performance absurd, but please try to realize that illusion has been my way of life for a very long time."

"I do realize, but wouldn't you like to indulge in a spot of reality for a change? I suggest you throw away those ghastly sneakers and dress as you want to. If anyone from the house should happen to find out about the tea-leaf reading, tell them it's your hobby. If they ask whether I know, tell them yes and I may be hitting you up for a job any day now. Oh, and one other thing. Did you ever actually meet Vangie Bodkin?"

"Is that her first name? No, I'm afraid it's just something that stuck in my head from the society pages. My required reading, you know."

"Perhaps you should start reading the obituaries, too," Sarah suggested gently. "It appears Mrs. Bodkin's been dead for quite some while. I think that's Miss Hartler's car stopping out front now. Good night, Mrs. Sorpende."

Chapter 21

Miss Hartler was in a state that fluctuated wildly between overwhelming gratification at the number of people who'd turned out to say good-by to dear Wumps and overwhelming grief at the thought of tomorrow's funeral. Charles got her into the house and strong-armed her into drinking enough brandy to quiet her down so that Sarah and Mariposa could put her to bed.

"Thank heaven that's done," sighed the weary landlady. "Has Mr. Bittersohn come in the back way, by any chance?"

"No, madam," said Charles. "The gentleman has not yet returned."

"Then we'd better leave the front hall light on and the night latch off."

"Mr. Bittersohn will be more apt to come through the alley, madam. As you may recall, you yourself gave him a set of keys to the basement door because of his necessarily irregular hours."

"So I did. Turn on the alleyway lamps so he won't fall over the trash cans and scoot along to bed yourselves. He'll show up sooner or later, no doubt."

Mr. Bittersohn did not show up. Mariposa reported at breakfast time that his bed had not been slept in.

"Maybe he slept someplace else, huh?" she suggested with an innocent smile.

"Go take Miss Hartler her poached egg," said Sarah crossly, "then get your mind out of the gutter and on to the dishes. If your niece's play starts at eleven, you'd better be out of here by ten. What if the subway breaks down again?"

She still hadn't told her faithful allies about the impending swarm, and she didn't want to start preparations in front of Mariposa for fear the helper would insist on staying and miss her big family event. There wasn't all that much to do, anyway. The house was clean, she had plenty of crackers and things for people to nibble on, and a whole case of sherry obtained at a substantial discount from a friend of Charles's who was alleged to have come by the wine honestly.

Uncle Jem, Dolph, and the invaluable Egbert had all agreed to lend a hand, and she was fairly confident Mr. Bittersohn would send that staff member he'd promised even though he himself had not appeared by noontime when Miss Hartler tottered out of her room swathed in musty black and quavered, "Marguerite should be here any minute. Aren't you ready, Sarah dear?"

"Whatever made you think I was going with you, Miss Hartler? How could I? One of us has to stay and get ready for all those people you've invited."

"But surely your servants—"

"It's their day off. Isn't that the car outside?"

The funeral was set for one o'clock. At half-past twelve, as Sarah was finishing a cup of tea and brooding about how she got herself into these things, the doorbell rang. That must be the person Mr. Bittersohn was sending. She answered it with a good deal of curiosity.

Sarah had vaguely expected a lantern-jawed individual in a trench coat with the collar turned up and the belt gutted in. What she found was an elderly lady in a slate-blue coat with a little gray mink collar, and a blue velour hat perched at a chic angle on her freshly coiffed silver hair. The woman was no taller than she. As they met face to face, Sarah thought she looked somehow familiar. Then light dawned.

"Why, Miss Smith! What a marvelous surprise, and how lovely you look. Do come in."

"Didn't recognize me, eh? Mr. Bittersohn said this would be the best disguise I could put on. I'm sorry I couldn't wear black since it's a funeral, but this is the only good outfit I own, and I didn't want to shame you in front of everybody the way I did before."

She took off the coat to reveal a matching shirtwaist dress with a pleated bosom and a row of tiny covered buttons marching down the front. "Is my dress all right? I bought it on my employees' discount at the going-out-of-business sale. Figured I might as well have a good one since I knew I'd never be able to afford another. He gave me the money to have it dry-cleaned and get my hair done. Such a fine young man. His mother must be proud of him."

"Actually I believe she's sorry he didn't become a podiatrist," said Sarah. "Your dress is exquisite. I only wish I had one as lovely. Can I give you some lunch?"

"Well—"

"Would you mind coming into the kitchen? I was just having a bite, myself."

As she was getting out another cup and plate, Miss Smith settled herself with a sigh of pure joy. "My, this is nice. I can't tell you how comfortable it feels to sit down at a real kitchen table again. Not that they don't give us good meals at the Senior Citizens, but it's always those long tables with some old codger jamming an elbow into your ribs and gumming at you to pass the ketchup. Not cozy, if you know what I mean."

"I shouldn't think it would be. Do you take milk and sugar in your tea? Or would you prefer coffee? I can make some in a second."

"No, tea's fine and I've got into the habit of taking it with just sugar. We always pinch those little envelopes out of the sugar bowls when we get a chance. They know we do, of course, but they make believe they don't see. I have a little hot plate in my room where I live and I can keep tea bags and sugar but not milk because it goes sour on me and who can afford it these days, anyway? But you shouldn't be waiting on me like this. I came to work, and don't think I won't. Mr. Bittersohn said I should keep my eyes peeled, too, just in case I recognize anybody."

"There'll be plenty to do in a little while, never fear. Eat your sandwich while you have the chance. I'm going to cut us a piece of cake." As Sarah had suspected, without her swaddling wraps Miss Smith was thinner than she ought to be.

Right now, though, she was supremely happy. "This reminds me of when my mother was alive, not that we lived in any such style as you but we did have a lovely flat in a three-decker over on Savin Hill Road. I wouldn't want you to think I've been a derelict all my life."

"I certainly don't think you're one now," Sarah assured

her. "You have too much gumption ever to be a derelict."

Miss Smith, she decided, must be a good deal younger than she looked in her working clothes; probably still in her late sixties. She'd treated her weather-beaten face to make-up from some carefully saved hoard, with pale pink lipstick and even a dab of blue eye shadow that intensified the somewhat faded color of her eyes. One or two small pieces of old gold jewelry that had no doubt been her mother's or grandmother's enhanced her well-chosen, well-fitted dress. She'd no doubt be one of the best-dressed people present this afternoon. Her manners were infinitely better than Professor Ormsby's, her conversation livelier than Mr. Porter-Smith's and far more sensible than Miss LaValliere's. If only she had some money!

The doorbell rang again. Sarah excused herself.

"Please go on with your lunch. That will be some more of my crew."

Uncle Jem and his long-suffering gentleman's private gentleman stood there, both of them got up as waiters. Jeremy Kelling had hung a massive chain and emblem from one of the disreputable chowder and marching societies he belonged to around his neck, and announced that he hosied to be wine steward. Dolph charged in as they were getting rid of coats and demanded to know what sort of tomfoolery the old idiot thought he was getting up to on a day of mourning. Jem retorted that any day Dolph showed up automatically became a day of mourning. Leaving them happily engaged in their usual exchange of pleasantries, Sarah went back to Miss Smith.

"My uncle and my cousin are here, along with my uncle's man, Egbert. If you're sure you've had enough to eat, you might as well come and know the worst."

Miss Smith gave a nervous pat to her impeccable hair-do, rinsed her hands at the kitchen sink, freshened her lipstick, and followed Sarah into the library.

"Miss Mary Smith, may I present my Uncle Jeremy Kelling, my Cousin Dolph Kelling, and Mr. Egbert Browne, who's the only sane one among us?"

Everybody claimed to be very pleased to meet everybody. As Dolph shook hands he said, "Mary Smith, eh? Seems to me I've heard that name before. Haven't we met somewhere?"

"I've heard you speak at any rate," Miss Smith replied, not sure whether Dolph was trying to be funny or not, which in fact he was not. "You spoke to a group at the North End Senior Citizens not long ago."

"M'yes, so I did. And you were there? Fancy that."

"Yes, I thought you made some interesting points about the needs of seniors, but there was one topic I was sorry you didn't address yourself to. What this city really needs is a chain of recycling depots where people can bring old papers and cans and bottles and stuff they pick up, and maybe get paid a small sum for their efforts. That would help solve the litter problem, cut down on the proliferation of rats and other vermin, aid the conservation effort, and provide employment and a little extra income for the elderly and the underprivileged."

"By George, that's brilliant! And the stuff they collect could be sold to recycling plants and before long the enterprise would be at least partially self-supporting."

"I don't see why it shouldn't. But it would need a good chunk of capital to get started, and somebody with a lot of drive and public spirit."

"And know-how."

That was an expression Dolph had recently learned and was using far too frequently. Jeremy Kelling started to make rude noises, but Sarah hauled him away by brute force.

"Uncle Jem," she hissed in his ear, "if you queer Miss Smith's pitch, I'll break your neck. Come help me fill some glasses."

He was in truth of little help, sloshing the jugs around, sneering at the labels, and howling, "Rotgut! Bellywash!" and similar expressions of connoisseurship. However, they managed to get a couple of trays set out and Sarah deployed her forces.

"Dolph, you're the biggest and burliest. You be doorkeeper. If you suspect anybody's trying to gate-crash, make it plain that this gathering is for relatives and close friends only. If diplomacy doesn't work, feel free to use crude and violent methods. Miss Smith, you hover in the dining room to let me know if the food starts to run out and keep an eye on the silver. I found one of Mr. Hartler's visitors trying to swipe a Coalport vase the other day. Egbert, you pass things around."

"What about coats, Mrs. Kelling?"

"Don't encourage people to take them off, and then they won't stay so long. If they must, they can dump them on Miss Hartler's bed. Uncle Jem, you stay with the sherry and make believe you're the one who has to pay for it. Restrain your natural generosity. We've got to break this thing up as quickly as possible. I'll be the odd-job man."

"I thought Mr. Bittersohn would be here," said Miss Smith.

"So did I," said Sarah rather worriedly, "but we'll have to manage without him."

They did. Egbert and Miss Smith were supremely competent. Jeremy Kelling was capable of serious effort in the dispensing of spirits, and adroit at insulting anybody who tried to get more than a fair share. Dolph's bulk and ferocious hauteur were enough to discourage the uninvited and perhaps some of the invited. They did have a mob as anticipated, but it was a well-controlled mob.

By half-past four the place was pretty well cleared out. Aunt Marguerite talked of ordering the limousine and Miss Hartler was soothing her nerves with a glass of cranberry juice. Then, at last, Mr. Bittersohn arrived.

Chapter 22

Max Bittersohn had not come alone. With him was a large woman wearing a hand-knitted coat of bright kelly green and a crocheted chartreuse tam-o'-shanter. Her face was kindly, her eyes brimming with sympathetic tears. She rushed up to Miss Hartler and engulfed her in a mighty embrace.

"Oh, you poor, poor woman! And you loving him so, and coming so faithful and trying so hard, and him giving you the slip and winding up in a coffin, God rest his soul."

Miss Hartler struggled to free herself. "Let go of me! Who are you, anyway? I don't even know you."

The woman released her clutch, stepped back, and nodded her tam-o'-shanter vigorously several times. "It's unsettled her wits, that's what. My mother went the same way when she heard about the ladder breaking and Dad almost to the top with his load of bricks, may he rest in peace. I'm Mrs. Feeley, Miss Green. You remember me. I took care of your brother these past two months and more. And a handful he was, I can tell you, always at me about that Iolani Palace of his and why hadn't I got him those sixty-two dining room chairs like he told me to? But a happy soul for all his notions and it was a terrible thing the way he went."

"I'm not Miss Green! I don't know any Miss Green!"

"If you don't, then who does? Be easy, now. If ever there was a sister that had nothing to blame herself for, it's you. Bringing him his supper in a paper bag, even, after he got it into his head he was being poisoned and both of you used to better things as anybody could see.

And no wrong done on my part and no offense taken, you know that. But as soon as I saw that picture in the paper I says to my husband, 'Phil,' I says, 'they've made an awful mistake. That's no William Hartler, that's our Mr. Green. I better go tell the police.'

"And Phil says to me, 'You keep out of it, Theresa. First thing you know the cops will start asking us do we have a license, which we don't.' So I didn't go, though the Lord knows nobody could have got better care than Mr. Green got from us, as you well know, Miss Green, and there's still three days' worth owing to us not that I'd be so mean as to press you for it at a time like this."

"The woman's out of her mind," Miss Hartler insisted. "Or else she's trying to get her name in the papers, or worm money out of me under false pretenses."

"Theresa Feeley is as honest as the day is long," said a voice from the dining room door. "I knew her for years in Dorchester."

"Mary Smith!"

Mrs. Feeley wheeled and smothered the smaller woman in her yards of knitting. "If you're not a sight for sore eyes! And look at you now, in your beautiful clothes with your hair dressed fit to meet the Queen of England, among all your swell friends. No wonder you never have time for the likes of your old neighbors anymore."

"Theresa, you know I'd always have time for you. It's just that—well, it's a long story."

"Ah, and you'd be the one to tell it. Such a gift of the tongue you always had. Many's the time I've said to Phil, you watch that Mary Smith, I said. She'll make her mark in the world. And never too busy or too proud—"

"Theresa, let's talk about me some other time. Right now, I'm sure these people want to know all about how you took care of Mr. Hartler. That was his real name, not Green."

"Oho, I see the way of it now. The sister told me Green because she didn't want her high-and-mighty friends to know her brother had gone soft in the head, see, not that I blame her and there's many another would do the same. Anyway, whoever he was, we gave him the big back bedroom that gets the sun and there he stayed most of the time, babbling over his books and his pictures and making believe he was writing letters to important people though no more could he write than a two-year-old, poor soul. Scrawls on a piece of paper is all they were.

"And here would come the sister almost every day after dark, maybe around suppertime or a little later, bringing him something to eat that he liked, which was mostly hamburgers and ice cream. He was losing weight because he wouldn't eat and she was trying to fatten him up, see. Then after he ate, she'd take him for a little walk just down the street and back. They'd be out maybe ten minutes, then back they'd come and off she'd go.

"But that night he died they didn't come back and they didn't come back and finally she came back by herself, crying her eyes out. 'He's given me the slip,' she says, 'knocked me down and ran away which I'd never have believed. The police are hunting him now but they say I can't bring him back here. They'll be taking him to a place where there's bars on the windows and locks on the doors so we'll have to pack his things and call for a taxi.' And we did and she took the suitcases and went off and that's the last I've seen of her till this very minute."

"That's a lie!" screamed Joanna Hartler.

"It's the honest truth and may God strike me dead on the spot if it isn't. And she forgot to pay me the three days that was owing, too. I didn't say anything at the time thinking she'd remember when she got him settled, see, but she hasn't so far, and now here she is calling me a liar to my face which I'm not and never was, as Mary here can tell you."

"Who else might be able to tell us something?" asked Bittersohn. "People who've seen Miss Hartler entering and leaving your house, for instance?"

"Well, there's my husband Phil and my son Mike and my daughter-in-law Rita and anybody that lives on the street, I shouldn't wonder, the nosy lot that they are. And there's my grandson Kevin that wants to be a news photographer and took some fine pictures of them unbeknownst, and here they are."

Mrs. Feeley had a sense of the dramatic. From the cavernous drawstring bag that matched her tam-o'-shanter, she whipped out a sheaf of photographs. They clearly showed the Hartlers in various poses: William writing at a desk in a room where a crucifix hung over the bed; Joanna walking up a wooden staircase wearing slacks, a long tweed coat, a trailing scarf, a crocheted beret that looked like a boudoir pillow, carrying the sort of smallish old-fashioned satchel that used to be known as a Boston bag; both Hartlers walking arm in arm under a street light with a sign on it that read, "Buses for Columbia Station."

"See, Mary." She showed them to Miss Smith. "That's them, plain as plain."

"But that's the man in the subway," cried Miss Smith. "The one who pushed Mr. Quiffen under the train. I remember now. I'd watched him coming down the stairs and noticed he was wearing elevator shoes. They looked so out of place on a man his age."

"Are you sure?" snapped Bittersohn.

"Quite sure. At least I know he was there when it happened."

"And when was this now?" said Mrs. Feeley.

"About a quarter to five on the afternoon of January 14, at Haymarket Station. The paper said he jumped or fell, but he was pushed and I'd be willing to swear this was the man who pushed him."

"Mary, love, far be it from me to give you the lie, but you see, dearie, that couldn't of been him. I'm not saying he wouldn't have done it. A man in his condition, who's to say what they might do if they took the notion. I'm not saying he couldn't have done it because didn't he turn up in the Public Garden with his head bashed in, poor soul, when I'd have said he'd barely wits enough about him to find his own way to the bathroom if your friends will excuse me for speaking so plain, much less all the way to Haymarket Station. But I'm saying he didn't do it because we never let him out of the house by himself. Those were the sister's orders and that's what we did. Either Phil or myself was right there to keep an eye on him every minute, Phil being retired now as you maybe didn't know. You can ask Mrs. O'Rourke on the first floor if you don't believe me, because that one never misses a move we make."

While she was talking, Bittersohn had taken the photographs and silently handed them to Sarah. "Wait a minute," Sarah interrupted after she'd puzzled over them for a moment. "That's not Mr. Hartler. I mean, it's like him but it's more like—if he and Miss Hartler had changed clothes—"

"And that's what you did, isn't it, Miss Hartler?" said

Bittersohn. "All the time your brother was supposedly staying here, you were masquerading in his place."

"Don't be insane! How could I?"

"Quite easily, I should think. For one thing, none of us knew Mr. Hartler except Mrs. Kelling, and she didn't know him very well. You and he must have been just about the same height when he wasn't wearing his elevator shoes."

"That they were," Mrs. Feeley interposed. "No taller than an elf he was in his dressing gown, but always in them uplift shoes when she took him out walking. Wouldn't pass the door without 'em. I made bold to ask herself once why she didn't wear high heels on her shoes the way her brother did and says to me, "Wumps would never stand for that,' she says. 'He has to be taller because he's the man of the family.' She always called him Wumps, don't ask me why, and a stranger name for a grown man I never did hear. And their voices were about the same pitch only he talked fast and loud and she always spoke soft and sort of pitiful like she's doing now when she isn't screeching her head off, not that you can blame her and I'd do the same in her place which I hope I never will be. And she could have put something in her cheeks and her clothes to make her look fatter the way the actresses do on TV, though they weren't so like in the face that you couldn't tell them apart when you got them together."

"That's why she had to bash his face in after she killed him," said Bittersohn. "As for killing Quiffen, she could simply have borrowed her brother's overcoat and shoes one day. He had more than one pair of those elevator shoes, didn't he, Mrs. Feeley?"

"Eight or ten of them, and all custom-made. He must have been a dressy man in his day. And she took the overcoat to be cleaned, I remember that, because she said she'd taken him in for ice cream and he'd slopped chocolate sauce all down the front which I didn't see myself because she had it folded over her arm when she went out."

"This is totally absurd," Miss Hartler insisted, her face whiter and more pinched than ever. "I adored Wumps! And I never even knew this—this Quiffen."

"Oh, come, Joanna," drawled Iris Pendragon. "You were absolutely certain you had old Barney hooked thirty or forty years ago, but he wiggled off the line. Beastly little man, anyway. I never could understand why you ever wanted him in the first place except for his money, and it's not as though you didn't have plenty of your own."

That was what got to Miss Hartler. "I did not! Wumps got every penny, and he doled it out to me in dribs and drabs as if he'd been Daddy Warbucks and I were Little Orphan Annie. And he was getting crazier and crazier, and squandering thousands upon thousands on stuff for the Iolani Palace that they wouldn't even accept, and there wasn't going to be anything left for me."

"All you had to do was go to court and have him declared mentally incompetent," Dolph protested. "You could have got yourself appointed conservator. That's what I did with Uncle Fred."

"Yes, Dolph, and then you had to play nursemaid to the old halfwit for the rest of his life, didn't you? Just because you're stupid, you needn't think everyone else is. I told Wumps once that I'd murder him if I ever got the chance, and I got it and I took it and don't expect me to pretend I'm sorry. My one regret is that I didn't kill Wumps forty years ago. And furthermore, you might have the courtesy to admit I did give him a lovely funeral."

Chapter 23

It was not an easy pinch. Miss Hartler had no intention of going quietly now that she'd had a taste of power, and Sergeant McNaughton had gentlemanly scruples.

Miss Mary Smith had none. She applied a superbly efficient arm lock and snapped at Sarah, "Get a blanket and a rope." By the time the police wagon arrived, the prisoner was well under control.

Once Aunt Marguerite managed to get it through her head that Sergeant McNaughton hadn't charged to the rescue in the nick of time but had simply been lurking in the back hall ready to close in when Max Bittersohn gave him the signal, and that the sergeant was a married man with five children and no inclination to attend parties in Newport, she yawned.

"Well, Sarah, if you've nothing in the house but this ghastly sherry, I think we'll pop on back to the hotel. Sweet of you to have us, of course, and I must admit this has been a more interesting afternoon than I'd expected. So Joanna actually killed old Wumps at last? Pity it wasn't the other way around. One can always use an extra man even if he is a little bit gaga. Iris, do you happen to recall what I did with my gloves?"

Mrs. Feeley rode off with Sergeant McNaughton to give her statement and present the evidence her grandson Kevin had so fortunately supplied. The few remaining gapers on the sidelines took Jeremy Kelling's broad hint that the entertainment was well and truly over. By the time Sarah's boarders began trickling back to the house, the used dishes were piled in the sink, the ashtrays emp-

tied, and the windows thrown open. Cold as it was, everybody felt a need for some fresh air.

"Miss Smith, you'll stay to dinner, won't you?" Sarah
coaxed.

"Er, h'mph." Dolph cleared his throat noisily. "I've
been hoping I might prevail on Miss Smith to join me for
dinner at the Ritz. This recycling scheme of hers wants a
lot of discussing. A lot of discussing."

"My God," gasped Uncle Jem. "To think I should live
to see the day!"

"What the hell, I'm human, ain't I?" snarled his
nephew. "I'll admit that living with Aunt Matilda all those
years was enough to put any man off women forever, but,
dammit, I—well, hell, I'm human, ain't I?"

"Maybe you are at that," Jeremy Kelling replied, gaz-
ing with a wild surmise upon this new facet of a man he'd
thought he knew and loathed. "Godspeed, my boy. The
speedier the better, I'd say. You know what happened to
those frogs of yours the minute you turned your back."

"I'm so sorry, Miss Smith, but they always go on like
that," Sarah explained, trying to conquer her hysterics.
"Dolph is an idiot in some ways and he's usually a good
deal slower off the mark than this, but he's honest, loyal,
dependable, and filthy rich."

"And I'm sixty-seven years old and lonesome as hell if
anybody wants to know," her cousin added without acri-
mony, "and that was the most beautiful arm lock I've ever
seen. How about it, Miss Smith? Feel like recycling an old
frog hunter into a Prince Charming? Hey, that's not bad.
Come on, you're a sport, take a chance. Mind if I call you
Mary?"

"Why, no," said Miss Smith after brief consideration. "I
don't think I'd mind a bit."

"Bless you, my children. Come on, Egbert, let's go
home and mix ourselves a large pitcher of martinis,"
crooned Jeremy Kelling. "Be sure to let me know the next
time you're throwing an after-the-funeral binge, Sarah. I
wouldn't miss it for anything."

"You certainly do know how to cheer a girl up."

Sarah kissed both her uncle and Egbert with a lifetime's
affection. "Thanks a million times. I'd never have got
through this afternoon without you. And Dolph, of course,
and—may I call you Mary?"

She gave her cousin about-to-be a hug. "Dolph does

need a wife desperately," she murmured. "Heaven knows what you'll be letting yourself in for—but you won't chicken out, will you?"

"I never have yet, have I?" Miss Smith rearranged her good velour hat on her nicely waved hair and fastened her little mink collar. "Then I expect I'll have the pleasure of seeing you again soon—Sarah."

"Why don't we make that very soon? Now that I have a vacancy, Dolph must bring you back here to stay."

"Damn good idea," said Dolph. "Keep an eye on her so she won't go hopping off."

"Oh, Dolph." Sarah suddenly remembered something. "Speaking of keeping an eye on people, have you any idea why Barnwell Quiffen put a detective on your trail?"

"Detective, eh?" Dolph was tickled silly by this news. "Why the hell didn't you let me know sooner? Have some fun with him, eh? Buy a false mustache. Leap in and out of—"

"Frog ponds?" Jeremy Kelling suggested innocently. "Hell of a lot of leaping you ever did, you great tub of lard. Sarah, where did you get this notion about detectives? Why would Quiffen do a thing like that?"

"Because he hated my guts," said Dolph promptly. "Kicked him off the Committee for Common Cleanliness. Had to. Tried to make a stink about me misusing funds because I wouldn't go along with that damn fool notion of Uncle Fred's. No disrespect to the dead, of course, and I realize Uncle Fred was a great man, but damn it, he did get some funny ideas in his later years. Went into Woolworth's and saw some parakeets wearing diapers, so he went ahead and ordered a hundred gross of 'em."

"Of parakeets?"

"No, damn it, of diapers. Going to make the pigeons wear 'em."

"What?" shrieked Sarah. "Dolph, are you seriously trying to tell us Uncle Frederick meant to put diapers on all the Boston Common pigeons?"

"Hell, no. He didn't mean to do it himself, he meant *me* to. That's where I drew the line. I mean, what the hell, I suppose I could go out with a few barrels of popcorn and trap the damn birds, but where would I go from there? Got to be changed, ain't they? Anybody thinks I'm going to spend the rest of my life hanging around the Common powdering pigeons' bottoms can damn well

think again and so I told the judge when I went to have
Uncle Fred declared mentally incompetent. And he agreed
with me," Dolph added triumphantly.

"But Quiffen kept yammering about that hundred
gross of parakeet diapers till I told him to shut up and get
out. Had it in for me ever since. Didn't dare risk a face-
to-face showdown so he sneaked in a detective. Wish I'd
known. I'd have shown him I'm a tough man to meddle
with. You remember that, Mary. Mary Kelling. Sounds
pretty good, eh? Where the hell have you been all my
life, anyway?"

As Miss Smith was making a prettily flustered good-by
to Mr. Bittersohn and Mr. Bittersohn was offering to drive
over and help her clean out the room she wouldn't be
needing anymore, Mrs. Sorpende entered the house. The
two former bag ladies exchanged startled glances, then
warm smiles.

"How delightful to see we have mutual acquaintances!
I don't believe we've met, though I feel I know you. I'm
Theonia Sorpende."

"And I'm Mary Smith."

"But she won't be for long," said Dolph cockily.
"Come on, Mary. Damn it, this is an important occasion.
A man doesn't get engaged every day."

"If you're going to be engaged to me, you'll have to
clean up your language." Mary Smith was getting off on
the right foot.

As they left, Mrs. Sorpende's gracious smile turned
to a twinkle of polite amusement. "Ah, me, I seem to
have been merely the plaything of an idle hour. How
wonderful they've found each other! Miss Smith has
great strength of character."

"She'll need every ounce of it when she marries
Dolph," Sarah replied. "Still, living with him can't possibly be much worse than scrounging in trash barrels."

"Oh, then you know?"

"Certainly I know. How do you think I found out about
you? We all have to get by as best we can, don't we?
Now why don't you nip up and get dressed for dinner?
Wear your lovely dress with that gorgeous red poppy,
will you? I need to look at something bright and cheerful for a change. Now I must fly. I'm head cook and assistant bottle washer around here, in case you hadn't
caught on, and dinner's going to be late and I'm counting

on you to keep Professor Ormsby from chewing the furniture."

When she got out to the kitchen, she found Mariposa in her new purple and fuchsia uniform, washing up glasses and fuming. "Why didn't you tell me everybody was coming back here this afternoon? I could have stayed."

"I didn't know myself," Sarah lied. "Miss Hartler asked them without telling me."

"Some nerve! Where's the old witch now? I'd like to give her a big, fat chunk of my mind."

"Never mind her, Mariposa, she's gone and she won't ever come back. Go set the table for six, will you? Then come and get a tray. We're going to be long on appetizers and short on dinner tonight."

Quickly Sarah furbished up the metaphorical funeral baked meats into an impressive array of canapés, and filled the decanter from the last jug of sherry. She opened cans of pea and tomato soup for purée mongole, made a fast exploration of the refrigerator and emptied everything she could find into a large casserole, spread cheese over the top, and thrust it into the oven to bake. She slashed a head of lettuce into serving portions and poured some of her premixed vinaigrette dressing over them. Mariposa could get their emergency cache of vanilla ice cream out of the freezer and spoon it into parfait glasses with crème de menthe and a few chopped nuts. It was the fastest dinner she'd got so far and please God it would be edible.

Then she ducked up the back stairs, took a fast shower, swept her light brown hair up into a knot, and put on the pretty gray satin Aunt Emma had given her. Running late, Sarah was not surprised to find her company already assembled when she got back to the library. Charles was doing the honors. Mariposa, she hoped, was back in the kitchen stirring the soup and fixing the desserts. Mr. Porter-Smith had on a black bow tie and a somber cummerbund in deference to what he'd obviously supposed would be a solemn occasion, and was looking askance at Mrs. Sorpende's flamboyant adornment.

Sarah soon fixed that. "Oh, you did wear your flower! How sweet of you. I told Mrs. Sorpende I needed something cheerful to look at tonight," she explained to the room at large. "You wouldn't believe what's been hap-

pening in this very room. Mr. Bittersohn, would you—"
His eyes turned battleship gray and she caught herself in
the nick of time. "Oh, you're already set for sherry. Forgive me if I act a bit flustered, everyone. It's because I
am. Charles, tell Mariposa to turn down the gas under
the soup and come in here, then I shan't have to go
through the whole performance twice. Professor Ormsby,
do have some more of those pâté things. Dinner's going
to be late, I'm afraid, though we'll hurry it along as best
we can."

"No rush," said that loquacious man with his mouth
full. "No place to go tonight. Where's Niobe? Her door's
open."

"So it is. I'm sorry, I forgot to close it. That used to be
the drawing room, as I may have mentioned, and we
had to open it up again this afternoon because a lot of
people came here after the funeral. That's why we're
running so far behind. It was Miss Hartler's idea to invite
them without asking permission. She appears to have
been full of ideas."

Sarah sipped at her own sherry until Mariposa joined
the group, ribbons aflutter and eyes wide. Then she told
her tale. What with numerous interruptions of, "How
ghastly!" from Miss LaValliere and trenchant questions
from Mr. Porter-Smith, the tale was long in the telling.
They were finished with the appetizers and the soup, and
well into the surprisingly tasty casserole before she got
through. Even then, nobody was satisfied.

"But what about all them strangers messin' up the
hall?" Mariposa put in despite the scandalized Charles's
attempts to shush her. "How come we found that woman
snooping through the china closet?"

"I simply don't know," said Sarah. "Mr. Bittersohn . . ." She groped for suitably noncommittal words
in order to avoid another blast from those boreal gray
eyes. "You know about antiques and things, and you
were awfully clever about leading Miss Hartler to confess
this afternoon. Would you have any ideas?"

"I wasn't so clever," he objected. "You were the one
who broke her down with that point about the clothes."

"It appears to me that the police sergeant who managed to track down Mrs. Feeley and stage that dramatic
confrontation is also in line for some well-deserved kudos,"
Mr. Porter-Smith added a bit resentfully, no doubt think-

ing that he himself would have been covered with Holmesian glory by now had not Cousin Percy required his services at the office.

"Sergeant McNaughton did a marvelous job," Sarah agreed, although she knew perfectly well who deserved the kudos. "But getting back to Mariposa's question, Mr. Bittersohn, couldn't you at least take a guess?"

"I could try. You may recall that I was talking with your aunt last night at the undertaker's? She told me then what Miss Hartler mentioned this afternoon, that the brother inherited the parents' entire estate on the understanding that he look after his sister."

"That was a risky sort of thing for them to do," said Mrs. Sorpende. "Look what happened to the Dashwoods."

"Who are they?" asked Miss LaValliere.

"Characters in a book by Jane Austen. Do go on, Mr. Bittersohn," Sarah urged before Miss LaValliere could ask, "Who's Jane Austen?"

"Evidently Miss Joanna didn't fare much better than Elizabeth and Marianne Dashwood, according to your aunt. Dear Wumps kept her short of cash. After he got too sick to function, she ought to have had herself appointed conservator, as your Cousin Dolph suggested, but that would have meant exposing Wumps's mental deterioration and that wouldn't have served her purpose. She might have forged his name to checks to keep them going, but there was a big element of risk in that. So what she did was to sell various antiques her brother had collected from people who were under the impression they were making donations to the Iolani Palace. That woman Mariposa mentioned was acting more like a customer than a sneak thief, wasn't she?"

"A pretty sharp customer," said Sarah. "She offered me fifty dollars for that pair of Coalport vases over there in the china cabinet. She tried to convince me they were reproductions."

"Which of course they're not," said Bittersohn. "Sounds more like a dealer, which would make a lot more sense though a lot less cash. Miss Hartler could drop into a shop with a nice little piece to whet their appetites and tell them she had plenty more like it at home. That could explain why she bumped off Quiffen when she learned he'd beaten her to your drawing room. A house like this is exactly the sort of background she'd need."

"And his having jilted her ages ago wouldn't make her any less reluctant to give him the shove," Sarah agreed. "Hell hath no fury, and so forth. That woman did act confused about whose house it was. Remember, Mariposa? And Mr. Hartler—I mean Miss Hartler—kept interrupting and fussing about what a nuisance he—I mean she was, which was certainly true. I'll bet he'd—oh, you know what I mean—given the impression he owned the place."

"No doubt," said Bittersohn. "Miss Hartler would have been posing as an old widower with a place too big for him and investments that weren't paying off as well as they used to, wanting to get rid of his stuff and move to a retirement home or somewhere. You couldn't blame outsiders for swallowing a story like that once they got a look inside this house. It was an ideal setup, and not a badly organized operation for an amateur."

"Don't you think, Mr. Bittersohn, that Miss Hartler must have been planning this whole thing for quite some time? Take that hotel stationery from Italy, for instance. She must have got hold of it ages ago, when she and her brother took a trip to Rome with Aunt Marguerite, just so that she could write a letter to leave around explaining why she'd been gone and why she was coming back at the right moment to be in on the obsequies. I wonder how she managed to find Mrs. Feeley to dump poor old Wumps on all that time?"

"Through an advertisement, I expect," Mrs. Sorpende put in. "People are always putting little ads in the classified section saying they're willing to board an elderly person who requires tender, loving care. Sometimes they mean it, sometimes they don't. This Mrs. Feeley sounds ideal. She lived close enough to Boston so that Miss Hartler could get back and forth easily. She was a kind, responsible, and also unsophisticated and sentimental sort of person who'd respond favorably to the picture Miss Hartler was trying to paint of herself as a loving sister trying to do her best for her senile older brother without committing him to an institution. Miss Hartler couldn't take him to a real nursing home because they keep records and wouldn't care to have her disrupt their schedules by taking him out for walks whenever it suited her purpose. Since the Feeleys were not only kind but also unlicensed, she thought she could depend on them to keep their mouths shut no matter what happened."

"But I don't get it," wailed Miss LaValliere. "I mean, you're saying that when Mr. Hartler lived here he was really Miss Hartler all the time, right? And when he went out to that Feeley place he was Miss Hartler because Mr. Hartler was already there, right? I mean, how could he? I mean, how could she? I mean I don't get it."

Sarah exchanged covert smiles with Mrs. Sorpende. "That's because you didn't see those photographs Mrs. Feeley brought with her. To begin with, the two of them were very much alike, even to their voices. You just didn't notice because he was so bouncy and jolly while she was droopy and whiny. He appeared taller and fatter but that could be done with elevator shoes and a pillow under the belt."

"Yes, but their clothes?"

"That was the easiest part. Mr. Hartler used to wear a poplin raincoat and one of those squashable tweed hats, as you've perhaps noticed. The coat was reversible. On the poplin side it buttoned at the right, like a man's. The other side was a dark tweed and buttoned left like a woman's. That's what Miss Hartler had on in the pictures, along with a trailing woolen scarf and a great floppy beret with crocheted flowers on it. She'd have left Boston wearing the man's hat and elevator shoes, with the beret and scarf stuffed down the front of the coat to give her a tummy. Somewhere alone the line, she'd reverse the coat to the tweed side, put on the beret and scarf and a pair of woman's shoes she had with her, and hide the man's hat and elevator shoes in a bag she was carrying."

"The point on which I crave elucidation," said Mr. Porter-Smith, "is where Miss Hartler kept her brother after she took him from the Feeley house until the time he turned up dead in the Public Garden. It would seem that he must have walked there since one could hardly picture that frail elderly woman carrying him; therefore, he must *ipso facto* have remained alive during the entire interval. However, your thesis as I understand it is that Miss Hartler took Mr. Hartler away from his lodgings, came back here by herself in an understandably boisterous mood, rejoined him later in the evening and remained with him until she walked him over to the place where his body was found, and killed him. That seems an incredible feat."

"Oh, Gene, you always have to make things harder," said Miss LaValliere. "She probably just dumped him at a movie. That's what I'd do."

"From the way Mrs. Feeley described the brother, I doubt whether Miss Hartler would dare leave him by himself in public," Sarah objected. "What I think is that she had a place all arranged to hide him in. When she came here disguised as Mr. Hartler that first time, she told me she was living at a rooming house on Hereford Street. I suspect the room was much closer to the Garden, perhaps around Arlington or Berkeley. She didn't give it up when she moved here pretending to be her brother. It hasn't been very long, after all, though it seems forever. I'd say she walked him from the Feeley house down to Savin Hill Station, brought him a few stops on the subway, then took a cab the rest of the way to wherever the hideout was."

"But why not take a cab the whole distance?"

"Because then there'd have been a cabbie working the Savin Hill area who could testify he'd picked up an old couple at that time and taken them to a Back Bay address," Bittersohn answered for her.

"And he might remember what that address was," said Sarah. "Aren't they supposed to keep logs, or tell their dispatchers where they're going?"

"Good point, Mrs. Kelling. By taking the cab from some other station, Miss Hartler would be cutting down on the chance of being identified."

"Then why take a cab at all? Why not stay right on the subway to Park Street and then transfer to the Green Line?"

"They were old people and that would mean climbing a lot of stairs as well as being exposed to the risk of meeting somebody who'd recognize them. The brother was unstable and excitable, and would be more apt than not to call attention to himself in one way or another if they stayed on the train for any length of time. A cab was faster and safer. Furthermore, if they pulled up at the rooming house in a cab and were spotted by some other resident, it would be easier for Miss Hartler to pretend she was just some good Samaritan bringing an old fool home from a party where he'd had too much to drink. She could then lock old Wumps in the room with those bogus Iolani Palace treasures to keep him happy for a while, get straight back into the cab, and be taken to South Station or maybe Columbia, ride to Savin Hill on the Red Line, do her act with Mrs. Feeley about having lost him, collect his stuff, and disappear."

"Where to? Back to the room?"

"No, I think she must have gone first to that big motel near Logan Airport and checked in under a false name with her brother's luggage, which also contained a good many of her own possessions. No doubt Mrs. Feeley found certain cases already packed and locked when she went to clear out his room. Since the Hartlers had been to Italy in the past, the luggage already had the sort of customs stickers on it that Mrs. Kelling would expect to see when Miss Hartler arrived here in an airport taxi."

"By the time she'd done all that," said Mrs. Sorpende in a tone that sent shivers down every spine around the table, "she mustn't have had long to wait."

"Not long," Bittersohn agreed. "She went back to the rented room on the trusty old MBTA, kept Wumps amused until the neighborhood quieted down, then took him over to the Garden and did him in."

"With what?" demanded Mr. Porter-Smith.

"I'm not sure you want me to answer that."

"Yes, we do," Miss LaValliere insisted.

"Okay, then. Apparently she took off one of his heavy elevator shoes on one pretext or another, hit him from behind with the heel, then put the shoe on her own foot and kicked in his face with the toe."

"Ugh!" Miss LaValliere turned an unbecoming shade of green. "Well," she added after some thought, "maybe at least that will be a lesson to brothers who go around sawing the high heels off their sisters' brand-new shoes."

"The saddest stories yield the profoundest morals," observed Mrs. Sorpende with a perfectly straight face. "And then Miss Hartler went back to the motel and enjoyed a sound night's sleep, no doubt. Do you know, Mr. Bittersohn, what puzzles me most is how the Feeleys were located so quickly. There must be scads of those little unlicensed private nursing homes in the greater Boston area."

"Just routine police work," Bittersohn replied with a jaw-cracking yawn he was unable to stifle.

"No doubt," said Sarah. "And while this routine police work went on all last night, all this morning, and most of the afternoon without a break, Miss Hartler beguiled the time mourning dear Wumps. Iris Pendragon told me Joanna had always been surprisingly good at amateur theatricals. Charles, we'll have our coffee here at the table tonight. And you'd better take away Mr. Bittersohn's ice cream. He's about to fall asleep in his plate."

Mysteries by
Edgar Award-winning Author
JOHN R. FEEGEL

"Feegel is a pro who knows how to write...his style
combines the best of Michael Crichton and Raymond
Chandler."—*Atlanta Journal Constitution*

THE DANCE CARD   58040-3/$2.95
During the autopsy of Navy Pathologist George Toll, Dr. Twig
Stanton discovers a coded card, sealed in plastic and surgi-
cally implanted in the dead man's abdomen. Stanton learns
that the Dance Card is Toll's record of what really happened in
the Bay of Pigs invasion, to be made public in the event of his
death. "A riveting spy novel that will keep you on tenterhooks
Philadelphia Inquirer

AUTOPSY   Avon Original   79681-8/$2.95
An Edgar Award-winning novel of passion, medical mystery
and electrifying courtroom drama. Only a famed pathologist
can solve the mystery of a dead man worth hundreds of thousands of dollars in insurance money if he was murdered—and
not a cent if he committed suicide. As he prepares to penetrate
the mystery, the hopes and destinies of ruthless men and
women are balanced on his decision.

Available wherever paperbacks are sold or directly from the publisher. Include $1.00 per
copy for postage and handling; allow 6-8 weeks for delivery. Avon Books, Dept BP, Box 767,
Rte 2, Dresden, TN 38225.

Feegel 2-83

Murder & Intrigue
FROM THE WITTY AND MASTERFUL
CHARLOTTE MACLEOD

MURDER ON LOCATION

GEORGE KENNEDY

Internationally renowned actor George Kennedy
finds himself playing both star and sleuth
in his own novel when murder stalks the set
in Mexico for the filming of a
major motion picture.
Whether the motive is sabotage
or personal vendetta, nothing is certain
except that everyone's a suspect—
even stars Dean Martin, Glenn Ford,
Raquel Welch, Yul Brynner and
Genevieve Bujold.   83857-5/$2.95

AN AVON PAPERBACK